CHESTNUT STREET

SIMON LANDRY

MILFORD
HOUSE

Milford House Press

Mechanicsburg, Pennsylvania

MILFORD HOUSE

an imprint of Sunbury Press, Inc.
Mechanicsburg, PA USA

For information about special discounts for bulk purchases, please contact Sunbury Press Orders Dept. at (855) 338-8359 or orders@sunburypress.com.

To request one of our authors for speaking engagements or book signings, please contact Sunbury Press Publicity Dept. at publicity@sunburypress.com.

ISBN: 978-1-62006-223-4 (Trade paperback)

Library of Congress Control Number: 2019952493

FIRST MILFORD HOUSE PRESS EDITION: October 2019

Product of the United States of America
0 1 1 2 3 5 8 13 21 34 55

Set in Bookman Old Style
Designed by Chris Fenwick
Cover by 100 Covers
Edited by Chris Fenwick

Continue the Enlightenment!

To Sophia and Marguerite;

Thank you for the long naps.

Love, Daddy.

North Philadelphia
July 10, 1969 – 3:30 a.m.

As he drank his fifth cup of coffee of the night, James Monroe was growing weary. He looked at himself in the rear-view mirror—he was a mess. His wavy brown hair was disheveled, he had bags under his eyes, and his usual boyish smile now replaced with a look of exhaustion. For the tenth night in a row, he was sitting alone in his car instead of being home with his wife; it was putting a strain on their marriage.

She was three months pregnant and working full shifts at the hospital during the day, so she was exhausted when she came home. They hadn't seen much of each other in the past few months, as he was spending most of his nights out on stakeouts, and friction had started building between them. He felt bad that he hadn't been around as much these past few weeks, but he told himself it would be worth it in the long run. He had a gut feeling that this was his big break. This was *his* scoop, from start to finish. This would be the story that would launch his career and propel him into the national spotlight and the best part was that he had done it all by himself, he wouldn't have to share any of the glory. It would be easy living for his family after that; they just needed to hang on for a little bit longer.

The car he'd been following from a safe distance for the last two hours came to a stop on the corner of Columbia and 22nd. The police captain in charge of the twenty-second district, who was sitting at the wheel, rolled down his window but kept his engine running.

James took out the camera he had checked out of the paper's photo lab and screwed on the high-powered lens. He double-checked that there was film in it and that everything was set up just right—he didn't want any slip-ups. He'd been working on this case for months and was almost ready to present it to his editor; there was no margin for error now. He lowered his window and set his camera in place. He was ready.

This story was every reporter's dream. The newly appointed police commissioner, a brutish Italian American, had been boasting for the better part of a year about his toughness on crime. There were already talks of the man seeking office in the near future. James had to give it to him—the man was a born politician. He knew just what to say to garner popular support. He was always saying that his job was to clean up the city and that he was the only man who could get the job done. The problem was that the Philadelphia Police Department's reputation for corruption, and sometimes sheer incompetence, was very much alive and well, no matter what the big man might claim.

James had been following some of the commissioner's subordinates around town for the past few months—precinct captains for the most part, just like tonight—hoping to capture proof that police corruption ran very high in the hierarchy.

If James could prove that some high-ranking police officers had their hands in the cookie jar, it would be a ground-breaking story. But if he could prove that the new commissioner had his hands dirty, too, it would be one of the biggest scandals this city had ever seen. Every reporter on the planet hoped to one day take down a lying politician or catch a dirty cop—this story might have both. There were only a few missing pieces to this puzzle, and James hoped to put them into place within the next few days. After that, he would submit all he had put together to his editor. Once it hit the press, James was sure the story would become national, opening doors for him. He knew this beat was only a stepping-stone toward something greater.

After waiting for what seemed like an eternity, he saw two very tall figures wearing dark clothes and hoodies approach the police captain's car. His camera was ready, but he still went over everything just in case. This was the fifth time in as many months he had seen this officer meet with these men under these circumstances. But this time, the police captain had made a crucial mistake—he'd parked his car under one of the few remaining streetlights that worked in this neighborhood. James' job had just become a lot easier. If he could get a good picture tonight, not only would the police officer be unable to deny it was him in the picture, but James could also identify who those two hoodlums were and keep digging into this story.

The two men walked up to the driver's side window. After exchanging words for a few minutes, the police officer passed a small bag to one of the men and gave the other one a piece of paper. He seemed to give the men instructions. James had already taken five pictures of them, including the exchange.

It was a well-known fact that street gangs around the city were bribing cops so they wouldn't be hindered in their illicit business, but this looked like the police officer was the one purchasing something. At first, he thought the police captain was buying drugs. It wouldn't be the first time a cop got caught using dope. The problem was, the cop did not receive anything in return. It had been the same thing for the past five meetings he had seen, and he had a good idea what this was about—but he needed to be sure before submitting anything.

James' car was parked on the opposite block, and he had turned off his engine to be as inconspicuous as possible. His good luck turned when three stray cats began fighting over a piece of food. In their struggle, they knocked over two metal garbage cans. The night had been very quiet, so the crashes seemed even louder as they split the silence. The three men talking on the opposite corner all turned toward his direction at the same time. James had been leaning out of his window with his camera lined up when it happened. He was surprised to find that the two tall figures talking to the police officer were not men but two lanky teenagers. His journalistic instincts made him snap off a few more pictures without even thinking, but he was positive they'd seen him and knew what was going on.

Without hesitation, James turned the key in the ignition, put the car into gear as fast as he could, and gunned the engine. It was time to get as far from this place as possible. The two teens had arrived on foot, so he wasn't worried about them. The cop, on the other hand, was still sitting at the wheel—if he caught up to him, it wouldn't end well. The only good news right now was that he'd been able to capture a perfectly framed shot of all the conspirators and that the cop's car was parked in the opposite direction, so he would have to turn around before giving chase. This bought him a few precious seconds to escape.

James ran a few stop signs and navigated through the streets recklessly, keeping his eye on the rear-view mirror as he sped across the neighborhood. He clipped the sidewalk when he turned a corner and almost lost control of his car. Every time he saw headlights in his mirror, his heart pounded in his chest, fearing that the police captain had caught up to him. James wasn't sure if the police captain had called in on the radio to get some support, but he couldn't take the chance. At this time of night, there was very little traffic, and if he drove too fast, he would draw too much attention. He needed to put as much distance as he could between himself and the spot where he had been seen, but afraid that if he kept driving this way he would crash or kill someone, he eased up on the gas when he finally made his way south on Broad Street.

Once he was out of North Philly, he eased back on the accelerator but kept driving, working a serpentine route that would take him back to South Philly.

He drove around town, looking for a place to hide. James parked his car behind a convenience store and took out his notebook, keeping the engine running in case he had to make a quick getaway. He quickly wrote down everything he had just witnessed and made a rough first draft of the article he would later submit to his chief editor. He wanted to record everything on paper while it was still fresh in his memory. James could review it and type a better version later when he got in the office.

Once he put everything down in writing, he stowed away his notebook and headed back out on the road. He figured that if he stayed mobile, there was less chance that someone would spot him.

At 9 a.m., he parked his car on the corner of 15th and Packer and stepped out. He walked into the building as soon as it opened and hid everything he had gathered so far, making sure it would all stay secure until he could come back to retrieve it. After being certain everything was safe, he sighed in relief as he headed for the exit. He could go back home and catch up on some sleep; he was looking forward to his bed and the much-needed rest that would come with it. Tonight, he would stay home with his wife. He could retrieve everything tomorrow and pick up work from there.

As he walked out of the building at the end of this very long night, he never saw the man behind him. Suddenly, a giant hand clasped over his mouth, and he felt the large knife being plunged into his back. James' scream was muffled as his heart was torn open, and he began to bleed out. It only took a few seconds for his body to go limp, and his entire world faded to black.

ONE

Center City
Corner of Chestnut and 22nd
Monday – May 6, 2013 – 7:25 a.m.

Samuel Brighton looked in the mirror as he stepped out of the shower. As he surveyed the fine lines in the corners of his eyes, he was still happy about the man staring back at him. He had an athletic figure, with only a few extra pounds around his waistline. His auburn hair was trimmed to a close crop as he tried to hide his emerging baldness. His eyes were a piercing blue and displayed an ever-present glimmer of curiosity. Even if his fifties were creeping toward him at an ever-increasing speed, he still felt blessed.

This day had started like every other weekday—he'd woken up at 5 a.m. to work out before the rest of his family had started stirring. He managed to keep a good physique even with age, but it was becoming increasingly difficult to maintain his standards.

Sam stepped out of the master bathroom and went to the closet to dress. He put on jeans and a t-shirt, strode into the kitchen, caught sight of the dining table, and smiled. His eleven-year-old daughter was eating her cereal while watching TV out of the corner of her eye. She was his little girl, and she was becoming a beautiful young lady. Sam wasn't in any hurry to see her become a teenager, but he knew he couldn't slow down time, so he was beginning to accept that she wasn't his "little girl" anymore. As he looked at her, Sam knew that Sofia would grow up to be special. Not only was she beautiful—she was at the top of her class and a very gifted basketball player even at her young age.

Sitting across from Sofia was the reason for her exceptional gifts. His wife Victoria was a beauty unto herself. Standing at six-two, she towered over most people, including Sam. Some folks assumed she was a fashion model, but just like with Sofia, it was her brain that set her apart from the rest.

Victoria was a highly specialized pediatric oncologist. She had developed some ground-breaking techniques for treating various forms of cancers in children, resulting in her being asked to speak at all sorts of medical conferences around the world. She was well-known and was sought after by many other hospitals. However, she had chosen to stay in Philly to work at the Children's Hospital because Philly was where Sam's job was. The hospital paid her well because they knew she could work anywhere else if she chose to. Her research attracted a lot of attention, and with attention came large donations—so they made every possible effort to keep her happy.

When Sam and Victoria had started living together, their home was a studio apartment only a few blocks away. When they began talking about having a child, they had considered moving into the suburbs and buying a house, not wanting to raise a child in an old apartment. As they were looking at houses, they'd learned that construction had begun on a brand-new condo tower just across the street, with all the modern amenities one could wish for.

Victoria's career was well established by that time, and she was making good money, so they opted to stay in the city. It would be a lot easier for both of them, and they didn't feel like putting up with traffic day in and day out. Sam could take the bus down Chestnut or walk to City Hall Station if the weather was nice enough and then take the Broad Street Line down to South Philadelphia High School, where he taught math. The entire trip took only twenty minutes if he took the bus or thirty-five if he walked, which he most often did. His wife, too, could walk to her research center on the corner of 36th and Market or to the hospital within thirty minutes.

Additionally, Sofia's school was right across the street, so Victoria could drop her off in the morning, and Sam picked her up on his way back from work. When Sam finished early, he could even hear the school's bell ring from his living room if he left the windows open. Now that Sofia was getting older, she was asking for more independence, and they had promised her that if she kept her grades up, she could get her own key when she started middle school next year. They enjoyed the simplicity of their life and never regretted opting for city life.

Sam went around the dining table, gave his daughter a kiss on the head, and wished her a great day. He told her that, if the weather held up, they could go out on the river path for a run that afternoon. Sofia had taken to running with her old man, and it was becoming increasingly difficult for Sam to keep up. He gave his wife a long kiss that made Sofia sigh in disgust. Luckily for Sam, Sofia hadn't yet developed an interest in boys, and he was in no hurry to see it happen.

He checked his phone for emails and saw he had a new one from work. It stated that there was a mandatory staff meeting today after class, so he told Sofia he would pick her up later than usual. He grabbed his keys, wallet, and phone and headed out the door.

TWO

Center City
Corner of Chestnut and 22nd
Monday – May 6, 2013 – 7:45 a.m.

Sam took the elevator down to the lobby, waved to the door-man, and went outside. The day's weather was nice and warm, so he decided he would walk down to the metro station.

He stopped at the Dunkin' Donuts on the next corner and was greeted by Norma, the cashier who worked the counter on weekday mornings. She asked him what he wanted, even though they both knew he always ordered the exact same thing—a large coffee with three creams and three sugars and a chocolate donut. His wife kept telling him that the sugar in his coffees and donuts was the main reason he was putting on some extra pounds, but Sam wasn't ready to give up his morning treats just yet. He smirked as he thought of the look his wife would give him at the sight of his breakfast and decided he would just have to exercise a little more to stay in shape.

After exiting the donut shop, he headed east toward City Hall Station. Sam needed some time to think and walking always helped him gather his thoughts. His mother had passed away a few weeks ago, and there was still a lot to be done, even though his grieving was pretty much over. The woman had been battling Alzheimer's for almost two decades, so Sam had seen that moment coming for quite a while; he had taken the time to visit her frequently at her apartment over the years. His childhood home was close to his school, so he would drop in a few times a week to check up on her and talk to her caregiver about her health. Her condition had gotten worse in the last year, and they both knew it was only a matter of time, so he'd had a while to prepare for her passing.

He had taken a few days off from work but went back quickly, even though he was still eligible for a couple more days of leave. Sitting at home wouldn't do much and keeping busy was the best way for him to move forward. After the burial, things got a little tougher for him—it was now time to organize her succession. Sam's mother had been a very proud and progressive woman. She'd given birth to Sam all alone in her apartment and had even given him her maiden name instead of his biological father's. She'd never remarried and had put all her energy into raising her only child. Since Sam had no siblings, there wasn't anybody else to factor in. Still, filling out the proper paperwork, paying taxes, and organizing everything was a hassle. He had enlisted the help of a young attorney to help him navigate through it all, but it was still a stressful time for him. Hopefully, it would all be settled in a few weeks, and he could move on with his life.

As he closed in on the metro station, he put in a reminder on his phone to go through the two boxes of possessions he had collected from his mom's apartment over the last weekend. They were crammed at the bottom of the hallway closet and were taking up unnecessary space. Victoria had been indulgent so far, but he knew it would start to annoy her soon. Anyways, he was sure there wasn't much in there he would want to keep, so it wouldn't take too long. Perhaps Sofia would help and find something she would want to keep as a souvenir of her grandmother.

Once he got on the train, he didn't even bother sitting down; his school was only a few stations away, and he would be at work within minutes. As the train was moving along, he only wished that today's staff meeting wouldn't go on for too long. He knew it was wishful thinking, but still, he hoped in vain.

THREE

South Philadelphia High School
Corner of Broad and Snyder
Monday – May 6, 2013 – 2:30 p.m.

The bell rang, and as students were racing to the door, Sam started picking up his papers and cleaning his desk. As he was putting away his pencils and pens in a drawer, he caught some movement out of the corner of his eye—one of his students apparently wanted to speak to him and was waiting for him to finish.

The school year was coming to an end, and his senior students were getting ready for graduation. Some of them were getting nervous about their grades, since they usually stopped putting in an effort once they got an acceptance letter, only to find out a few weeks later that the school year wasn't actually finished and they needed to get back to work—they always discovered, to their horror, that grades still mattered, even at this point. He imagined this would be another plea for lenience.

Vanessa Stanford was a gorgeous young lady. She had long, blonde hair and an athletic figure that drew a lot of attention. She also had the habit of testing the limits of the school's dress code on a regular basis and proved to be quite a distraction to her male counterparts. Those boys were overflowing with testosterone, and Sam knew that she used it to her advantage to get what she wanted. A senior like all of Sam's students, she could easily pass for a college student, or even a young professional when she dressed accordingly, but that almost never happened.

Even though he had never actually been able to prove it, he knew Vanessa had some of the boys in class do her homework from time to time, especially when it was a harder task that needed more time and effort. Sam didn't mind, as he knew that she was shooting herself in the foot—when the time for testing came around, she wouldn't have done any of the work to get prepared, and it would show on the final result. So, he let it slide.

As Sam looked up, he noticed that her outfit today was particularly racy. She was wearing a very short jean skirt that he was sure didn't respect the school dress code and a skin-tight, low-cut red shirt that showed way too much skin in Sam's opinion. He found it sad that a girl this young felt the need to dress like this as if her body were the only thing worth noticing. His thoughts went to Sofia. She was about to become a teenager herself, and hopefully, she would have a little more respect for her body and her self-worth. He told himself that it was his job as a father to teach her about those things and to make sure she grew up a wholesome person. Sam kept putting his things away and when Vanessa saw she was the last remaining student in the classroom, she got up and walked up to his desk.

"I need to talk to you," she said, holding her books to her chest and looking a bit worried.

From her expression, Sam figured she was anxious about her grades and wanted to discuss them with him.

"I can't right now, Vanessa. I'm sorry," he answered. "There's a staff meeting in a few minutes I have to get to."

Sam kept busy putting his things away and avoided looking directly at her. Being alone in his classroom made him uncomfortable. If anyone were to walk by, they might misinterpret things, especially given her flirtatious reputation.

"Please, Mr. Brighton…" she whined. "I need to talk to you. It's important!"

Sam struggled to hold in an annoyed sigh. "Sorry, Vanessa, not today. Like I said, I have a meeting I need to attend. We can talk Thursday after class," he finished. He turned his chair toward the classroom door, motioning for her to leave.

"But Mr. Brighton, it's important. We have to talk!" she pleaded.

Sam sighed. He was getting irritated by her stubbornness. If this kept up, he would be late for the staff meeting, and all the good seats in the back of the auditorium would be taken. He'd be forced to sit down in the front rows with the vice-principal and the suck-ups.

Just then, Vanessa noticed his irritation and changed tactics. She sat on the corner of his desk, crossed her legs, and leaned in to show as much cleavage as she could. When she noticed that Sam had finally looked up at her, she smiled at him and said, "What if I wait for you here until your meeting is over?"

Sam couldn't believe what was happening. "You are being very inappropriate right now, young lady," he responded, flustered. He stood up but kept looking down at his desk. "Now, please shut the door on your way out," he said as he walked out the door. When he got to the hallway, he turned back to see Vanessa still sitting on his desk, looking bewildered.

As he glanced at his watch, he saw he didn't have time to drop by the teachers' lounge to grab his stuff before the meeting. Now he wouldn't have his phone with him to pass the time and would have to listen to whatever they would be talking about. He sighed as he made his way down the corridor. This day couldn't end quickly enough.

FOUR

South Philadelphia High School
Corner of Broad and Snyder
Monday – May 6, 2013 – 2:35 p.m.

As Sam walked into the school's auditorium, he dreaded being stuck in the front rows. But as he looked up, he saw someone waving at him—his friend Dean had saved him a spot way back in the last row. Sam waved back in relief; finally, there was some good news. He walked up the steps and found his seat.

"Hey, buddy. Thanks for saving me a spot," Sam whispered to his friend.

"No problem," Dean replied, still fiddling around with his phone. When he lifted his head, he noticed that Sam's hands were empty.

"You didn't bring anything?" he asked. General assemblies were usually a pointless waste of everyone's time, so most people brought things with them, either grading papers, reading books and magazines, or playing with cellphones as the speaker droned on. It was all done hidden from plain sight so they wouldn't appear disinterested to the bosses who led these meetings. Nevertheless, the principal and vice-principals knew very well what went on but didn't say much unless it was too overtly apparent that someone wasn't paying attention. The employees made a conscious effort to hide their disinterest. It was just the way this game was played.

"No, I didn't have time to stop by my desk. One of my students wouldn't leave my classroom. Wouldn't leave me alone."

"What happened?"

"I'll tell you later," Sam replied, still rattled over what Vanessa had done.

"What are you up to?" he asked Dean, peeking at his screen.

"Catching up on some reading. Latest developments in artificial intelligence," the man replied.

Dean Ashton was the school's computer lab teacher, but you wouldn't know by looking at him. A former linebacker at Rutgers, Dean was a six-foot-four amateur bodybuilder. He weighed in at a very lean two hundred and forty pounds. When the freshmen walked into South Philly High at the beginning of a new school year, at first, they thought Dean was a security guard. Upon closer inspection, they noticed his shaved head, sweatpants, tight workout shirts, and flashy sneakers, so they assumed he was a gym teacher.

Even the parents were fooled. On most parent-teacher nights, Dean's desk was deserted because they were looking for a computer nerd and didn't think twice to look toward the massive African-American male sitting across the gym at his tiny desk. Dean didn't mind a bit since it meant those events were quiet for him, while Sam's desk had a long line-up of parents worried about their kids getting into college.

Even though his appearance was deceptive, Dean was a virtuoso with any type of electronic machine. After his football scholarship allowed him to get his degree in computer engineering, Dean had worked for a few years in Silicon Valley. Even though the pay was good, and he enjoyed working on the newest technology, Dean had decided to give it up and move back east. The competitive environment out west wasn't for him; he'd hated always battling with his colleagues, constantly trying to prove to one another who was best. Dean was more laid back and didn't care a bit who was number one. So, after two years of putting most of his money aside, he moved back to Philly, bought himself a nice little townhouse in West Philadelphia, and found his calling as a computer lab teacher. The job meant that he could still play with computers all day while keeping a more relaxed schedule and enjoying long summer vacations and good benefits. Sam thought himself pretty good with phones and computers, but he knew he was light-years behind Dean.

The man could write code in his sleep and could hack his way into anything if he so chose without ever being caught.

As the meeting started, Dean was deeply invested in whatever was on his phone's screen and was already out of it, so Sam decided not to bother his friend. He would be forced to listen.

After thanking everyone for their attendance, as if they were there by choice, the vice-principal did a roll call. Sam elbowed Dean in the ribs when his name was called out so his presence could be accounted for. Dean raised his hand, and as soon as he saw that the vice-principal was looking for the next name on the list, he put his head back down and continued playing with his cell phone. Sam raised his hand when his name was called then settled into his very uncomfortable seat as best he could. This was shaping out to be a very long afternoon.

Today's meeting was titled "Statistics on the Perception of Violent Behavior in Our School." The large projection screen on the auditorium's stage began showing slide after slide of statistical tables. As Sam looked around, he saw that no one seemed to understand what these tables meant. Even Sam, as a math teacher, couldn't decipher what the vice-principal was trying to explain. It seemed the man himself didn't quite understand what he was talking about. Eventually, one of the goody-two-shoes sitting in the front row asked what would happen with these statistics and what precise measures would be taken to lessen the perception of violent behavior. The vice-principal answered that today's meeting was only meant to present the statistics and that no actual measures were in the works for the time being. Upon hearing the answer, Sam tuned out, and his thoughts began to wander.

Sam found it odd that the school's principal wasn't the one conducting the meeting. Usually, this type of mindless drivel was right up the man's alley. The principal could talk for hours without saying anything concrete and could drown you in statistics until you were bored out of your mind. A career politician at heart, Donald Jackson had been the principal for the city's largest high school for the last decade.

The imposing African-American was a mountain of a man. He stood at six feet and seven inches tall and weighed over three hundred pounds. His head was bald and wrinkled, causing his eyebrows to scrunch up above his deep-set eyes—the man looked perpetually upset. He had taught for only a few years before moving on to the administrative side of the job. Students and staff members alike were afraid to go into his office.

If you looked up the word "windbag" in the dictionary, you would probably see the man's picture next to it. He could always be counted on to deliver a long and boring speech. He just loved to hear himself talk, and he was fond of using allusions to his glory days as a basketball player at Penn with his twin brother Davis to illustrate any kind of point. To hear him talk, you would think his brother and he had been the most valuable players on a team that had won the national championship four years in a row. The fact that he'd ridden the bench for all those four years, on a team that had never even qualified for the national championship tournament, didn't seem to be relevant to Donald Jackson. In his own mind, the man belonged in the Hall of Fame, and his wisdom was only rivaled by that of God's.

At sixty-six years old, Donald Jackson had been eligible for retirement with a full pension for a few years now, but he had remained on as principal. Many thought it was because he was waiting for his brother to position himself on the political chessboard.

Davis Jackson had been far more successful than his brother and seemed to be the humbler of the two. A brilliant law student, he had risen through the ranks over the years to eventually become a very well-respected district attorney for the city of Philadelphia. Eight years later, he was elected mayor and was currently finishing his second term in office. A political animal in his own way, Davis Jackson was now bidding for a seat as a US Senator. The current Senator had resigned a few weeks before because he was fighting a losing battle against lung cancer.

Davis Jackson had seized the opportunity and tossed his hat in the ring. Davis Jackson was running a very well-orchestrated campaign on the back of his record as district attorney and mayor. He had virtually no opposition. He was already considered by some political analysts as a presidential hopeful for 2024. Even though he was running as a Democrat, his tough stance on crime was his main political asset, and that bought him support from Democrats and Republicans alike. He was always bragging about the number of criminals he had helped put away and that he was the man who cleaned up the city.

Sam felt that Philadelphia wasn't such a bad place to live in and didn't see his hometown as the cesspool of criminal activity that Davis Jackson seemed to describe, but he had to admit, the man was very convincing and was a brilliant orator. Right now, there didn't seem to be a single opponent on any side of the aisle that could stand up to him, and some people were already calling him Senator.

Donald Jackson, on the other hand, was the opposite. Even though it was his brother who was the candidate for the election, Donald made political speeches whenever the opportunity arose. He was his brother's fiercest supporter and relayed his slogan—*Dedicated to Justice!*—every chance he got. Donald remained in his posting as principal of South Philadelphia High because being the head administrator of the city's largest high school was a good jumping board to another political assignment. Rumors were already circulating that he had locked in the chief of staff's position inside his brother's future political cabinet.

Even though the man was annoying beyond belief, Sam had tremendous respect for Donald Jackson. He thought he was a very good principal, always running a tight ship. Sam knew he could always count on him to back him up and thought Jackson felt the same about him. If he could only dial it back a few notches on the political speeches, the man would be tolerable.

Sam came out of his day-dreaming as the meeting was coming to an end. He turned to Dean, gave him a nudge, and said, "Holy crap, I didn't understand any of this. How about you?"

"Every single word!" Dean replied with a beaming smile.

They both chuckled. Sam looked around and noticed that pretty much everybody was just as confused.

"Let me grab my keys from my desk, and I'll meet you downstairs in a second," Sam told Dean.

As he was turning to leave the auditorium, he saw that Dean had been accosted by a colleague, a young geography teacher whose name he hadn't yet learned. South Philadelphia High School was so big, it was almost a city in its own right. It was pretty impossible to know everyone.

Dean's impressive physique attracted a lot of attention from the ladies. He knew there was a herd of students who were madly in love with him and signed up for his classes even though they had no interest in computers. The female staff members were just as eager. Their computers always seemed to break down, and he was the one they asked to help them fix it up. Dean always gave them the cold shoulder, though, and refused to fix their computer problems, which drove the ladies at school even madder. It made them try that much harder to get some of his attention; it also meant that he was constantly solicited by them.

Sam chuckled at what he was seeing. Being Dean's best friend, he was the only one at school who knew that Dean's hard-to-get attitude was because his friend "played for the other team," a closely guarded secret that Sam swore he would protect. Dean had been living with his partner Paul for the last decade. Paul was the opposite of Dean. A man of small stature with a receding hairline and big, wire-framed glasses, there was nothing athletic about him. He worked as an accountant and wasn't in the least interested in technology. It was hard to understand how they could form a working couple, but somehow, they made it work. Dean and Paul came over to Sam's house for supper at least twice a month, and they even helped look after Sofia from time to time. Sam and Victoria considered them family.

Sam saw that Dean was caught in a conversation that he was trying to get out of, so he gestured to his friend to meet him outside. It would buy him a few minutes, so he could walk all the way across the school to get his keys, wallet, and phone out of his desk in the teachers' lounge. He turned and hurried out of the auditorium.

As he stepped out, he felt a hand grasp his arm. He whipped around and saw Vanessa standing right in front of him. She had a look of fierce determination in her eyes.

"Mr. Brighton, we need to talk, now!" she said sternly.

"Jesus freakin' Christ!" was all Sam could say, as he whipped his shoulder sideways to break free from her touch. "Get the hell away from me!"

Vanessa looked stunned by Sam's reaction. For a second, she just stood there, mouth agape and eyes wide.

Her reaction calmed Sam down. She no longer attempted to look flirtatious; rather, she looked anxious, even sad.

He also noticed that a few colleagues were staring in their direction, some of them whispering to each other. People could very easily get the wrong idea about what was happening here, seeing a teacher and a student standing so close to one another, the young girl looking distressed and the teacher looking annoyed. Vanessa's reputation of using her physical attributes to her advantage was well known, and the way she'd chosen to dress today didn't help at all.

"Mr. Brighton! It's important! We need to talk! Right now!" she said loud enough for everyone around to hear.

"Alright! What's so important you have to follow me around like this?"

"Not here. We need to talk in private."

"That's not going to happen."

Sam leaned in a whispered to her ear:

"Especially not after the little stunt you tried to pull in my classroom earlier."

"But…"

"No 'but!'" Sam snapped back. "You either say what you have to say right now or get lost!"

Vanessa just stood there, and her breathing became labored as she fought hard to hold back tears.

He noticed that a lot of staff members were now standing around, watching their argument.

Sam took a few steps back, sucked in a deep breath, and in a calm voice, said, "Vanessa, I apologize for my reaction. I shouldn't have snapped at you. I'm sorry. But you can't keep harassing me this way. We'll talk some other time. Now, please leave."

Sam turned around and walked to the teachers' lounge without looking back.

When he got to his desk, he unlocked his drawer, grabbed his keys, wallet, and cell phone, and locked his desk. He hurried outside, hoping to catch up to his friend.

He walked out of the school's front entrance and saw Dean waiting for him. As he walked up to him, his friend noticed the worried look on Sam's face.

"What took you so long? Is everything okay?"

Sam sighed as they both started walking toward the subway's entrance.

"Student of mine won't leave me alone. You know Vanessa Stanford?"

"Yes, I do," Dean answered with a sympathetic look. "She took my class last year. She didn't even know how to turn on a friggin' computer when she started the semester, and she didn't seem the least bit interested in technology. Why? What happened?"

"She wouldn't leave my classroom at the end of class. Said she needed to talk to me about something. I told her a bunch of times that it would have to wait until Thursday, but she wouldn't take no for an answer. She even had the nerve to flirt with me, too!" Sam answered.

"You wouldn't be the first one," Dean replied.

"What? You, too?"

"No, not me... not in an obvious manner, anyway. She always dressed more provocatively on the days when she had a class with me, but she must have sensed that it wasn't working because she never tried anything overt. But there are rumors going around..."

"What rumors?" Sam asked, even though he was sure he had already heard most of them.

"Well, I know for a fact that she had a few kids do her work for her in my class. I heard those boys brag about getting laid in exchange for doing it. Can't say I blame them. I probably would've done the same if I'd been in their shoes. But I also heard that she's slept with a couple of teachers over the past few years. Can't say for sure if it's true. Might just be gossip."

They kept walking at a brisk pace. They knew the subway's schedule, and if they hurried, they might make the next train. If not, they'd have to wait fifteen minutes.

They went down the stairway, passed the turnstile, and hopped on the train just as the doors were closing.

Sam exhaled and allowed himself to relax in his seat.

FIVE

Center City
Corner of Broad and Chestnut
Monday – May 6, 2013 – 4:15 p.m.

Sam said goodbye to Dean. After riding on the Orange Line together in silence for a few stations, they both got off the train. Dean would transfer to the Blue Line and head back to his house in West Philly; Sam wanted to walk home and enjoy the warm spring weather.

He would be at Sofia's school in about fifteen minutes. It was such a beautiful day that Sam decided he would pick up some takeout on the way to his daughter's school, and instead of watching TV while he cooked dinner, they could go out for a run before Vicky came home.

As he was walking back up Chestnut, Sam reflected on his day. The incident with Vanessa was troubling him. The fact that she had attempted to flirt with him after class was more than alarming, and the incident after the staff meeting didn't help a bit. That type of situation could be very dangerous if not handled the right way, as it might very well be misinterpreted. He told himself he needed to get ahead of this. He should write an email to the vice-principal, informing him of what had happened. Maybe it wasn't the first time Vanessa had done such a thing.

After the way he'd yelled at her, Sam was worried that Vanessa would try to lash out at him. If he wrote an email to the relevant people informing them that Vanessa had tried to flirt with him and that her behavior bordered on harassment, there would be written proof, and he would feel secure in his handling of the situation. He also needed to talk to Vanessa about this, but not before informing the administration.

Sam thought for a second about using his phone to access his school's email account. It was easy enough to do. But Sam had a very strict *"no work after work"* policy, and he intended on respecting it. So, he put a reminder on his calendar to email his bosses first thing tomorrow when he walked in. For now, he would try to put this incident out of his mind and focus on spending time with his family.

He stopped in at DiBruno's on the corner of 18th and picked up lasagna, some bread, and a chocolate cake. He knew the cake wasn't a good idea and wouldn't help his waistline, but this had been a crummy day, and he felt that he deserved a little pick-me-up. Besides, he was going out for a run with Sofia, so he reasoned that he would burn pre-emptively whatever he would ingest later.

He walked out of the shop and picked up his pace. There was no need to keep Sofia waiting any longer, and he was looking forward to going out for a run with her—it would help take his mind off things.

SIX

Center City
Corner of Chestnut and 22nd
Monday – May 6, 2013 – 5:52 p.m.

The Brighton family was sitting at the dining table enjoying their copious meal. Victoria had finished early today and was able to join her family for dinner. Usually, her work demanded long hours, so Vicky would finish late and come home after dinner. She didn't want to miss a single minute with her family whenever she could, but sometimes, when she was on call, she didn't even manage to come home before Sofia went to bed. When their little girl was younger, Sofia would punish her mom for a few days by ignoring her, but now that she was getting older, she understood that Mommy wasn't being absent on purpose—she just had a very demanding job. Sofia had begun to respect her mom for the time and sacrifice she put in to help cure young children of disease, even if it meant she was busy at times.

Victoria rarely made it home for dinner but she made sure to be home every night before Sofia went to bed. Today, they were lucky—a patient had canceled his appointment, and she'd been able to come home early.

As the three family members were digging into their meals, there was a moment of silence around the table. Sam was lost in thought, still attempting to get a grasp on what had happened that day.

His thoughts were interrupted as Sofia piped up, over the clattering of knives and forks, "So, Dad, how are ya' feeling after that little run today?" She grinned mischievously, and he rolled his eyes, chuckling.

"Hey, I saw you slowing down at the last quarter-mile—I was just catching up!" He winked at her, and she giggled before continuing her dinner.

Sam and Sofia had set out for a vigorous four-mile run after school. Sam had kept up with his daughter for most of it, but the last mile had proven to be too much for him. He let Sofia finish at her own pace while he switched back-and-forth from running to walking for the remainder of their course. When he had gone up the steps that led back onto Chestnut from the Schuylkill River Path, he had found Sofia waiting for him, and it looked like she hadn't even broken a sweat.

Sam felt a mix of emotions. He was feeling old, and today's run only served to prove that he wasn't a young man anymore. Perhaps he should take his wife's advice and cut back on the sweet stuff. On the other hand, seeing the way his daughter was growing up filled him with great pride. Upon reflection, he told himself that he had a good life and that if raising such a wonderful child came at the cost of old age, it was very much worth it.

After stretching and cooling down, they had gone home to find that Victoria was already there. They had all agreed that everyone should get in their pajamas before dinner and that tonight would be a family movie night.

"So, how was your day at school, sweetie?" Victoria asked.

"Pretty good," their daughter answered.

Sam chimed in. "What'd you work on today?"

"Nothing," she replied blandly.

"Really? You did nothing today? And you learned nothing?" Sam asked, laughing.

"No, that's not what I mean… Okay, we worked on grammar today, but it's so boring!" she said, rolling her eyes.

Sofia was ahead of her class in most subjects, so if they'd spent the entire day working on something she'd already mastered, it wasn't surprising she felt like the day had been wasted.

"Hey, there's the big basketball tournament in two weeks, remember?" Sofia asked her mom.

"Yes, I remember, honey. I already told you I would be there," Victoria answered, giving her a wink.

"I know, Mom. But I saw on the news that it would be sunny and warm on Saturday, and I want us to go out so we can practice my shot."

"Sorry, sweetie, I'm on call Saturday. I'll be at the hospital all day," Victoria said, already reading the disappointed look on her daughter's face.

"I'll shoot hoops with you," Sam offered, hoping that Sofia's mood would change.

"You? Dad, you stink at basketball! You can barely hit the backboard!" Sofia replied, annoyed.

Sam knew he wasn't his daughter's first choice for a basketball coach. Her mom had been a prolific college athlete, getting a full scholarship during her four years at Temple and using her basketball skills to pay for her education. Sam couldn't hit the side of a barn no matter how hard he tried.

"I resent that!" Sam chuckled. "It's not my fault they make those backboards so darn small!"

Sofia giggled at her father's self-derision, and she smiled.

"Tell you what—I might not be a great shooter, but I'm the best in the city when it comes to running after balls and passing them back to you."

"Okay, Dad. You can come shoot hoops with me Saturday," she said, giving him a mock sigh.

Sam snorted. "Geez, thanks for including me."

Victoria turned to Sofia. "I have an idea. How about your father makes a video of you making a few shots then sends it to me? I can look it over and give you a few pointers when I get back from work. I should be back around dinner time."

"Okay. Thanks, Mom," Sofia said with a smile.

"And if the weather holds up and I'm able to finish up early, we could go out again after dinner. What do you think, Sam?" she asked her husband.

"Sounds like a plan!" Sam replied enthusiastically, shoving a huge piece of lasagna in his mouth. "So, how was your day, hon'?" he asked through a mouthful of pasta, snickering as he noticed the disapproving looks on both his wife and child's faces.

"Pretty good day. Nothing unusual," she said.

Victoria never really talked about her work, except for saying she had a good day. She didn't like to talk about sick kids at the dinner table because she felt that Sofia didn't need to be exposed to that.

"How about you?" she asked him in turn. "Anything interesting happen today?"

"Yeah, you could say that," Sam muttered.

"What happened?" she asked curiously. Working with teenagers, Sam often had a bunch of quirky incidents happen daily, and his family loved to hear about some of the crazy stuff these kids tried to pull throughout the school year.

Sam talked about his boring meeting and how he felt that an hour of his life had been wasted. But as he finished his sentence, his voice trailed off, and he looked down at his plate.

"What's wrong?" Victoria pressed.

"We'll talk about it later," Sam replied, looking down at his plate, suddenly not feeling as hungry as he had just a second before.

"Come on, Dad!" Sofia pleaded, throwing her father an annoyed look. "I'm almost twelve. I can handle it." She understood that when her parents said they would discuss something later; it was because they didn't want her to hear about it.

Sam didn't tell his family about the incident with Vanessa. He figured it would blow over once he had rectified things tomorrow and that it might prompt his daughter to ask questions, he just wasn't ready to answer yet. They all finished their plates in silence and started picking up.

Sam put the dishes in the dishwasher, Victoria prepared the dessert that would be eaten on the couch, and Sofia surfed through the TV's On-Demand menu, looking for a movie to watch.

As Sam was finishing up in the kitchen, there was a loud knock on the door. Everyone froze in place, and they all looked at each other. Nobody was expecting company. After another loud knock, they heard someone yell, "Philadelphia Police! Open up, please!"

They all stared at each other for a second, wondering what this could be about. Finally, Sam stood up and opened the door. Two patrolmen were standing in front of him. One was a very young man, and the other one was older and had sergeant's chevrons on his uniform. The latter had a mean look to him, and he held a sheet of paper in his hand. He glared at Sam and asked, "Are you Samuel Brighton?"

"Yes, sir, I am," Sam answered cautiously. "Can I help you with something?"

"Sir, I have a warrant here to search the contents of your cellular phone. Can you get it for me, please?"

"My phone? What for?" Sam asked, bewildered. "What's this all about?"

"Sir, if you could just get the phone, please. Now," the other cop said abruptly. The first one handed Sam the letter he was holding.

Victoria and Sofia were now standing right behind him; Sofia was holding her mother's hand and seemed intimidated by the two police officers.

"Sam, what is this about?" Victoria asked quietly.

"I don't know, sweetie. This is a search warrant for my phone. I have no idea why, though. Could you go and get it for me? I think it's on the kitchen counter."

Victoria went into the kitchen, and when she came back, she saw that the cop had his hand stretched out, expecting her to give him the device straight away. Victoria handed Sam the phone and looked at the man with an air of suspicion.

Sam took the phone and reluctantly handed it over to the young officer.

"Is there a combination to unlock it, sir?" the officer asked politely.

"No, you swipe the screen," Sam replied. "Can I know what this is all about? What are you looking for exactly?"

The sergeant took the phone from his younger colleague and started fiddling with it. After a few seconds, he turned the phone over and shoved it right in Sam's face. Sam gasped. He was looking at a picture of Vanessa, stark naked, sitting on a desk with her legs crossed and blowing him a kiss. A second later, he heard Victoria gasp then shout, "Oh my God!"

She took Sofia's face and buried it in her chest so she couldn't see the picture anymore. It was too late, though—she had seen it, just like everyone else in the room.

"What the hell?" was all Sam could blurt out.

The officer took out a clear plastic bag, dropped the phone in it, took out a marker, and wrote on the bag. Once he was done, he put the bag inside his pants' pocket, turned to his rookie colleague, and grunted, "Cuff him and read him his rights."

The younger man began, asking Sam politely to turn around and place his hands behind his back. Sam was too stunned to even hear the man's commands. He was just standing there, his mouth agape. The police officer turned Sam around and handcuffed him. He then started reading Sam his rights from a little plastic card he held in his hand. After he was done cuffing Sam, he turned him toward the door and started escorting him to the elevators.

Sam still hadn't said a single word since seeing the picture on his phone and was desperately trying to figure out what was going on. When he finally started coming out of his stupor, he heard his daughter crying, clinging to her mother's waist. He looked at Victoria, who also had tears in her eyes and was asking, "Sam, what the hell is going on? How could you?"

Sam was already out the door, being pushed forward by the old sergeant, but he managed to yell out, "Vicky, I don't know what's happening! Call a lawyer! Please!"

Victoria stepped out of the apartment, but when she got too close to Sam, the sergeant put one hand in front of him and the other on his holster.

"Ma'am get back inside right now!" he growled menacingly.

Victoria just stood there. She didn't dare come closer, but she refused to go back inside the apartment. She just stared at Sam while the cops were waiting for the elevator to come up.

"Honey, I have no idea what's going on here. I don't know what that picture is all about. You've got to believe me! Please help me! Call a lawyer!"

As he was pleading with Victoria for help, the elevator dinged, and the doors opened. The old sergeant asked the woman who was standing in the elevator to exit the cabin, and the woman obeyed immediately. Sam could see by her eyes that she recognized him, but she didn't dare say anything. She just considered him with a fearful gaze as she scurried past, and he was sure the news of his arrest would be known across the building in a matter of hours.

As the doors were closing, all Sam could think to scream was, "Vicky, help me!"

SEVEN

Center City
Corner of Chestnut and 22nd
Monday – May 6, 2013 – 6:15 p.m.

The elevator finally arrived at the lobby after a few minutes. It had stopped twice to pick up someone who had called it. Every time, the old policeman barked at the people to step back and wait for the next one.

When they exited the cabin, he pushed Sam forward, who stumbled and almost fell. The young cop managed to catch Sam by the elbow and prop him back up. He held onto Sam's arm as they walked toward the front door.

As Sam was being escorted out, he couldn't help but notice that everyone had stopped whatever they were doing and were just staring at him. The doorman, a friendly Latino fellow everyone called Angel, looked at him with a disapproving stare, already presuming his guilt.

Sam crossed the large lobby and saw other people that he had seen daily. Everyone seemed to be gawking at him, but when Sam tried to meet their gazes, they all suddenly dropped their eyes to the floor.

Just as they were opening the front door, Sam asked, "What the hell is this about? Why are you arresting me?"

The older cop answered. "We got an anonymous tip that you were in possession of child pornography on your phone. So, we got a warrant to confiscate and search your device. Looks like we got you, you little pervert!"

"That's impossible! I didn't take that picture! I have no idea how it got on my phone… This is a huge mistake! I'm innocent!" Sam was shouting as the young cop bowed Sam's head and helped him sit down in the back of the squad car.

"Yeah. That's what they all say," the sergeant replied. "Now shut the hell up. I don't want to hear another word out of you." He put the car into gear while his colleague took a seat on the passenger's side.

As they rolled down Chestnut Street toward Old Philly, Sam just looked out the window as if in a trance. He was still trying to wrap his head around what was happening. He had no clue how that picture had ended up on his phone. His first thought was that Vanessa had felt some need for revenge after their confrontation and that this was the way she had found to punish him. But to him, it seemed like an exaggerated vengeance for such a little incident. Even if that were the case, he still couldn't understand how she would have done it.

The only thing he knew for certain was that he hadn't taken the picture himself. He thought maybe Vanessa had sent it to him, but he didn't know how she would've known his number. Sam was a very private person; he was one of the remaining few people on the planet who didn't have a Facebook account. Aside from his family and a few close friends, no one knew his cell phone number. Not even the school's administration had it, so it seemed unlikely that she could have sent it to him.

Could she have stolen his phone and planted the photo? That scenario seemed even less likely. Sam kept his phone under lock and key inside his desk when he was working and, otherwise, kept it on his person when he wasn't at school. He couldn't think of a single moment when Vanessa could have gotten her hands on his device. For a second, he contemplated the idea that she had hacked his phone remotely but quickly dismissed it. The only person he could think of that could pull off something like that was Dean, although he couldn't think of a reason why his friend would do such a thing.

As the squad car turned north on 7th Street and headed to the police headquarters, Sam tried to run down every possibility in his head again and again, but every time, he seemed to hit a brick wall. He was unable to grasp what was going on. He didn't even notice when he was taken out of the car and escorted inside. They took his fingerprints and his personal items without him being conscious of any of it. He was so lost in thought, trying to make sense of the situation, that he didn't feel himself being walked down the long hallway that led to the holding cell.

Sam snapped back to reality as he heard the metal clang of the cell door closing in front of him. As he looked around, he saw that he was standing in a large cage with a dozen other men. Most of them were sitting, but a few were standing—they all glared at him when he turned around, and some had murderous looks in their eyes. He heard the old sergeant call, "Enjoy the rest of your night, perv'! They're gonna love you in there!"

The cop walked away laughing as Sam looked for a place to sit. All the benches were occupied, so he sat down in a corner, looking at the floor in front of him, trying to make himself as small as possible.

EIGHT

Philadelphia Municipal Court
Corner of Chestnut and Broad
Wednesday – May 8, 2013 – 10:23 a.m.

Sam was sitting at the defense table next to his lawyer. Right behind him was Victoria. She had moved patients around so she could attend his hearing, but she'd left Sofia at school. There was no need for the child to be witness to this.

Sam had spent the last two days locked inside the police station. The nights had been restless, as the accommodations were far from luxurious. His mind was still attempting to comprehend what had happened and why. There was also a steady flow of men being led in and out of the holding area, and every time someone new walked in, Sam feared being attacked by the newcomer.

The morning following his arrest, he had been allowed to make a call. He called his wife on her cellphone and asked if she had found a lawyer. The only one she could think of on such short notice was the young man who was helping Sam with his mother's succession. She'd left him a voicemail telling him what had happened and asking him to come down to the police station as soon as he could.

A detective had tried to interrogate Sam right after he had placed his phone call, but Sam had refused to talk unless his lawyer was present. After thirty minutes of questioning, during which Sam declined to answer every single question, the detective had given up and returned him to his cell.

His lawyer had shown up late on Tuesday afternoon. He was a young go-getter who had been recommended by the one who was handling his mom's succession. He had talked to the officer in charge of Sam's case and relayed the information to Sam. For some reason, the police's computer crime department had received an anonymous tip that Sam was in possession of child pornography and that he'd kept some of the pictures and videos on his phone. They had gotten a warrant from a judge allowing them to search his phone and had immediately gone to his apartment to conduct a search. Upon seeing the first incriminating picture, they had seized the phone, and the police's computer technicians had gone to work digging through the device to look for more.

They had sent another patrolman to his apartment the following morning to recover his laptop, which Victoria had reluctantly given up. She had asked politely when she would get it back, as it had some files for her job and all the family photos on it. The patrolman told her he didn't know and to call the police department to get answers. Now, the cops were combing through all his possessions, trying to find more incriminating material. Sam knew there was nothing there, but after witnessing with his own eyes what was on his phone, he thought maybe something had been planted on his laptop as well. He still wasn't any closer to understanding how and why this was happening, and his lawyer didn't provide any answers to those questions either. Although he was constantly reassuring Sam and told him he was handling things, it didn't seem to Sam that he had done much of anything so far. Every time Sam asked his lawyer about his plans or his strategy, the only answer he ever got was: "Don't worry Sam, I got this."

Sam was regretting hiring this kid.

The prosecuting attorney was showing the judge the evidence that had been collected. There were only three real pieces of evidence for him to show.

The first was a transcript of the tip that the police had received. Someone had called the police and told them about the picture on the phone. This person had also stated that Sam was very good with computers and that the phone should be seized as soon as possible, lest he destroy the file for good. Whoever had called the cops had also said it wasn't the first time Sam had done this and that this was their chance to catch him red-handed.

The second piece of evidence was the picture itself. The prosecution had the picture enlarged to poster-size and put it up on an easel for the judge to see. Although Vanessa's private parts had been blacked out, her nudity was undeniable, and the picture was clearly designed to be very sexual in nature.

At first, Sam couldn't bring himself to look at the picture, merely concentrating on what the prosecuting attorney was telling the jury. His gaze was fixed on the rough, wooden desk in front of him, and his ears burned as he listened to the prosecution explain to the jury the implications of what they were witnessing. As the opposing counsel was finishing up, Sam glanced up and looked at the over-sized image that had started all of this. The bailiff was removing it from the stand, but just before it whipped out of his view, Sam thought he noticed something strange about it, perhaps something in the background. Squinting, he craned his neck to get a better look, but it was too late. However, he was suddenly distracted by the last, most poignant bit of evidence.

The final nail in Sam's coffin was the worst of them all. The prosecuting attorney turned to the judge and said, "Your honor, we would like to call Vanessa Stanford to the stand."

All heads inside the courtroom turned as Vanessa stood up and walked up to the witness stand. She was wearing sensible, black leather shoes, a knee-high navy skirt, and a white blouse underneath a red wool cardigan. Her hair was held back by a white headband, and her makeup was barely visible. Sam couldn't recall her ever dressing so conservatively. Vanessa looked like a preacher's daughter. It was clear that the prosecuting attorney had told her how to dress in order to look as innocent and vulnerable as possible, and even Sam had to admit that she'd pulled it off admirably.

After being sworn in, the opposing counsel approached the witness stand and asked, "Miss Stanford, how old are you?"

"I'm seventeen," she said in a quiet voice. Her eyes seemed to be looking in the distance, not making eye contact with anyone. She never even turned toward Sam's table when she got up to the stand.

"And can you please tell us who took that picture we just saw?"

"It was Samuel Brighton."

"Would you care to describe your relationship with Mr. Brighton?" the lawyer asked while looking at the members of the jury.

"He's my math teacher," she stated.

"What else? I'd like to remind you that you are under oath," he said, turning back to her to emphasize this point.

"We were lovers," she said, looking down at her feet.

"What?" Sam screamed, shooting up from his chair upon hearing Vanessa's statement.

There was a hush in the crowd as people inside the courtroom reacted to her last statement.

"Would you mind, for the jury's sake, elaborating on the subject? Could you describe how you became Mr. Brighton's lover?"

Vanessa took a long breath.

"It started last October. Mr. Brighton told me I needed to stay after class because he needed to talk to me."

"What happened then?"

"He said that he thought I wasn't applying myself enough in class and that my grades weren't up to par."

"Is that it?" the lawyer asked, turning once again to the jurors.

"No. He said that I had to stay after class for remedial work at least once a week if I wanted to pass."

"Were there other students during these so-called *remedial classes?*"

"Never. I was always alone."

"So, what happened then? Please describe to the jury how Mr. Brighton seduced you."

Sam was fuming. It was all completely fabricated. He had never asked her to stay after class, not even once, yet the opposing lawyer had now planted the idea in the jury's head that he had seduced and taken advantage of her.

Sam turned to his lawyer and said:

"This is bullshit! She's lying! Do *something*!"

"Don't worry" was all his lawyer replied.

Vanessa resumed her testimony.

"At first, he just complimented me, you know, saying I was pretty and stuff…"

"But then what happened?" the prosecution interjected.

"Then he started touching me, placing his hand on my thigh when he leaned in to explain something, rubbing my back, things like that."

"Did you ask him to stop?"

"At first, I tried. I told him I felt uncomfortable, but then over time, I got used to it, and I even started to like it. Eventually, we started by just kissing, but it quickly moved on to more physical stuff."

"What do you mean by *physical stuff*?"

"When we were kissing, he would touch my butt, caress my breasts, that kind of thing."

"Is that it?"

"No… After a few times, he told me he wanted more."

"What do you mean by that? I'm asking so the jury can better understand the relationship between you two."

She paused. "He said he wanted to make love to me."

Again, a hush fell over the crowd.

Sam couldn't help it. He jumped up once more from his chair and shouted:

"She's lying!" he yelled, pointing a finger at Vanessa.

The judge banged his gavel hard.

"Silence! Mr. Brighton sit down and be quiet or I'll have you removed from these proceedings."

Sam reluctantly sat down. He turned to his attorney and noticed the man had not taken down a single note on his legal pad so far.

Once the courtroom got quiet, the prosecution resumed interrogating Vanessa.

"And did you? Make love, I mean."

"Yes," was all she said, her eyes fixed on the floor in front of her.

"How did it happen, if I may ask?"

"One day in early December, he asked me to stay after class. Once everyone was gone, he shut the door, and we started making out. After a few minutes, he pulled out a condom from his pocket and asked if I was ready," she said with a tremor in her voice. "He took off my clothes, then he took off his pants. He propped me up on his desk, and we had sex," she finished, her eyes brimming with tears.

At this point, Sam couldn't believe what he was hearing. He bowed his head and closed his eyes, praying that it was all some sick prank or a nightmare he would eventually wake up from.

"Was it the only time?" the lawyer asked.

"No," she said shortly.

"How often would you meet for these little sessions?"

"Once a week, sometimes twice," she replied, her breathing becoming labored as she attempted to keep the tears at bay.

"Did you ever try to end the relationship?"

"Yes, I did, but…" Her voice trailed off.

"But what?" the lawyer pressed, as everyone leaned forward in their seats, anxious to hear her answer.

"He said that if we stopped seeing each other, then I wouldn't pass his class."

Sam couldn't help himself. He stood up and yelled, "That's a load o' crap! That never happened! She's lying!"

The judge banged his gavel again and told Sam to sit down. Sam was warned once more not to interrupt because he would be held in contempt. He sat down but trembled furiously.

Although he didn't dare turn around to see, he could hear his wife sobbing behind him.

"And what about the picture? Why did he take it?" the lawyer asked after the room had settled down.

"He kept asking me to take sexy photos and send them to him. He said he wanted some souvenirs. I didn't want to because I was scared he would show them off."

"So, what made you finally change your mind? Why did you let him take this photo of you?" the attorney asked, pointing to the spot in the courtroom where the enlarged copy of Vanessa's picture had been propped up earlier.

"Last month, I decided that I wanted to end this. I told Mr. Brighton that we couldn't see each other anymore, no matter what he said. I told him he couldn't flunk me because I wouldn't sleep with him anymore and that if he tried, then I would tell on him."

"And how did he react?"

"At first, he got mad, but eventually, he said it was okay, as long as I would let him take one picture of me so he could remember all the good moments we'd shared together. I thought it was kind of sweet, so I agreed."

"Did you ever meet up with your teacher after that?"

"No. Although I got the feeling that the door was always open if I ever wanted to hook up with him again; he never actually asked," she answered. She had regained her composure, and her answers were short and straightforward.

"One last question, Miss Stanford, if I may?" the prosecutor asked his witness as he approached her. "How do you feel about your relationship with Mr. Brighton?"

"I feel awful," she whispered, her tears starting up again. "He was my favorite teacher, and he took advantage of me!" she said, her body shaking as she cried.

The prosecuting attorney thanked her, and the judge asked Sam's lawyer if he had questions for the witness.

"We don't at this time, your honor," he replied.

"What the hell do you mean?" Sam asked. "Do something! Ask her questions. She's lying!"

"Now's not the right time, Sam" his lawyer whispered.

"What? Of course, it's the right time! What the hell are you doing? Get up there and do your… cross-examination thing!" Sam replied with an angry tone.

"Don't worry Sam. I know what I'm doing. Trust me" was all his lawyer answered.

"But you're not doing anything! What am I paying you for?"

"Sam you've got to trust me on this."

The judge looked over at Sam's table and asked his attorney:

"Do you have any questions for the witness or not?"

"We don't your honor."

Sam couldn't believe it. His lawyer hadn't done anything yet. He didn't even attempt to cross-examine Vanessa, trying to poke holes in her story. He felt like leaping over his table and running across the courtroom to shake the truth out of her.

Vanessa was asked to leave the witness stand, and Sam glared at her angrily. If his eyes could have killed, she would have dropped right where she stood.

After Vanessa's testimony, the prosecuting attorney then gave a long speech, describing Sam as a sexual predator who had taken advantage of a vulnerable student while in a position of power. Sam had to be put away for a long time for the safety of all the children of the city, he said.

Sam couldn't believe what he was hearing. He was being depicted as some sort of deviant. He turned to his attorney and said, "Are you going to do anything?"

His lawyer said. "I know what I'm doing, trust me."

"It's getting kind of hard to trust you when you won't tell me what it is you have planned. You're not even taking notes!"

His lawyer sighed and looked down at his watch. Sam couldn't believe it. Was the man bored? Was this trial keeping him from a more important engagement?

Sam's attorney waited for his turn to talk. When it was time for the defense to argue, he gave a short and unconvincing speech. He told the judge that Sam had no prior criminal record. The young man tried to convince the judge of the weakness of the evidence against his client, but to Sam, the only thing that looked weak was his attorney's arguments. The prosecution had been relentless, and it almost looked like his lawyer had given up before this thing had even started. Sam regretted hiring him.

Sam was all but convinced he would be found guilty and was already thinking about appealing the verdict. One thing was sure to him, he would have to hire someone else if it came down to that.

After the closing arguments, the judge only took a few minutes to render his verdict. He declared Sam guilty of all charges against him. Sam put his head down between his knees and broke down crying. He couldn't believe it. He heard Victoria burst into tears behind him. A few seconds later, she got up, and he saw her run out of the courtroom.

Sam's lawyer put away his files inside his briefcase and turned to Sam:

"Sorry Sam. I thought I had it."

"Had what? You didn't do *squat*!"

"Can't win them all Sam. Sorry. I'll get to work on an appeal."

"No, you won't. You're fired!"

"Suit yourself. Best of luck to you" was all he replied before heading towards to exit.

The judge gave his final instructions and set the bail at fifty thousand dollars. He banged his gavel and told the bailor to return Sam to his cell.

But Sam couldn't move his legs—he was catatonic. The bailor asked for help from a colleague, and they dragged Sam back to holding.

NINE

Center City
Corner of Chestnut and 22nd
Friday – May 10, 2013 – 3:31 p.m.

Sam had been released on bail the following morning. Victoria had emptied their savings account and posted the money for his release. He was due in court the following Tuesday for his sentencing and was given only a few days to put his affairs in order. Since he had fired his lawyer right after being found guilty, he needed to find a new one. After the way his trial had gone, he wasn't feeling very confident about the outcome of his appeal. He had tasked Victoria with finding a new attorney as quickly as possible.

As soon as his sentencing hearing was over, he would be on his way to jail, and that idea terrified Sam. He was gentle by nature and didn't have an ounce of malice in him. He had heard, like everyone else, about what happened to sex offenders in jail, and he feared he wouldn't last very long in prison.

The first gruesome task was to clean out his desk at work. He had been fired the very next morning after his arrest by the school board, receiving an email from his employer informing him of the procedures for his termination. They had issued a public statement to the press condemning his behavior, reiterating how they worked hard to ensure a safe and healthy environment for the children of the city and that what had happened was a deplorable but isolated incident.

Sam had to call the police department to ask for an escort, as he wasn't allowed to set foot inside the school without a police presence. By the time he showed up with the police officer escorting him, it was lunchtime, and all the kids were out of class. Everyone had heard about what had happened only a few days ago, and Sam could hear the whispers and almost feel the fingers pointing at him when he wasn't looking. He also had to deal with the looks from the staff as he walked up to the teach-ers' lounge.

When he stepped inside the room, it fell silent in an instant. Everyone stopped what they were doing and looked at him. Sam figured they hadn't known about his little visit. No one even dared speak to him or wave hello. It was almost as if he had never existed to these people, even though he had been a teacher here for the past two decades.

Sam pointed out his desk to the officer, and they walked to-ward it together. Sam grabbed a cardboard box and gathered his things. There wasn't much to take; Sam had been one of the teachers on the forefront of the digital revolution, and most of his professional possessions rested inside a few portable data storage keys.

As he was looking through his drawers, Sam glanced again around the room, at the people he'd once thought of as friends. Now, they all looked too afraid to meet his gaze but kept on staring at him without saying a word in support. Sam grabbed his data keys, a picture of his family that he kept taped inside his drawer, and his favorite pen. It had been a gift from Victoria and had cost a fair amount of money, so he didn't feel like leav-ing it behind for someone else to take. He took one last look around and decided that he didn't need anything else from work. The sooner he could get out of the school and away from the gawking, the better he would feel.

While he was coming down the stairs, Sam came across Dean, who was waiting for him at the bottom of the stairway. The news of Sam's presence at school had spread like wildfire. Sam asked the cop escorting him to wait for a second. He ap-proached his friend and whispered, "I'm sorry you had to see this. I don't know what the hell happened, but I'm innocent. You have to believe me."

"I believe you. You hang in there, my friend. This has to be a mistake, and I'm sure it'll be set straight soon enough. If you ever need anything, you know how to reach me—don't hesi-tate."

"Thanks, Dee." They shook hands, and Sam nodded to the cop standing a few feet behind him. It was time to leave.

As he was walking out with his police escort, he saw Donald Jackson giving an interview to a TV outlet in front of the school. Sam wondered what they were doing there, but then he understood—Principal Jackson was publicly condemning Sam on live television. He caught the last part of his speech.

"I have to admit that I'm ashamed all this took place right under my nose. The only good news that came out of all this is we caught the perpetrator before he made any other innocent victims."

Sam froze in his steps. He just stood there, dumbfounded. He couldn't believe what he was hearing, just steps away from him.

A reporter asked what the principal planned to do to prevent similar incidents from happening in the future.

"That's a very good question. The first thing we need to do is discourage people from posing such disgusting acts. This can be done by reinforcing harsher sentences for sex offenders like Samuel Brighton. Criminals such as that man shouldn't get away with a slap on the wrist. Hopefully, if the fine citizens of Pennsylvania elect my brother Davis, we could see those changes put in motion pretty quickly." Jackson paused for an instant, allowing the reporters to jot down everything he was saying. As he waited to get the press's attention, he turned his head and saw Sam watching him. Upon meeting his gaze, Jackson simply turned back to the media crowd in front of him and resumed speaking.

"The second thing we need to do is establish a good working partnership between the school board and the city's police force to implement stronger and more extensive background checks for all the city's teachers and other school employees. As we speak, we only do a background check when we first hire an employee. My brother and I believe we need to be a lot more thorough in that aspect. We want to make sure all children can learn in a safe, wholesome environment. Hopefully, we can all learn from this horrific incident as we move forward and make this city and this country a better and safer place," Jackson finished his speech and turned again toward Sam's direction, staring right back at him.

Sam tried to read his former boss's facial expression, but the man gave nothing away. It was as if Sam were a complete stranger. Jackson never even came close to defending his long-time employee; rather, the man utilized the situation to gain political traction for his brother's campaign.

Sam was disgusted by what he'd just heard. Jackson had thrown him under the bus without blinking an eye, discarding years of trust between them to gain political capital. The man's ambitions had no limit.

Sam mumbled: "You son of a bitch."

One of the reporters heard him and spun around. When he recognized Sam, the reporter ran toward him to ask him questions, only to be followed a few seconds later by all the other journalists present. Sam was bombarded with questions as microphones were shoved in his face. He looked at Jackson once more, but the man gave no discernable reaction to his presence, so he pushed through the crowd of reporters, his head low, cardboard box in his hands. Slowly, the policeman helped him navigate toward his cruiser. After putting the box in the trunk, he opened the door for Sam and let him in the back seat. They moved away from the school and headed back to his apartment.

After returning home with the few things he had picked up from work, Sam felt like crap. He left the building and just walked around aimlessly for a few hours. He stopped at his usual donut shop from pure force of habit and approached the counter. Norma was still manning the register at this hour, but when she saw him, she didn't have her usual friendly smile. Now, she looked annoyed and was just waiting for him to order, tapping a finger on the counter.

Sam asked for his typical coffee and donut. When it came time to pay, he left a large tip, hoping Norma would see it as a friendly gesture, but her facial expression didn't change. He waited by the end of the counter, and when he got his order, he left without anyone wishing him a great day.

He walked around the Schuylkill River Path for a while, finally walking back up the stairs to Chestnut Street after about thirty minutes. He checked his watch; Sofia's school was about to finish. He wasn't allowed to pick her up anymore, as he was banned from school grounds. The judge had given very clear instructions, stating that Sam wasn't allowed anywhere near children except for his daughter. Sofia's school had sent an email to the family's account asking for Victoria to be the one picking Sofia up after school or to make other arrangements. That email account was linked to both Sam and Victoria's smartphones so they could both have access to important messages from school at the same time. However, since his phone had been confiscated as evidence, along with his laptop, Victoria was the one who broke the news to Sam.

Now, Sam waited on the next corner, as close to the school as he was legally allowed, waiting for his daughter.

Suddenly, he caught sight of Sofia trudging toward him, her face downcast. She wouldn't meet his eyes. Trying to feign cheerfulness, he called out, "Hey, kiddo! How was school?"

There was no sign of a smile, and she looked to be on the verge of tears. Sam quickly strode over to her and crouched down, trying to meet her gaze.

"Sweetie, what's wrong? What happened?"

With a shuddering breath, Sofia finally looked up, her eyes brimming with tears.

"Dad… They called you…" she hesitated, taking another deep breath. "They called you 'pedo' today."

"What? Who's they?" Sam pressed gently, taking her hand. "Who said that?"

"Some of the other kids at school. They said some mean things about you. I even heard a few teachers whispering in the school yard."

Sofia fell into Sam's arms, quietly sobbing.

Sam felt like rushing over to the school yard and going berserk, but his daughter's well-being took precedence.

He tried to appear calm, but he was furious when he mulled over what his daughter had just told him. How did the children from her school even hear about this? Did an adult at Sofia's school talk out of turn, or was it a parent who had heard about it and told their child? And teachers? Didn't they know any better than to run their mouths? It broke his heart to see his normally cheerful daughter look so devastated.

Sofia broke free of her father's embrace and wiped the tears from her eyes. She looked at him, still crouching in front of her. Then, she turned around and saw some of the kids from her school pointing and giggling.

"Dad... I don't want you to pick me up after school. I'd rather go straight home and not have to wait for you."

Sam was heartbroken. His little girl was innocent, and yet, she had become a victim. He loved picking up his daughter after school and talking with her about her day as they walked across the street to their home, but he understood his daughter not wanting to spend a single second too long after class. He thought about discussing it with Victoria when she got home from work later. Maybe Sofia could go to a different school.

"Honey, it's fine. I understand. How about I give you a key and tell the doorman? From now on, you can go home all on your own after school."

He gave her a hug, and they walked home in silence. He tried holding his daughter's hand, but she would have none of it.

TEN

Center City
Corner of Chestnut and 22nd
Monday – May 13, 2013 – 7:55 a.m.

The Brighton family was sitting at the breakfast table, but no one said a word. Sam, trying to break the silence, looked at his daughter and asked, "You want to go work on your jump shot after school today, honey?"

"No," was all Sofia said, staring down at her bowl of cereal.

"Come on, sweetie… It's going to be a gorgeous afternoon. We could walk down the river to the basketball courts and shoot hoops before the sun sets. What do you say?"

"I said no!" Sofia replied in an annoyed tone.

"Why not?" Sam pressed.

"Let it go, Sam," Victoria butted in.

Sofia pushed her bowl away and got up without saying another word. She headed to her room and slammed the door shut.

"You need to give her some space, Sam. It's been a rough couple of days for her," Victoria said to her husband, picking up her daughter's breakfast and heading to the kitchen.

"I know that. But spending all her free time locked inside her room isn't going to help," he replied as he got up and cleared the rest of the table.

"Maybe, but that's her choice. She didn't ask to be put through all of this, you know."

"And you think I did?" Sam snapped back. How could his wife even hint that all of this was somehow his fault?

"Don't you bark at me, Sam!" Victoria growled right back. "We've all been through hell because of what happened, and none of it is our fault!"

Reporters had been hanging around building for a few days, and some of them had even managed to bother Victoria at work. The constant pestering since the story of his conviction had broken out was affecting every aspect of her life, and it was putting a strain on their relationship. Sofia, too, had been the recipient of constant mockery at school and had been shunned by all her friends.

"Well, it's not my goddamn fault either!" Sam replied swiftly, raising his voice a little louder.

It wasn't the first time they had argued over what had happened. Sam had tried to explain over and over how all of it was just one enormous setup. Victoria did her best to understand and forgive, but what she had witnessed in court couldn't be erased from her memory. No matter how often Sam attempted to convince her of his innocence, she just couldn't get over what she had seen and heard.

"Vicky, I keep telling you, I don't know what happened. You have to believe me!"

"I want to Sam. You have no idea how much I want to believe you," she trembled out as she began crying.

"But you don't, right?" Sam asked angrily.

Just then, Sofia burst out of her room and shouted at both her parents, "Will you two stop fighting? I can't take it anymore!" She started crying as she screamed at them, then she slammed the door back shut.

"You see what you just did?" Victoria asked, pointing at her daughter's bedroom door.

"What *I* did? So, I guess this is my fault, too, right?!" Sam shouted.

Victoria didn't bother answering her husband. She grabbed her keys and went to her daughter's room.

"Come on, sweetie. I'll walk you to school," she called, trying to regain her composure.

They both walked past Sam, who was still standing by the dinner table, dishes in his hands, breathing hard and trying to control his anger.

"Sofia, go call the elevator. I'll be there in a second," her mom told her, before closing the hallway door so she could be alone with Sam.

"I think you should find another place to stay for tonight," Victoria said. She stared at him for a few moments before turning around and walking out of the apartment.

Center City
Corner of Chestnut and 22nd
Monday – May 13, 2013 – 12:57 p.m.

The apartment was eerily silent. Victoria had gone to work after seeing Sofia to school.

Now, Sam was just standing alone in his living room, still wearing his pajamas because he had nowhere to go and nothing to do. He looked around his place with tears in his eyes. He hadn't shaved in days, so he now had the makings of a full beard. Looking at himself in the hallway mirror, he couldn't believe the mess he had become. His life had fallen apart. He'd lost his job. But even worse, his family was being torn to shreds. He still couldn't understand what had happened or why, and every time he tried to make sense of it, his mind went blank.

As he stared out the window, he saw that the kids at school were outside during their lunch break; it only took an instant for him to spot Sofia. Normally, she would have been playing basketball with her friends or just running around the yard with a big smile on her face. Now, Sam saw his little girl standing by herself in a corner, just watching the other kids playing. The other children seemed to make a conscious effort to avoid her, and even the teachers monitoring outside stayed away from her. Sofia had become an outcast, and it wasn't even her fault. She had done nothing to deserve this.

Watching Sofia sitting alone in the school yard's corner, Sam clenched his fists. What had happened to him? To his life? A couple of days earlier, it was the comfortable, simple life he'd always known. And then…

"Gone," he whispered. His hands were shaking now. Sam couldn't believe how messed up all of this was. He'd been thrown away by the justice system, his coworkers, his friends, and now, his own wife had asked him to move out. He didn't have anyone anymore.

Then, a thought slowly surfaced in his mind—*I'm the only person who can make this right, now.* He realized that if anything was going to get better, *he* would have to do something about it. He sat down on the couch and dropped his head in his hands, a plan forming in his mind. Raising his eyes to look out the window at the clouds drifted across the clear spring sky, he knew what he had to do. Sam would *not* let his family down. He took one last look around the apartment and stood up, a feeling of purpose coursing through him.

Sam walked around his home, gathering everything he would need, and put it all in an old backpack. He left a post-it note on the fridge that simply said, *"I'll make it right. I'll see you soon. Love you."* His wife and daughter wouldn't understand what he meant and would obviously be worried about him, but he was doing it for them. There was no turning back now. These people, whoever they were, had screwed up his family's life, and he would make things whole again—even if it was the last thing he did.

Taking one last look at the family picture in the hallway, Sam turned around and headed out the door.

TWELVE

Center City
Corner of Chestnut and 22nd
Monday – May 13, 2013 – 1:12 p.m.

As his plan was taking shape, Sam made a mental list of everything he would need to ensure its success. He had a lot of errands to run and only a few hours before the sun would go down and the shops would close. Fortunately for him, not owning a car meant that he walked around the city quite a bit, and he was very familiar with his surroundings. He knew from memory that all the places he would need to go were on Chestnut Street or just nearby. He would most likely be able to knock off his entire list before the day was done.

But before heading toward the center of the city, Sam went across the river. His first stop was crucial. He crossed Market Street and headed to the train station. He always found the massive building quite impressive, with its huge columned porte-cochères on the west façade. Every time Sam went inside that station, he was awestruck. When he reached the main hall, he stopped and took a minute to look at his surroundings. He stared at the massive coffer ceiling, with its red and gold trimming and huge marble columns. This place could almost be a temple if it weren't for the constant announcements on the intercom system and the throngs of people milling about twenty-four hours a day. His journey to redemption would begin right here, right now.

The first thing he did was hit the ATM machine. He had left his wallet at home and had only brought three items with him: his debit card, credit card, and access card for his building. The access card was blank and had no inscriptions on it or any discernable aspect that would allow someone to identify its use.

He would need it in case he ever wanted to walk back into his building.

He withdrew as much money as possible from his bank account and his credit card. Victoria probably wouldn't even notice, as he was the one in charge of the finances in his household. Sam thought it unlikely that someone was watching his bank accounts and credit cards, but he didn't want to take any unnecessary risks, so he would pay for everything in cash whenever possible.

He now had almost two thousand dollars on him. Sam stowed everything away in his pocket; he wanted to be sure that no one else would find items with his name on them and somehow retrace his steps, so he destroyed both his bank cards and tossed them inside the waste disposal attached to the ATM. This was the reason he had left his wallet at home, too. Now, he had no piece of identification on him, nothing that could be traced back to Samuel Brighton.

Feeling all this money on him, Sam felt the need to find a more secure way to keep it on his person. Walking around a large city where crime occurred on a regular basis with a stack of bills in his pockets didn't make much sense.

He crossed the great hall and headed inside a drugstore. He asked an employee where all the traveling accessories were, and the young man told him which aisle to head to. After searching for a few minutes, he found what he was looking for. Being inside a very busy train station with thousands of travelers heading in and out daily, the drugstore had an extensive array of travel accessories. Sam grabbed a money belt from one of the racks and went to the register. After paying for his item, he looked around, searching for a sign that would show him where the nearest restroom was.

When he got to the restroom, Sam stepped inside a stall and opened the box with his new money belt. After lifting his shirt and strapping the belt on, he put away all his money and his access card in the various pockets. He pulled his shirt back on and stepped out. Although it felt strange on his body, when he looked in the mirror, he noticed that even though he knew he was wearing the belt under his shirt, he could barely distinguish its presence. He figured that people who didn't know to look for it wouldn't notice at all and felt safer now.

After discarding the belt's packaging and receipt in the trash bin, Sam walked out of the restroom. He had one last stop to make. He went all the way across the station to the Southeastern Pennsylvania Transportation Authority counter. There, he purchased a monthly travel card that would allow him to take the bus or ride the subway if he ever needed to get from one point of the city to another fast.

As he was heading toward the exit, Sam looked at one of the huge clocks on the wall of the main hall. It had only taken him thirty minutes to get everything he needed from the train station. As he was crossing the hall, Sam stopped to look at the massive Hancock sculpture, depicting the archangel Michael lifting the body of a dead soldier from the flames of war. The World War II memorial was surrounded by the names of all the old railroad employees who had been killed in the war.

Looking at the hundreds of names inscribed on the marble base of the statue, Sam's resolve only grew stronger. He reflected on the sacrifice that the brave men and women in service had made for their country, and his thoughts shifted to the many homeless veterans he saw roaming the streets as he walked around the city—another idea struck him as he headed out the door.

THIRTEEN

Center City
Corner of Chestnut and 16th
Monday – May 13, 2013 – 1:57 p.m.

As Sam was walking east to keep shopping for all the supplies, he would need in his attempt to clear his name, he had to pass his building. He couldn't help but stop and look up at the windows on the floor where his condo was situated. A part of him wanted to head back inside, crawl into bed, and wait to wake up from this nightmare. But the harsh reality was that he wasn't dreaming, and his life was going down the crapper. He had a mission to complete if he ever hoped to get back to his normal life—now was not the time to be sentimental.

Sam stopped on the corner of 18th Street and strode inside the offices of the Philadelphia Teachers' Union. He asked to see the advisor who had been working on his case. When he sat down with the man, Sam learned that there had been no new developments. The union had tried to get the school board to change their minds and suspend him without pay instead of firing him, but he explained that the public outcry was too big for the school board to back down. The media coverage of his situation had been unexpectedly large, and the administrators didn't want to look too lenient in the public eye. His union had tried to appeal the decision, but since his trial had taken place in a matter of days and he had quickly been found guilty, there wasn't much that could be done now.

Sam's advisor suggested that he appeal his verdict. If the decision was reversed, he could call back and they would try to get him his job back. For now, there wasn't anything they could do. Sam thanked the man for his efforts and told him he would take his advice under consideration. The advisor shook Sam's hand and apologized for not being able to do more. He wished Sam luck and escorted him out. Although he had been professional, Sam felt like the man was almost in a hurry to get him out of the building, lest they be seen together.

Sam started walking again, heading for his second stop of the day. As he crossed Broad Street, he passed one of the many entrances to the metro station located beneath City Hall. He couldn't help but reminisce about the hundreds of times he had gone down those staircases on his way to work, where he thought he was well respected and appreciated. Now, he was a pariah. People he had considered peers had shunned him and pretended he'd never existed. He would show them, and everyone else, how sadly mistaken they were. He was not a man to be underestimated.

Arriving on the corner of 13th, he went inside the large Army surplus store. The first floor was lined with all sorts of equipment, mostly used for camping. Sam had visited the store once before because Victoria had wanted to take Sofia camping for a weekend near Valley Forge. At the time, Sam didn't feel like splurging for brand new camping equipment that might only be used once, so he'd purchased a used tent and an inflatable mattress to limit the cost of the expedition. His instincts had been right on the money—Sofia was very much like her old man and hated being outside, except to play sports. Just like Sam, she was a city girl and was more at ease in the creature comforts of home than out in the woods. Sam had gone to the store again after their trip to sell back the camping equipment and salvage as much money as possible. This time, he wasn't going camping.

He climbed up the stairs to the second floor. The entire space was lined with row after row of used clothing, much of it surplus military clothing. Sam started searching through the aisles, looking for the items he needed. At the end of the second aisle was a rack of desert camo pants. It had the newer digital camouflage pattern armies around the world now favored. Sam found his size and looked the pants over. They were pretty worn but had no discernible holes in them, and they had a large cargo pocket on each side. Sam didn't know if he would need so much storage space, but he figured it was better to have it and not need it than the other way around. He put the pants on his shoulder and kept browsing.

A bit further, he found his second item. It was an old army jacket with the same desert camouflage pattern. Sam tried it on over his t-shirt, and although it was a bit too large for him, he took it anyway.

At the end of the row were racks of boots of all shapes and sizes. It took over ten minutes for Sam to find what he wanted. He found a pair a size eleven tan boots. Sam wore size ten shoes, but it had been very hard to find a pair of the right style and color; he figured it wouldn't matter much. He didn't even bother trying them on and told himself that if they felt too big, he could always wear two pairs of socks.

On the opposite wall, Sam saw dozens of shelves with hats and caps. He found a boonie hat with the same camo pattern he was going for. It had a military unit symbol on the side, but he had no idea what it meant. Hopefully, he would never come across someone who might recognize it and engage him in conversation.

Sam looked at the price tags of all the items he had picked out and calculated it would cost him just under two hundred dollars. He went inside one of the fitting rooms, and after making sure that everything fit, he took out just enough money from his belt for his items. It didn't seem like a good idea to let everyone at the register see he was carrying cash strapped to his waist. You never knew who might see it and decide that it would be a good idea to relieve Sam of it all.

He went back downstairs to pay for all he had picked out. When the cashier asked him if he needed a bag, he declined and told her he would put everything away in his own backpack. He stuffed it all in and put his change in his pockets, thanked the cashier politely, and stepped out onto the street.

FOURTEEN

Downtown Philly
Corner of Chestnut and 13th
Monday – May 13, 2013 – 2:31 p.m.

Just a few doors down from the Army surplus store was Sam's next destination. As he walked into the House of Beauty, he felt suddenly very out of place. The hair shop was packed with all sorts of wigs and extensions, but the clientele was exclusively comprised of women, all of them African-American. As they saw the middle-aged white male walk in, with his bushy beard and tired eyes, they all froze. No one seemed to be able to understand just what the heck he was doing there.

The heavyset woman behind the counter had a very mean look about her, and she kept eyeing Sam as he perused the store, following him around with an icy stare as if she thought he was doing something suspicious. She was filing her nails and chewing loudly on a piece of gum as she waited for the next customer to walk up to the cash register, but she remained focused on Sam.

Sam felt the woman's stare on the back of his head and decided it wouldn't help him to linger here for too long. The media coverage of his arrest and the debacle at the school when he'd gone to pick up his things had given him a lot of unwanted notoriety. Even though he'd let his beard grow in since last week, people still stared at him when they crossed his path. They knew he was someone they'd seen before but weren't able to pinpoint exactly where or when they had. If Sam hung around this place for too long, the woman watching him from across the room might eventually put two and two together and recognize him. Sam had no wish for that to happen, so he scanned through the inventory faster.

He settled for a wig of medium-length black hair. The hair looked almost like it could belong on a woman of Asian or Hispanic descent, but Sam didn't feel like being picky right now. The sooner he could get out of this place, the better he would feel. He put the wig on his head to assess the general fit, and though it was a bit tight, he decided it would have to do.

He went up to the register and paid for his item. The cashier didn't say a single word to him; she just pointed at the amount on the screen and held out her hand. The wig cost forty-five dollars, so Sam took out fifty and told the woman to keep the change. Just like the previous week at the donut shop, he had hoped that leaving a large tip would land him in the woman's good graces. Unfortunately, it didn't seem to work this time either. He told himself to stop being so generous, as it didn't seem to help and only made him burn through his money faster. Sam thanked her, and the woman mumbled a few syllables in return. He walked out of the store, took in his surroundings, and located his next stop.

FIFTEEN

Downtown Philly
Corner of Market and 10th
Monday – May 13, 2013 – 2:42 p.m.

Before going out to get the countless other items on his list, Sam wanted to check on his progress. He needed to get a general idea of what he was trying to accomplish to make sure that everything worked according to plan; otherwise, the entire endeavor would just be a huge waste of time and money.

He headed north onto Market Street and turned right. A few blocks later, he was standing outside the large shopping mall that occupied the entire block. The main occupant was a K-Mart superstore. Before going up the escalator, Sam tried to decide if there was anything here, he would need to purchase. For the moment, he couldn't think of anything, so he went up to the second floor. Reading the signs, he located the restrooms at the very end of the store and went inside the men's room. He walked all the way down, and after making sure the last stall was empty, he stepped in.

Once inside, he started undressing. Sitting on the toilet, he took off his pants, hung them up on the hook on the door, and removed his shoes, which he placed at the bottom of his pack. Sam put on the Army pants, then the boots. He laced them up, and although they were a size too large, they still felt very comfortable. Sam put on the jacket he'd bought, and after buttoning it up, he removed his Phillies cap, replacing it with his new wig and boonie hat. He tried to adjust his headgear as best he could, but without a mirror, it wasn't easy. When he felt like everything was in the right place, he put his old pants and cap inside his backpack and stepped out of the stall.

As he stood in front of the mirror, he was amazed at the sight—the man staring back at him didn't look at all like Sam. Where he normally shaved daily, he now had a full beard, with hints of gray on the chin. He'd kept his auburn hair very short for the past few years in a futile attempt to mask his bourgeoning baldness, but now, he had shoulder-length black hair. As he was standing there, he didn't see Samuel Brighton anymore.

In front of him was one of the hundreds of disenfranchised veterans who had fought for their country in the middle east and now roamed the city. Sam needed to be an entirely new person for what he was trying to accomplish. Not only did he want to move about the city hidden from public scrutiny, but if what he was planning worked out, the authorities would soon look for him—so he needed to disappear. He was very satisfied with the results of his outfit; he took one last look in the mirror and whispered, "Good."

Pleased, he went back inside the stall and removed everything he'd just put on, placing all the items in his backpack. He put on his jeans, sneakers, and Phillies cap again and took out a few hundred dollars more from his money belt. His next stop would be the most expensive of all. As he walked out of the store, his eyes caught a glimpse of the rack of impulse items lined up near the cash register.

Using a few dollar bills and some loose change he had left on him from what he'd spent so far, he bought four granola bars. He hadn't eaten all day since breakfast, and his stomach was growling. His appetite had pretty much vanished over the past few days, and he was already starting to lose weight. But now, all this walking around seemed to have brought back some of his appetite. He paid for his food and walked out onto Market Street.

SIXTEEN

Downtown Philly
Corner of Chestnut and 8th
Monday – May 13, 2013 – 2:57 p.m.

As Sam walked through Old Philly, he tried to remember where the shop he was looking for was located.

One of the perks of his now-former job was that he'd had free periods from time to time in his schedule. Being so close to a metro station, Sam could finish the class he was teaching and be downtown or in Old Philly within fifteen minutes. He spent his free periods out of school whenever possible. Just being outside could recharge his batteries and give him the energy needed to go through the rest of his day. He loved walking around Old Philly, often with a large coffee in his hands, creamed and sweetened just the way he liked it, enjoying the lush greenery and general ambiance of the neighborhood.

Just a few streets away were a couple of blocks known as Jeweler's Row. These blocks were populated by dozens of jewelry shops, antique stores, and pawn shops. Sam had spent quite a large amount of time over the past few years going inside various shops just looking at merchandise, sometimes searching for a gift for Victoria or Sophia or just a little gadget for himself.

He knew from memory that there was a highly specialized pawnshop in this area, but he had forgotten the exact spot. It took him about twenty minutes to find the place he was looking for, on the corner of 8th and Chestnut. As he walked in, a small chime rang, and he waited for someone to greet him at the counter. An employee stepped out from the backroom; Sam told him about the two very specific items he was looking for. The first was a very particular pair of eyeglasses. The employee showed him a few pairs from a display case, and Sam chose some with thick, black frames. As he tried them on, they looked like the cheap glasses nerds wore in movies; it was exactly the look he wanted. He then asked the young clerk about his second item.

"I need to see some ID first, sir," the clerk told him.

"I don't have any on me, sorry."

"Then I can't, sir. It's against the law," he said firmly.

"I don't care, son. I'll pay cash, so there won't be any traces," Sam said, trying to convince the young man.

"Even if you did, sir, I'm not permitted by law," the young man replied, looking nervous. Maybe he thought Sam was an undercover cop attempting to entrap him.

"There's an extra three hundred bucks in it, just for you. You can claim it as stolen," Sam muttered, showing him a wad of cash.

The young man hesitated, and after a few seconds, he scurried into the backroom to retrieve the key to a large wooden display case, showing Sam the selection in front of him. Sam pointed to the one he wanted.

"Are you sure about this? If the cops find you with this, you'll be in big trouble," the clerk warned.

"I'm already in trouble, son," Sam replied, as he felt the item in his hand. He set it down next to the register and inquired about the price.

"It'll be one hundred and fifty, sir. Plus, you know…"

"Yeah, I know," Sam said as he counted four hundred and fifty dollars and handed the cash over.

The young man rang up the amount on the cash register. He put the money into the register, but his commission went inside his own pocket.

The clerk looked around and said, "Now, please exit the store before someone walks in on us. If the cops catch you, you were never here. Understand?"

"Don't worry, I got you," Sam replied and quickly walked out.

When he stepped outside, he headed west on Chestnut. He only had one last stop to make to clear his list, and he was getting tired. He took out a granola bar from his backpack and started eating as he walked.

SEVENTEEN

Center City
Corner of Chestnut and 16th
Monday – May 13, 2013 – 3:11 p.m.

Sam took a second to rest before arriving at what he thought would be his last stop. Although he only had a few purchases left, he realized that this would be the easiest part of his day. What was waiting for him after this last errand would prove to be much more difficult.

Although he'd walked past it at the beginning of his run, he chose to stop here last because what he needed to purchase depended on what he was able to gather beforehand.

While he was walking up Chestnut, he started paying more attention to the homeless men and women around him. His plan counted on the fact that he could pass as one of them and just blend into the general landscape of the city, becoming one of the many faceless humans other folks ignored on their way to work. But if he wanted to blend in, he first had to see how they went about so he wouldn't stand out.

The first thing he noticed was that pretty much all of them held an empty coffee or soda cup in the hopes that some gentle soul would be generous enough to help them out with a little spare change. He figured he would have to go through a garbage bin or two to find one. While Sam wasn't germophobic, the thought of rummaging through trash and holding onto a dirty cup all day made his stomach turn—but he knew he would just have to suck it up.

He stepped into the RadioShack on the corner of Chestnut and 16th and went right to the mobile phone section. If they didn't have what he was looking for, he knew there was a

Staples only a few blocks over and even a few drugstores that might have what he needed, but his best bet was to start here.

He started by picking up a Bluetooth earpiece. There were a lot of them, so he chose the cheapest one on display. He didn't plan on wearing it all day, so comfort and battery life weren't issues. He then picked up a prepaid smartphone. Looking at it, he saw that it was a late model, two or three years old, like all the other prepaid smartphones on display.

He checked the back of the box to make sure it had all the features he was looking for. It wasn't a high-performance machine, but it would get the job done. He also grabbed two charging sticks after making sure they were compatible with his new phone. The last item he put in his basket was a USB female-to-female adapter so he could connect his various devices to each other without using a computer to link them.

The police had confiscated his phone upon his arrest, along with his laptop, but now, he would have the ability to go online and, more importantly, call and text people with complete anonymity. Even though he still had no clue who was behind all this, they might have the capabilities to monitor his home and phone. This way, he could stay in touch with the world without fear of getting caught.

It was at that precise moment that Sam realized there had been something missing from his list. He cursed himself for not thinking about it earlier but was glad that the realization had come to him now and not when he would be in desperate need of it. The smartphone he was purchasing had a limited number of minutes and data usage already programmed into it, so he would need a credit card to purchase more if he ran out. Sam had no intention of returning here on a regular basis to buy a new phone every time it ran out since that would be a huge waste of time and money, so he would need to refill its usage plan from time to time.

The problem was that Sam had destroyed his credit card earlier today at the train station. He started to panic but quickly regained his composure, thinking about his options. He knew his credit card's number by heart but didn't want to use it in case someone was tracking him through his financial account. The same logic eliminated Victoria's card. Suddenly, an idea came to him, and he walked out of the store and looked around.

After a few seconds of reflection, he remembered there was a drugstore just a few blocks from where he was standing. Sam walked over to it and went inside. He approached the cash register, where he saw a display case full of gift cards. Sam wasn't looking for gift cards, but after turning the case around a few degrees, he saw what he needed—he grabbed four prepaid Visa cards. Each card was redeemable for an amount of fifty dollars. Sam figured that if he ever needed more than two hundred dollars' worth of data usage, he would already be in a heap of trouble, and more data probably wouldn't be the solution to his predicament.

He crossed the street and went into Starbuck's, where he snuck into the bathroom, locked the door behind him, and proceeded to change once more.

Sam took off his jeans and sneakers and replaced them with the cargo pants and boots he'd bought. He then put on the jacket, wig, and boonie hat. The final touch was putting on the thick, black eyeglasses he'd bought a few hours earlier. Sam kept the rest of his gear inside his backpack but made sure that everything was packed in the right order, with the most important items on top of the pile for faster access.

He tore open the smartphone's box, turned it on, then threw the box in the garbage bin. After a few minutes, the phone was active. Using the coffee shop's Wi-Fi network, Sam created a phony email account and user profile so he could access the various apps on the phone. When he was sure everything was working as it should, he powered the phone down to conserve battery life and put it away in his pants' pocket before leaving the bathroom.

Sam drew a lot of attention and realized that no one had seen a bum walk into the coffee shop, yet there was one walking out. Sam smiled and waved at the pretty redhead behind the counter then went outside. Now that the easy part was over, the difficult one would begin—Sam needed to find a place to spend the night.

EIGHTEEN

Center City
Schuylkill River Path, underneath Market Street
Monday – May 13, 2013 – 5:45 p.m.

As the sun was going down, Sam was on his quest to find a suitable place to spend the night.

At first, he thought about checking into a cheap motel. There were a few of them across the river, near the train station and around University City. But upon reflection, he decided to disregard that idea; checking into a hotel or motel meant that he had to show his face at the counter. Most of the hotels he knew asked for a piece of identification and a credit card so they could charge the guests for amenities that weren't included in the original payment. In accordance with his plan, Sam didn't have any form of identification on him now. If the authorities were ever to find him, they wouldn't be able to positively ID him instantly, and that might just give him a little wiggle room.

But even if he'd somehow managed to get his hands on a counterfeit piece of identification, there was still the problem of payment. The employee at the front desk was sure to raise an eyebrow upon seeing a fellow who looked down on his luck pull out a wad of cash to pay for a hotel room, no matter how cheap it was. Sam wanted to disappear, so that meant leaving as little trace of his presence as possible. He also wanted to limit his spending—he only had a few hundred dollars left in his money belt, and if he spent it all on a place to sleep, he'd be out of cash within a few days.

He then thought about trying to find a place to stay at one of the homeless shelters around the city, but again, he came up with the same problem: people would remember seeing his face, even if he was in disguise. The volunteers at the shelter might want to engage him in conversation, trying to be as help-ful as possible in the hopes of giving the homeless men they graciously hosted every night a chance for a better life. Sam was looking to be invisible, so he had to find a way to spend the night as far away from other human beings as possible.

He wandered around the neighborhood, running through his options. His stomach was still growling, and he was down to his last granola bar. As he approached the bridge that spanned across the river, he saw the train station a few blocks away; there were a dozen restaurants inside the main hall that called out to him. He crossed the bridge and started heading toward the station.

As he came close to it, Sam was standing on the corner of 30th and Market, waiting for the light to change so he could cross over. When the "Walk" sign started flashing, Sam froze in his tracks. He saw two Amtrak Police SUVs parked in front of the building. Looking around, he spotted no less than ten Amtrak Police officers patrolling the grounds around the sta-tion. He figured there had to be at least as many of them inside. He was in the middle of the end-of-the-day rush hour, and the SEPTA metro line and Amtrak trains that ran underneath the station would be packed with travelers, so it was entirely logical to have a large police presence at this hour.

Not wanting to attract any unwanted attention, Sam turned away and crossed the bridge on Market, heading back east to-ward the city. When he was halfway across, he stopped and looked at the river running underneath him. He spotted the Schuylkill River Path about a hundred feet from where he was standing. The path ran along the river for miles in each direc-tion; he'd used it hundreds of times when he'd gone out jogging, like many other residents of the area. It was one of the most popular spots in Center City.

He remembered there were benches all along the path, and he'd noticed when he sometimes went out for a jog very early in the morning that most of those benches were occupied by homeless men sleeping. He figured that since the weather was nice and warm and it didn't look like it would rain anytime soon, he might as well do like his comrades and find a nice bench to crash on for the night.

As he descended the stairway and walked along the bike path, looking for a bench, a cautious thought suddenly flashed through his mind. Sleeping on a bench would be his fall-back plan, but Sam didn't know the dynamics of homeless life at night. Did some of them claim specific benches as their own? Was there a pecking order? Were they territorial by nature? Would they try and jump the new guy and go through his stuff when he was asleep? He had no answers to these questions, and his stress level was growing as nightfall approached. But he had another idea, and hopefully, it would work out.

The Chestnut Street Bridge was one of the two bridges built at the end of the nineteenth century to link Center City and West Philadelphia. It spanned over the Schuylkill River with a set of arches that had been widened when it had been rebuilt in the fifties, but the original stone arches that were set on firm ground remained untouched. On the eastern bank of the river, the bridge was supported by three massive arches. The first one passed over the bike path that followed the river for miles in each direction. The second arch was over a train track that ran alongside as well, used by merchandise trains daily. The final arch merged into the small hill that led up to street level. This final arch was not easily accessible, as there was a fence running alongside the train track to keep people away, but if you managed to bypass that obstacle, you could use the arch as cover. The small alcove created by the stone arch was small and dark, but still large enough to fit a man comfortably. Sam had always wondered through the years, as he passed underneath the bridge on his runs if anyone used it as shelter. It would make sense for someone to figure out a way in to stay warm and dry. He was about to find out.

He approached the fence and noticed signs of human activity in the vicinity of the alcove. There was an old mattress ripped to shreds lying right outside the entrance and trash littered everywhere. He would have to tread carefully. Upon closer inspection, he saw that years of neglect had rendered the fence pretty much useless, as it was rusty and torn open in multiple places. It wouldn't take much effort to get through it and walk across the train track.

Sam couldn't fathom the idea that no one before him had thought to use that space, so he advanced very slowly. He waited for a few minutes, hoping for a break in the foot traffic along the river path. It wouldn't do him any good for folks to see him cross the fence and head up the slope. After a little while, he had a few seconds where there wasn't anyone in his vicinity, so he quickly went to the fence and found a small corner that had been ripped loose. He bent down and crawled through the tiny hole as fast as he could and ran up to the alcove's entrance, but he paused before going in further.

When he got close, he realized it was extremely dark inside the alcove, and he still wasn't sure if anyone was living inside. The place was large enough to offer shelter for one person, two at the most, and he had no intention of having a roommate.

Sam took out his phone and powered it up. Once it was up and running, he used its flashlight to light his path inside and began searching for signs of occupancy. If he saw anything that might indicate someone had used the space recently, he would move on. There was still about an hour of daylight left, and the river path was illuminated, so he was in no rush. The last thing he needed was to pick a fight with someone over a piece of real estate.

Scanning around, he saw some trash lying about and quite a bit of rubble. The concrete underneath Chestnut had started to pull away. Hopefully, he wouldn't be hit on the head with a rock as a truck went over the bridge.

He'd expected to see a sleeping bag, some plastic bags, empty food containers, or any other signs that someone had stayed there. There were a few pieces of trash, but otherwise, the space looked unoccupied. He crept to the very end of the cave to check things out. The place was pitch black, so the further he advanced, the less he saw. When he was sure it was empty and felt confident he would be alone, he settled in.

He had just found his hideout. Here, he could sleep while shielded from the elements. As summer was fast approaching, the late afternoon thunderstorms were getting more and more frequent. If there was a downpour, at least here he could keep dry. But the main attraction for him was the total darkness. As Sam moved in further, he became invisible to the outside world. Even if another person walked in, they wouldn't be able to spot him unless they had a flashlight. It wasn't a five-star hotel, but for Sam, it was perfect. He was now safe and away from prying eyes.

After hiding his backpack underneath a pile of concrete rubble, he settled down with his back against the wall created by the stone arch. He tried to get as comfortable as possible, but it was far from easy. There was cracked rubble everywhere, so lying down to sleep would be impossible without some sort of mattress. He thought about retrieving the one he'd seen lying outside, but since it was ripped up in pieces and most likely soaking wet from rainfall or God knows what else, he decided against it. Sam tried stretching out his legs, but as the slope in the ground in front of him was going up, not down, he was unable to sit this way. Sam sat down with his knees folded underneath him; he would have to try to sleep sitting up.

Sam wasn't the outdoors type, to say the least. He had trouble sleeping in a tent, lying down on an inflatable mattress. The only time his family had gone camping, he'd had to take sleeping pills to help him get through the night. Now, he was attempting to sleep in a seated position underneath a dilapidated bridge—if his wife could have seen him, she would have been impressed.

The sudden thought of his family brought a knot to his stomach, and he sighed and leaned his head back against the stone. Tonight, he wouldn't come home, and his wife and child wouldn't know where he was or what he was doing. It broke his heart to think of Victoria worrying through the night, wondering what was happening to him, but he kept telling himself it was for the best. He needed to shield his family from himself as much as possible. The worst part of it was that he was just two blocks away from them, but they would never know it.

He could see it was getting darker outside, so Sam told himself that he needed to try and get some rest. Today had been exhausting. The physical aspect of walking around the city all day wasn't bothering him, but the stress of his situation was getting to him. He felt like he had hundreds of pounds of weight on his shoulders. Even though he had a general plan in his head, he wasn't a hundred percent sure on how it would all play out, so he kept telling himself to get some rest.

It proved to be difficult. His mind was churning at incredible speed, his thoughts going from his family to his day, to his all-important plan. Even though his brain was still racing, Sam forced himself to rest. He lowered the brim of his boonie hat down to shield his eyes from the light outside his little cave, and sat motionless, with his eyes shut. He was convinced that sleep would eventually come.

Center City
Underneath the Chestnut Street Bridge
Tuesday – May 14, 2013 – 7:11 a.m.

Sam woke abruptly, surrounded by thunderous noise. It took him a few seconds to get his bearings and remember where he was. The noise that had shaken him out of his sleep was the rumble of a merchandise train passing by just a few feet away from him. Sam felt the stone arch he was leaning against vibrate and hoped that nothing would detach from the road above and crush him.

Sam didn't know exactly how long he'd been asleep, but he knew for certain it hadn't been more than an hour. He remembered seeing the first rays of sunshine creeping in the cave's entrance.

Sam had spent most of the night thinking about his family, trying to make sense of how he'd gotten here, and going over every part of his plan to get his name cleared. The deafening sounds of cars and trucks passing over his head made his ears hurt. The incessant buzzing of city noise, with its tire screeches and cabs honking, had made it impossible for him to sleep. He'd fought the urge to check the time on his phone to conserve as much battery power as possible. He didn't know exactly when he would be able to plug it in, or where for that matter, so he'd kept it powered down for the entire night.

Stretching painfully, he knew he must have fallen asleep out of pure exhaustion. Pulling out his phone, he turned it on to get an idea of the time. He knew from the light streaming into his hideout it was still early in the morning, but he had a lot to do today, and knowing the exact time would help him set things in motion.

His first thought after turning on the phone was to check if he still had his things. He got up painstakingly and tried to stretch a bit more. He walked a few feet and uncovered his backpack; so far, everything seemed to be just as he'd left it, but not wanting to take any chances, he opened his backpack and went through his inventory—everything was there. Once more, his stomach growled, and he realized he'd scarfed down his last granola bar the previous evening. He would just have to do without food for now and find a way to get some grub later. Right now, it was time to get moving.

As he was gathering his stuff, he felt some previously unknown admiration for the homeless people that populated the city. He had a cushy life, and he knew it. His condo had soundproof windows and central air, so he wasn't used to the sounds of the city at night anymore. He slept on a soft mattress and had never gone hungry for more than a few hours. He admired the men and women who put up with such horrid living conditions daily. Sam wasn't sure if he was cut out for this lifestyle or just how long he would last in the elements, but he didn't have much of a choice—so he resigned himself to put up with it as long as he could.

Checking the time on his phone, an idea popped in his head. It was a risky play, but somehow, he just couldn't let the opportunity pass.

Sam climbed up to his hideout's entrance and waited for a break in the pedestrian traffic. There weren't many people around at this hour, except for the occasional jogger or dog walker. When he saw an opening, he stepped out of the shadows, crossed beneath the fence, and walked up the ramp back onto Chestnut. As he moved, all his joints and muscles ached like crazy. His body wasn't used to staying so long in such an uncomfortable position. Hopefully, walking around would help get rid of the stiffness.

He went down the street and sat down at a bus stop on the corner of 24th, pulling the brim of his cap low to hide his eyes as much as he could while keeping an eye on the street.

A few minutes later, he saw his wife and daughter exit their building just two blocks down. He fought the urge to yell out their names and run after them but stopped himself—it would be better for everyone if they didn't know what he was up to. If things went wrong and what he had in mind didn't work out, at least they wouldn't be accused of knowing about his plans and considered an accessory. The only way for him to keep his family safe right now was to stay as far from them as he could. If he succeeded and cleared his name, they would see him soon enough as a free man. If they didn't, they would either go see him in jail or visit his grave.

Even from a distance, he could tell that Victoria didn't have the usual spring in her step as she walked Sofia to school. Normally, she was happy to get a new day underway, excited about furthering her research or looking forward to dealing with a patient that presented challenging conditions. What Sam saw was far from what he was accustomed to.

Vicky spent a fair amount of time getting ready in the morning. Her hair had to be perfect, her makeup was discreet but always well applied, and she dressed according to the latest trends. She kept saying that what her young patients and their parents saw was their first impression of her, long before she even started talking, so she always made a conscious effort to look her best. Sam had been the opposite, always wearing jeans and t-shirts to work, and that irritated Victoria to no end. But after years of trying to change Sam's wardrobe, she had finally given up.

It was obvious that Victoria's night hadn't been any better than Sam's; they'd probably waited for him to come home for hours. Since Sam didn't have his phone, they had no way to reach him anymore. It must have been torture for her not to know where he was.

Victoria was wearing faded blue jeans, sensible brown shoes, and a light blue blouse, instead of her stylish dresses. Her hair had been tied up hurriedly in a ponytail and was a bit disheveled.

Sam couldn't tell from where he was sitting, but he was sure she wasn't wearing any makeup.

She had most likely spent the entire night up, hoping he would come home, wondering what the note he'd left on the refrigerator meant, only to get ready for work at the last second. Sofia was holding her mom's hand, something she'd stopped doing long ago, as they turned the corner on the way to school. The poor kid must have been scared out of her mind, wondering where her daddy was.

It broke Sam's heart to see his family in such a pitiful state. What he had just witnessed reminded him that there wasn't just one victim in this entire mess—his family had been collateral damage, and they were suffering the consequences of what had happened to him. It infuriated him to see the impact it was having on those he loved the most. All for something he hadn't done, even though no one seemed to believe him.

Once he saw his wife and daughter turn the corner and disappear from his line of sight completely, he got up and started heading downtown.

Unconsciously, he walked into the Dunkin' Donuts to grab coffee and a donut. Once he realized where he was, he understood that he'd walked in out of pure force of habit. He was famished, and his stomach had guided him in without him even realizing it.

Warily, Sam walked up to the counter and said hi to Norma. He asked for a large coffee and a chocolate donut. As he finished up ordering, Sam noticed that a lot of people were staring at him. It took him a second to remember that was disguised as a vagrant from head to toe and looked nothing like the other patrons. They were probably wondering what the heck a homeless vet was doing in this part of town, ordering coffee just like any other customer.

Norma stared at him for a moment. The tattered army jacket, long black hair, and thick glasses made him stand out from the crowd. Sam was terrified for a second that she would recognize him. He'd even ordered the same items he did every morning without thinking. If Norma saw through his disguise, she would be sure to ask him just what the hell he was doing there dressed that way. Worse still, it was well known in Sam's entourage that he stopped here every single morning, sometimes even in the afternoon when he felt the need for a little boost of energy, so if the authorities went looking for him, they would surely come to check out this place. If Norma told the cops he'd been in here and gave a description of his new appearance, it might ruin everything.

Sam felt a drop of sweat pearl at the top of his forehead. Norma looked at him quizzically for a few more seconds, but she shrugged and told the man standing in front of her the total amount that was due. Sam paid but kept all the change. He figured that the homeless probably weren't good tippers, and if he left a fair amount behind, it would look suspicious. Sam also remembered that, so far, his generous tips hadn't garnered any sympathy.

He quickly moved down to the end of the counter. As soon as Sam was handed his coffee and the paper bag containing his donut, he bolted out the door and walked as fast as he could away from the place. He'd just made his first mistake. Sam told himself that he had to fight his instincts to behave as he normally would because Samuel Brighton didn't exist anymore. He was a ghost and needed to work very hard to remain unseen.

The good news was that he had walked into a place where he was well known, talked to a person he'd spoken to every single weekday of his life for the past decade, and had grabbed some food and a drink without anyone recognizing him. It made Sam very confident about his choice of costume and his ability to blend in. Although he now knew he could move about the city without being noticed, he told himself that there was no need to take unnecessary risks. He would try to stay away from public spaces as much as humanly possible. For now, Sam enjoyed his donut and coffee as he walked eastbound toward Broad Street.

He had a lot of time before his first real task would begin. Once he finished his donut, Sam downed his coffee in one long gulp. He threw away the paper bag, but remembering what he had seen the previous day, kept the paper cup. Sam crumpled it in his fist and put it away in one of his cargo pockets.

He started walking slowly, pretending to have a small limp in his right leg. Sam had noticed that homeless people were never in a hurry to get anywhere and that quite a few of them had some serious health issues. He couldn't start walking at his usual brisk pace, or he would stand out too much. Sam grew tense—it was very hard for him to walk this slow, pretending to have a serious injury, because everything Sam was now doing went against his nature. He started paying a lot more attention to his surroundings, the sounds, smells, and sights around him that his mind usually ignored as he walked blissfully to work. If he wanted to hide in plain sight, he would need to travel around unnoticed.

He had a lot of distance to travel, and he found it easy to get lost in thought, but he tried to keep his mind focused on the task ahead. In his attempt to clear his name, he would have to start where it all began—Sam was going back to school.

TWENTY

South Philly
Corner of Broad and Snyder
Tuesday – May 14, 2013 – 3:07 p.m.

As he walked down Chestnut, Sam realized he would need some help with the next part of his plan. Since he'd been fired from school, the administration had revoked all his access codes; Sam couldn't check his work emails or even see the amount of his last paycheck. As he was planning his next move, he reflected upon how he could obtain the information he needed. So, he enlisted some help.

He stopped on the corner of Broad and Chestnut and sat on a bench. He was a bit nervous since there was always a little bit more police presence in this part of town. It was also one of the busiest intersections in the city, so he hoped to get lost in the crowds. He pulled out his phone and inserted the battery. Years of reading spy novels and watching television series had taught him that cell phones were traceable even when they were powered down; the only effective way to keep them off the grid was to take out the battery. He was steadily growing paranoid and didn't want to take any chances. Once he snapped the cover back on, he powered up his phone.

He recalled Dean's cell number from memory and sent him a text message:

"Need your help. Locked out of system. Need contact info for Vanessa Stanford. Send it to this number only. Don't tell anyone. Thanks. S.B."

Once he saw that the message had gone out, Sam turned the phone off and took out the battery again, placing everything back inside his jacket's breast pocket for easier access. He would check his phone from time to time to see if Dean had answered.

Dean, or "Mr. Dee" as the students called him, was one of the few staff members who could get away with using his cell phone in class. Most teachers kept them in the teachers' lounge in silent mode because they felt it was hypocritical to be seen with an electronic device in class while asking their students to do the opposite. Sam felt the same and had made it a habit to put away his phone in his desk in the teachers' lounge while he was in class. The only time he'd broken that rule was when Victoria was pregnant, but his students understood his reason for doing so and hadn't complained. Dean's situation was quite different. His students sent their homework by email, and since the school's internet connection was so pitiful, he used his own 4G network to read messages and reply to students.

Sam intended to corner Vanessa and confront her. She was the first step in his long quest to understand what was happening. He still couldn't believe that she would have done such a thing purely out of spite. Despite their last argument and his opinion on how the young lady conducted herself, he felt that their relationship as student and teacher had been anything but hateful. Sam knew that someone else had to be involved if only to snap the picture they'd found. The angle of the picture implied that the girl hadn't taken the photo herself—someone else had been holding the phone.

The other thing that bothered Sam a lot was the speed with which all the events had taken place. It had only taken a few days from his arrest to the start of his trial, to his conviction. His previous lawyer's feeble attempt at getting Sam free hadn't helped. Sometimes Sam felt like his lawyer had been working for the other side. Someone had to be pushing things along behind the curtains—he was sure of it. Now was not the time to dwell on the past, though. He had to focus on what lay ahead.

He had to find whoever was behind all of this and make him pay. The problem was, he had no idea who that person could be.

Sam had taken a huge gamble in contacting his friend. He'd tried and tried to push the thoughts away, but the fact was,

Dean could very well have pulled something like this off. He was one of the very few people Sam knew who could hack a phone remotely. And it didn't help matters that he was one of the only people who knew Sam's phone number. As the thoughts chased themselves in circles around his head, Sam took a deep breath and looked at the message he'd sent his friend. His *best* friend.

He shook his head—no, no matter what, he needed to trust Dean. He needed someone he could rely on, and he just couldn't bring himself to believe that Dean would betray him like this. But Dean knew Sam's number and knew Vanessa from his class a year before. Although he wouldn't—couldn't—believe that his best friend would betray him, the thought still found a way to creep through his brain from time to time.

Even if his friend hadn't set him up, which he sincerely hoped was true, he couldn't be sure that he would help him. He didn't know if Dean truly believed in his innocence or not. After the trial and Vanessa's very convincing testimony, Dean might have decided to break ties with Sam. He could only pray that Dean knew he wasn't the monster everyone else was portraying him as; he just had to wait and pray that his friend would remain by his side in his hour of need.

Sam started heading south toward the school. If Dean came through, he would send over Vanessa's file. The file would include her picture, date of birth, class schedule, but most importantly, her contact information, like her home address and her parents' phone number and email.

If Sam had Vanessa's address, he could plan her most logical route home. He would be able to know if she took the bus, public transit, or simply walked. Sam could then find the most logical place to have a little chat with her. He didn't have a clue what he would say to her or even if he could manage to keep his cool around her after what she'd done to him, but he knew she was the key to unlocking everything else.

After about fifteen minutes of walking, Sam turned left, about halfway to the school. He knew there was a park a few streets away, so he found a place to sit in the shade. It was another hot day in Philly, and Sam was wearing a jacket on top of his shirt. Sam felt the sweat dripping from his armpits and down his ribs; he needed a few minutes to cool down. He assembled his phone and waited for it to come online. A few seconds later, he heard a tiny bell ring and an icon appeared, informing him he had a new text message. He opened the messaging app and read:

"1598 Porter St. W. 267-987-3564. Tinast56@hotmail.com. Hope u ok."

Sam was relieved. His friend had come through for him, and he had everything he needed to get started. He opened the map application on his phone and typed in the address. Sam knew where it was, having grown up in South Philly himself, but still, he had to be sure. He examined the directions to her house and tagged the location so he wouldn't need to type it in every time he wanted to map out a route. Once he was finished, he disassembled his phone once more and put it away. He walked to the fountain in the park, took a few sips to keep hydrated, and resumed walking.

He continued traveling southbound on Broad Street until he was right across the corner from the school. It felt funny to him. The place had always been like his second home, yet here he was feeling like a stranger. He sat down on the sidewalk just outside a drugstore, where he had a clear view of the school's front entrance.

As he looked around, he saw a little coffee shop right across the street. He thought about how all coffee shops now had free wireless access for their customers. If he ever ran out of data, he could always just squat there and log on. But he hadn't seen many homeless folks using cell phones as he traveled around the city, so he thought it would be risky to do so and decided to only use his phone discreetly unless it was an emergency.

After looking up her address on the map, Sam felt confident that Vanessa would walk home since it was only about ten blocks away. But since she might be the kind of girl who would go out with a boy only because he had a car, he kept an eye on the parking lot as well. His position offered him a wide view of the front of the school, and he was sure he would eventually see her go by. If he didn't, he would try to find another vantage point tomorrow.

His plan was to follow her home from a distance. If he found a place suitable for an ambush, he would take note of it and wait for her there the following day. If not, he would think of something else.

As Sam made his plans, another thought hit him—how far was he willing to go to find out the truth? Or could he force himself to go far *enough*? He'd always been a mild-mannered person, someone whom violence was foreign to. He'd never been in a fight, even when he was a boy in school, so he was worried he didn't have the guts to do what needed to be done to find answers. On the other hand, the way he'd been acting the last few days and the drastic plan that was already forming in his head had made him worry, too—what if he went too far during his fight for redemption? Already, he could feel a fierce fire burning inside him, pushing him to do whatever he could to clear his name and reunite with his family. His life had gone down the crapper in a matter of days, so who knew what this change had done to him, what he was capable of now? He pushed the thoughts away for the moment. Sam needed to focus and trust himself if anyone. He was on a time crunch, and he couldn't waste any precious minutes worrying about what he would and would not do—he just needed to try.

Fifteen minutes later, he saw Vanessa from a distance. Her long, blonde hair made her easy to spot, even from across the street. She appeared to be walking home, as he'd expected.

Sam felt the urge to run straight at her, tackle her to the ground, and shake the truth out of her, but he willed himself to sit still. He should have been standing in front of a judge at the very moment, hearing his sentencing and being sent to jail. He was now officially a fugitive, and once the judge was done pronouncing his sentence, the police would be on the lookout for him—he needed to keep a low profile until he solved this mystery.

Watching Vanessa, he expected her to turn left on Broad Street and head south toward her home, but she went right and headed north toward Snyder Station. As he watched her go down the stairs, he had only a few seconds to decide—he could stay put, let her go, and try again tomorrow or get up and follow her into the subway. Sam reasoned that his chances of getting caught increased by the hour, and wasting an entire day waiting wasn't a good option; so he stood up, crossed the street, and descended into the station about a minute after she did. Hopefully, he could board the same train; otherwise, he'd have to wait until tomorrow and try again, wasting precious time.

Fortunately, as he was scanning his card, he heard the *whoosh* of an incoming train, so he knew he hadn't missed her. He kept his distance, and when he saw her board her wagon, he jumped inside the one right behind her. Now, he could keep her in his line of sight without being too visible. He saw Vanessa put in her earbuds and pull out her phone, just like pretty much every other passenger. She seemed oblivious to his presence.

Every time the train approached a station, Sam looked up to see if the girl would stand, but for now, she was staying put. As he kept his eyes on her, he noticed the people aboard his wagon were staring at him. He remembered that the homeless didn't ride the subway often and favored walking around so they could spend what little money they had on food, drink, or various sins. He made a mental note to avoid the metro and buses as much as possible from now on, so as not to draw too much attention to himself. Even though he was sure that nobody could recognize him, some people might still call the cops to alert them of an undesirable person on the train, which was the last thing he needed right now.

TWENTY-ONE

Downtown Philly
Corner of 15th and Market
Tuesday – May 14, 2013 – 3:41 p.m.

As the train was pulling into City Hall Station, Sam saw Vanessa stand up and walk to the door, getting ready to exit. Sam stayed put but kept a close eye on her. He waited until the doors started closing again and quickly got out, keeping a safe distance behind her. He watched her climb the stairs, but he stayed behind and pretended to rummage through a trash bin.

When she was out of sight, he raced up the stairway and scanned the street for her. Her hair was unmistakable, so he kept further back without fear of losing her in the crowd. He followed her onto 15th Street, walking one hundred feet behind on the opposite sidewalk. He figured she'd gone downtown either to shop or maybe to work a part-time job, as so many seniors did.

She turned left into an alleyway, so he jogged to the corner to avoid losing her. Peeking around, he saw the alleyway was lined with dozens of doors and staircases. Those doors were most likely the backdoors of the many businesses that lined Chestnut and Market Streets, two of the busiest streets in the city. Fearing that following her down the narrow alley would be impossible without being spotted, he remained on the corner and quickly put his phone together. He was getting very agile at this task, and it took him only a few seconds to power it on.

As soon as the phone was ready, he opened the camera app and used the video recorder to see down the alley while remaining out of sight. Looking at the screen, he noticed Vanessa ringing at a door on her left, about sixty yards away, so he took a picture, figuring it might help him identify where she was going.

He went back on Chestnut Street and made a rough calculation of the distance Vanessa had traveled from the corner of 15th to figure out which business the door belonged to. It wasn't easy in this part of town, as there were dozens of shops, both large and small, lining the street. From his estimation, he thought the most likely targets were either a Five Guys burger restaurant, a thrift shop or a Dunkin' Donuts. There was also a blank metal door under some scaffolding, but since there weren't any windows, he figured it led to some apartments upstairs.

Sam was sure she wasn't working at the donut shop—he stopped in from time to time when he was itching for an afternoon sugar fix on his way back from work, so he would surely have seen her. Eliminating that possibility, he was now focusing on either the burger joint or the thrift shop. The store had large, unobstructed windows to display its merchandise, so it would be easy for him to spot her while remaining on the street, but the burger place's windows were elevated from street level, so he couldn't see inside from where he was standing.

Logically, a pretty girl like Vanessa wouldn't be working in the greasy kitchen. Any manager worth his salt would put her up at the register to keep her in plain view for the male customers. Sam wasn't ready for a confrontation, though; he wanted to do more recon and learn her daily routine in the hopes of finding a weak spot to exploit. He needed to talk to her in private, not cause a scene in public. So, Sam crossed the street and sat directly opposite the thrift shop. From where he was seated, he could see well inside the store. If she was in there, he would spot her easily and plan his next move. He told himself that if she didn't appear within an hour, he would rule out the place and move on to the restaurant.

After waiting for more than an hour, he still hadn't seen Vanessa in the thrift shop, so all that remained was the burger place. He didn't have the luxury of time on his side, and he needed to act right away. He decided to be bold and just walk inside. As he pushed open the door, he pretended to be lost, keeping with his act, and looked all around the dining room. He didn't see her at any of the registers. The kitchen was in full view of the customers, as was the standard for restaurants nowadays, but she wasn't there either.

Sam was confused. He remained standing in place for a few seconds then noticed some of the patrons looking at him, so he shrugged and walked back out. The men and women sitting down to enjoy their meals would dismiss him as just another lost cause, drunk or drugged out of his mind, who had mistakenly walked in the wrong door. They would forget about him and go about their day.

As he was trying to figure out what had gone wrong and how he'd lost her, Sam had an idea. He deduced that the girl would have to go home at some point, which would mean she would have to take the subway back to her house. Sam would wait for her to come out and pick things up from there. He walked to one of the benches around the massive City Hall building on 15th Street and sat down, pulled out his empty paper cup from his pants, and put his head down. Sam willed himself not to move, but it was nerve-racking.

There was always a large police presence around City Hall. Sam wondered if they'd already been alerted and were on the lookout for him. He knew they couldn't chase him away from his bench since he wasn't breaking any laws by sitting there, but he was still a convicted criminal and fugitive. It all added a layer of pressure he could have gone without.

TWENTY-TWO

Downtown Philly
Corner of Chestnut and 15th
Tuesday – May 14, 2013 – 7:09 p.m.

After three stressful hours, Sam finally saw, out of the corner of his eye, Vanessa's familiar silhouette emerge out of the alleyway she'd entered earlier. He wasn't used to sitting still for such a long time. Now, his butt hurt, but on the plus side, he had about two bucks in loose change in his paper cup now.

Once he saw Vanessa go down the staircase, he sighed in relief and searched the alley and check things out, now that he knew she was traveling in the opposite direction. He walked along the alley, still limping until he was in the general vicinity of where he'd seen her. He noticed that all the backdoors were the same generic metal doors, and it was hard to tell them apart from a distance. Fortunately, most of them were labeled with the identity of the business they belonged to, presumably to help delivery men get to the right place.

Sam checked them one by one. Between the burger place and the thrift store was a door with *"Shikoku"* inscribed in magic marker on it, and he stopped and examined it curiously. He had just spent four hours sitting on the opposite sidewalk on Chestnut and didn't remember seeing that name. Remembering the scaffolding he'd seen earlier, he figured that maybe it was a Japanese restaurant about to open, but the fact that he hadn't seen any windows or signs in front had ruled it out as a place the girl could be working at.

As he approached the door, he noticed the video camera sitting on top of it, aiming down. Not wanting to be captured on film, he turned around and exited the alley. As he was leaving, he noticed a gap between two large garbage containers on the opposite side of the alley. Looking around more attentively, he saw that there weren't any cameras aimed in that direction. It might prove a good spot to take Vanessa aside for their little talk. But it was also dangerously close to City Hall, and if she screamed, it wouldn't take long for the cops to be on top of him. He dismissed the thought. There had to be a better way, but time was against him, so he'd need to figure it out soon.

He had some time to kill before sundown, so he returned to his spot on the sidewalk and observe for a few more hours. Maybe he could even gather enough change to buy a bit of food without having to draw from his money belt.

As he was watching the opposite side of the street, Sam paid more attention to the door under the scaffolding. His eyes still scanned the entire scene, going from the thrift shop to the burger place, but now, he fixated on the door nestled between those two.

As time went by, he started noticing a few men going through the blank metal door underneath the scaffolding. This was odd—it didn't look like a place that was open for business, but maybe there might be some offices upstairs. Still, that wouldn't explain why Vanessa had come in through the back. Why didn't she use the front door like everyone else? He focused his entire attention on that site for the rest of the evening. As the evening rush hour started, the streets became more and more crowded. It was getting difficult for Sam to keep watch, as people were walking in front of him, blocking his view. But he was still able to keep an eye on the door. In the last two hours, he had seen twelve more men go in. He noticed that these same men were exiting the building about thirty minutes later. Since he knew there was no chance he would bump into Vanessa now, he decided to be bold and go check it out himself.

He got up and stretched, his joints cracking; he wasn't made to sit around for hours without moving, and his body was letting him know. After shouldering his backpack, he crossed the street in the middle of traffic, since he'd noticed that the homeless didn't seem to bother with crosswalks or traffic lights. He was almost run over by a sedan and cursed by a few drivers as he limped across.

He told himself this would only be a quick peek because he needed to go all the way back to the river before sunset. Even though he'd been able to go inside his hideout unhindered the night before, he couldn't be sure that tonight would be just as easy, or any other night for that matter. He had to get there early and have a contingency plan in case he needed to find another place to hide out for the night.

The door opened onto a stairway. Sam went up to the second floor and arrived in front of another sturdy door surmounted by a security camera. He didn't dare look up. There was a bell on the doorframe, so he pressed it. He heard the chime through the other side of the door, but no one answered. Sam examined the entrance closely, but there was no handle— it was impossible to go in unless someone inside let you in. He rang the bell a second time, but the result was the same. Sam tried a third time, and as he was pressing the button, he heard a buzz, and the door unlocked.

Sam's relief was short-lived as a monstrous black man appeared in front of him. He towered over Sam, standing close to seven feet tall, with massive arms the size of Sam's thighs.

"Get lost, old man! This is private property!"

Sam was taken by surprise and couldn't think of anything to say.

"Did you hear me? Get the hell out before I throw your ass out!"

Sam regained his composure and stammered, "H-Hey man, you got any change? I'm hungry."

The bouncer took Sam by the lapel of his jacket and lifted him off the ground as if he weighed little more than a feather. He threw Sam against the opposite wall, knocking the wind out of him. Luckily for Sam, his backpack absorbed most of the impact from the fall, but he panicked, thinking of the items resting inside. Hopefully, nothing was broken.

The bouncer picked Sam up from the ground, lifted him once again so their faces would line up, and hissed, "We ain't got no change here, and if you ever show your face again, I'll mess you up good. Understood?"

Sam was genuinely scared, so he mumbled, "Yeah. Sorry man, I won't bother you no more."

The bouncer put Sam down and pointed to the stairway. Sam scrambled back down and out the door, and as he pushed it open, a man was entering. Sam looked at him from head to toe, but the man refused to meet his gaze, cringing away from him. He was in his mid-thirties and was clad in a fashionable pink shirt with a black silk tie, black dress pants, and brown leather shoes. Sam continued to watch the man as he went up the stairs. The bouncer had retreated behind his door, so the man had to ring the doorbell and look up at the camera. It only took a few seconds for the buzzer to sound, and the door was opened. The man was escorted in, and the door closed behind him.

TWENTY-THREE

Center City
Corner of Chestnut and 19th
Tuesday – May 14, 2013 – 7:43 p.m.

As Sam slowly limped his way back to his hideout, he thought about what he'd just witnessed and tried to make sense of it all. His back hurt from being thrown against a wall like a ragdoll, and the prospect of spending the night in his uncomfortable position didn't help brighten his mood. As he replayed the events of the day, he understood what had gone wrong.

The problem was his appearance. While his disguise helped him blend in as he walked around the city, it also limited his movements. He couldn't walk into a place as he pleased or take public transit to move around. The people who lived in the city had gotten used to homeless men and women roaming around and generally didn't pay much attention to them. Sam had been just the same. He rarely gave any change to them, except for the moments when he felt a twinge of guilt at the sight of their hunched forms sitting on the sidewalks. Maybe if a bum opened a door for him, he might give the man a bit of change, but otherwise, he just acted like they didn't exist.

Folks didn't mind them until they impacted their daily routine. No one wanted to ride the metro sitting next to a man who smelled like piss or wanted to eat next to a woman in dirty rags. These aspects of a normal life weren't accessible to the less fortunate, and it incited some unpleasant reactions when their activities disrupted the routines of others.

When Sam replayed in his mind the observations he'd made while sitting on the sidewalk, it all became clear. The men he'd seen walk through the door were pretty much all the same— they wore suits and ties and had well-kept appearances. Even the ones who wore more casual clothing looked like their wardrobe cost a fortune. It all made sense since Market Street, which was home to all the big banks and trading firms, was just a block away. Add to the mix the hundreds of bureaucrats that milled around City Hall, and it was no wonder he didn't fit their profile and had received such a warm welcome.

The place was probably some private club for the wealthy and affluent men of Philadelphia. The bouncer was just doing his job, preventing a panhandler from harassing the rich folks of the city.

Sam stopped into a convenience store and bought two power bars and a Gatorade with the money he'd gathered in his cup. He'd pulled in almost five bucks while sitting on the sidewalk. Even though he still had a few hundred dollars on him, he was reluctant to spend any of it. He might need that money at some point, and if he spent it all on food, he would be in trouble when times got tough. Even though he was famished and could have bought enough food to satisfy his hunger, he told himself to suck it up and only spend the change he'd gathered that day.

As he reached 24th Street, he stopped and looked back before heading down to the river. He stared at his former home for a few seconds and considered calling Victoria to let her know he was okay. She must have been present at his sentencing today, and when he had failed to show up, she would have become even more worried. Perhaps they thought he'd killed himself and that they would fish his body out of a river in a few days. He would use his time in his hideout to think of a discreet way to let her know that he was okay, but right now, it was time to move. It was almost dark, and he needed to plan his next step. His gut told him he was onto something, but he didn't know what yet.

Once he made sure no one else was using the far recess of the alcove, he moved in all the way to the back, once again using the flashlight on his phone to help him navigate through the rubble.

After hiding his backpack and settling in, Sam closed his eyes and reflected on what he'd learned that day.

TWENTY-FOUR

Center City
Corner of 22nd and Chestnut
Wednesday – May 15, 2013 – 9:18 a.m.

Sam had just suffered through another restless night. He was feeling the fatigue accumulate, and the aches and pains hadn't subsided. Even though he still wasn't anywhere close to understanding what was happening to him or why, at least he'd been able to plan out his next step. If everything went right, today was the day he would start getting some answers. But first, there was a lot to do.

He hiked up to street level and took a seat on the bench inside the bus stop until he saw his family exit. Victoria was walking Sofia to school even though they hadn't seen him in two days. She figured the girl needed some sense of normalcy and that being busy at school would keep her mind off things. After following his wife from a distance to make sure she was heading to the hospital, he wandered around the block. He had some time to kill but staying in one place for too long might draw some unwanted attention. Sam was trying his very best to do the exact opposite.

He waited until morning rush hour had passed, walked down to 22nd Street, and turned right. Sam sat down on the sidewalk, right beside the massive parking garage door that let drivers in and out of his building. After waiting a few minutes, he heard the garage door starting to roll up, and a black BMW sedan exited and turned into traffic. When the door started rolling back down, Sam waited for it to get halfway to the ground before slipping underneath it. He was now back inside his building. Sam didn't dare go in through the front door, as he was now a wanted man; he had no idea if his decision to skip bail had made the news or not, but now wasn't the time to take chances.

If he remained in disguise, the doorman would never let him inside the building. On the other hand, if he changed his appearance back to its normal state, everyone would be aware of his whereabouts. He had no choice but to find another way inside his home.

Sam walked across the parking garage. As he heard another engine start, he took cover behind a large SUV and waited for the car to pass. When the coast was clear, he resumed his progress and reached the elevators. He thought about calling the elevator down but was afraid of being stuck in a cabin with someone else. Looking like he did, they would surely call security. So, he opened the door that led to the stairway and started climbing.

He walked up a flight of stairs and opened the door slightly to peek outside. The stairway that led to the residential floors was separate from the one that led down to the parking garage because part of the ground floor was occupied by a dental clinic, a dry cleaner, and a yoga studio. The architects who had designed the building had thought things through and separated the stairways to avoid giving visitors access to the condos without passing by the front desk first.

Sam waited for the doorman to be distracted by a delivery man ringing at the front door and ran across the main hallway. He tapped his access card against the reader, allowing him to access the staircase and the elevator banks. He waited for what seemed an eternity for the tiny light to turn green, opened the door to the stairway, and hurried inside.

When he got to his floor, he was out of breath and dripping with sweat, having just climbed up twenty-six floors. He opened the door slightly, checked to see if the hallway was empty, and ran to his apartment door. Sam found the emergency spare key they kept taped to the top of the doorframe and unlocked the condo before slipping inside and locking it once again. He sighed in relief; after spending a couple of days outside, being in a clean room with air conditioning felt like paradise.

He got undressed and put everything he had in the washer. Even though he wanted to appear like a bum, he wouldn't be able to stand smelling like one for much longer. He plugged his phone into the outlet over the kitchen counter and headed for the bathroom, where he took a long, steaming shower and washed from head to toe twice. After toweling down, he examined himself in the mirror. His beard was bushy, but his hair was still short. He took out his hair clippers and proceeded to trim his beard. Once he was finished, he went back in the shower and rinsed off. After drying himself once more, he cleaned the entire bathroom to make sure there wouldn't be a single hair left anywhere. He didn't want to leave traces of his presence.

He heard the chime of the washer, so he tossed everything in the dryer, adding his bath towel to the mix so it wouldn't still be damp when Vicky came back home. While he was waiting for the dryer to finish up, he laid down on top of the bed and allowed himself a nap.

He was awoken by the chime of the dryer as it finished its cycle. He'd only slept thirty minutes, but that half-hour had been more restful than the two previous nights put together. His body was yearning to stay in bed, but he knew he couldn't afford that luxury.

He got up, tugged on the bedspread to erase his body's imprint and went inside the closet; he needed to find some clean clothes that would help him gain access inside the mysterious place Vanessa had gone into. As he was browsing through all his clothes, he asked himself what Victoria would suggest he wear. He smiled as he imagined her. She would tell him to wear some tight-fitting jeans that would complement his slim figure, with a light blue dress shirt that would bring out the color of his eyes. She would insist on keeping the top button open so as not to look too stiff. For the final touch, she would most likely pick out a nice silver watch and a pair of brown, leather loafers. Sam took out all the items but decided not to put on the watch—he wouldn't pass as homeless if people caught a glimpse of silver on his wrist as he walked around, and some of his fellow vagrants could be tempted to cut his hand off to take it away from him.

He put on his fancy clothes and placed his loafers inside his backpack. He then took everything out of the dryer. After hanging his towel back into place, he put on his cargo pants and jacket on top of what he was wearing and retrieved his phone from the kitchen, stowing it away in his pocket after removing the battery. He put the charger inside a pocket of his pack, too, and drank long gulps of water straight from the tap.

For a moment, he felt tempted to raid the fridge and eat every single scrap of food inside, but he knew that wouldn't go unnoticed. Searching through the cupboards, he found a box of granola bars used in Sofia's lunches, but there was only one remaining. Victoria had an uncanny ability to remember exactly how much of everything was left in the house at any moment and would wonder why the box was now empty. It wouldn't matter much, but there was no reason to leave any hints he'd been there, so he put the bar back in its box.

After making sure twice that everything was back in its place and that there wasn't a single trace of his presence left, Sam put on his boots and went to the door. After closing it behind him, he got on his toes to tape the spare key back in its place. As he was walking back toward the staircase leading down to the basement, a door opened on his left and bumped into someone.

"Oh! Excuse me!" a woman said.

Sam was stunned. He froze in place and didn't know what to do. The woman was in her late thirties, with long, curly, brown hair and wearing a tight summer dress.

She looked at him from head to toe with a curious stare.

"Do I know you from somewhere?" she asked.

Sam was panicking. It was Heather Simms. His condo tower was a small community and Heather was the town gossip. She'd married a rich trader fifteen years older and she spent her days going to the gym, the spa, or shopping. She was the typical trophy wife, with nothing to do all day but nose around and talk about other residents of the building.

Sam and Victoria had spent all their life savings to afford one of the more luxurious units on the second-to-last floor. Heather's husband had shelled out over two million dollars to purchase the corner unit that occupied a massive part of the twenty-sixth and twenty-seventh floors. Heather considered herself royalty inside this place and never shied away from letting folks know just how rich they were. Nothing happened in the complex that she didn't know about. If she saw through his disguise and recognized him, all the residents would know it by the end of the day. The police would be on site shortly after, and they were bound to question his family, which was the last thing Sam wanted.

He walked past her and mumbled, "Sorry, ma'am," as he headed for the door. He heard her shout, "Wait a minute! Who are you? What are you doing here?"

Sam didn't waste a second—he rushed to open the staircase door. As he was leaving, he turned around and saw Heather take out her cellphone. She was probably calling the front desk to alert them of an intruder in the building.

He bolted down the stairs two at a time. He had twenty-six floors to go down, and then he had to get to the other staircase that led down to the basement. As he was rushing down the stairs, he almost sprained his ankle twice but reached the ground level in record time. As he ripped open the door, he saw the doorman talking on the phone when the man raised his head and looked in his direction. Sam had been spotted.

The doorman was still talking on the phone, most likely asking Heather for a description of the man she'd seen. Sam knew he had to leave as soon as possible. He could run thirty feet toward the door that led down to the basement, but the front desk was in his path and if they locked the building down, he would be trapped inside the garage. His other option was to sprint fifty feet right out the front door. The way was clear, but he would have to run past everyone in the lobby. He knew the guard manning the front desk would probably be able to intercept him if he went for the basement, so he only had one real choice—he ran as fast as he could for the front door.

The doorman jumped up, but it would take time for him to round his desk and catch up. Sam pushed an elderly man out of his way and kept running. The doorman, Angel, turned out to be surprisingly quick for a man his age. He caught up to Sam and grab him by the jacket.

"Hey! What are you doing here?" Angel asked gruffly.

Sam whipped around and shouted as he struggled to break away. "Let go of me!" He freed himself from the man's grip and pushed him back. Angel fell backward and knocked his head on the marble floor with a dull *whack*. Sam felt awful about what he'd just done, but there wasn't time for remorse. He only had a few seconds to choose where to go. Sam made up his mind and bolted out the door.

He ran toward the river. Sam ran across the street, barely avoiding getting killed by an oncoming truck. He heard someone scream for him to stop. He didn't dare look back; instead, he ran down the staircase that led to the river path. He crossed the fence and scurried inside his hideout, hoping no one had seen him. Hopefully, no one on the path had caught sight of him because if they had and told the authorities, he'd be trapped inside.

As he gasped, trying as best he could to catch his breath, Sam waited in the furthest recess of the alcove for time to pass. He had a few hours ahead of him, so he'd let things cool down before heading back out.

TWENTY-FIVE

South Philly
Corner of Broad and Snyder
Wednesday – May 15, 2013 – 3:10 p.m.

After waiting for what seemed like an eternity, but, was only an hour and a half, Sam came out of hiding and proceeded to his next stop. He walked down another street that ran parallel to Chestnut for a few blocks. Undoubtedly, Angel had met the police by now and given them a description of the intruder who had assaulted him.

Even though a fair amount of time had passed since he'd escaped Angel's grasp, the police might still be patrolling the area.

Sam's instinct proved correct as he saw a patrol car park on the curb in front of his building, so he went southbound down a block before walking towards downtown.

Once he was all the way down to 17th Street, he rejoined the foot traffic on Chestnut and tried to blend into the crowd. He still had a long walk ahead of him, but now that he was far away from his building, he relaxed a little.

He was back in South Philly, sitting at his improvised observation post outside the drugstore and waiting for his target to appear. As soon as he saw Vanessa exit from the school and walking north, he got up and went to the metro station to get ahead of her.

He ran down the stairs and swiped his card on the reader to open the turnstiles. Sam was lucky enough to see that a train was still waiting to depart, so he ran to board it just as the doors were closing. He wasn't happy about taking the train again, but he felt he had no other choice. Walking to the farthest corner of the wagon, he sat out of view of most passengers. He had a good idea where she was heading.

As the train's intercom system announced that the next stop was City Hall Station, Sam got up and waited by the door. If he wanted to stay ahead of Vanessa, he needed to exit the station before she did. As soon as the doors started moving, Sam forced them open and sprinted for the stairs. He emerged outside and found his bench on the corner of 15th and Market. To his surprise, there were two teenage boys sitting on it, and he cursed his bad luck. He tried to think of another place to sit when he remembered the spot he'd seen in the alley the previous day. It wasn't perfect, but it would have to do. He walked as fast as he could without attracting too much attention and headed down the alley. When he reached the large trash dumpsters, he feigned falling and took a seat between the containers. Anyone passing by would assume he was just another drunk who had passed out.

He heard the faint sound of footsteps echoing down the alley and resisted the urge to look up. When he saw a pair of white sneakers stop in front of a door, he looked up just enough to confirm that it was Vanessa and that he had spotted the right door. She rang the doorbell and looked up at the camera. After a few seconds, the door opened, and she was let in.

Sam let a minute pass before he stood. He crept closer to the door to check it out, and it was indeed the one labeled "Shikoku." Now that he was sure of where she was, it was time for them to have a chat.

Sam walked back to the corner and turned right. On the corner of 15th and Chestnut was Wendy's fast-food restaurant, and he pushed through the door and headed straight for the bathroom. A young man at the counter said something to him, but he ignored him. Once in the bathroom, he found an empty stall and changed in a hurry, pulling out the loafers and his special glasses from their case. After putting his shoes and glasses on, he stuffed everything else inside his bag and left the bathroom. Walking past the sinks, he glanced in the mirror and saw that the transformation had been a success. He now looked respectable, but that also meant he could be recognized with greater ease. Sam would need to revert to his homeless state as quickly as possible, but for now, all he could do was keep his head down, using the brim of his baseball cap to shield his face.

He went back into the alley and hid his backpack behind one of the large trash dumpsters he'd used as cover. Hurrying back onto 15th, he turned right on Chestnut. Now, it was time for a big decision—for action.

Sam went to the metal door under the scaffolding and noticed it, too, had the word "Shikoku" written in small letters with a magic marker. Apparently, this place wasn't too keen on advertising. He tried to hide the trembling in his hands and hoped they would let him in this time around.

He climbed up the stairs and rang the doorbell, looking up just enough to show a bit of his face but not enough for them to get a good glimpse of it. A few seconds later, he heard a buzzer sound, and the door opened. The very large gentleman who had manhandled him the day before now motioned him inside and pointed to a large white counter on the other side of the tiny lobby.

Behind the shiny, white Formica counter was a small Asian woman who looked to be about sixty. She was sitting on a stool and waved him over. Sam's nostrils were assaulted by the smell of cheap scented candles and as he approached the counter, he started looking around. He'd been so nervous about finding a way to get inside, he didn't know what to expect, so his mind was only just starting to take things in. His body was shaking from stress—he was inside, but now what?

The woman looked over at Sam and asked with a thick accent, "What you want?"

Sam's brain took a few seconds to process the question. The only thing he managed to say was, "Uh…?"

"What you want, mister?" the lady asked again, but as she said so, she pointed at the three large monitors behind her, above her head.

When Sam finally noticed them, what he saw stunned him. Displayed on each screen were pictures of three different young women, posing in sexy underwear. Next to each picture was a brief bullet-point presentation of the lady in question. After ten seconds, the images cycled, and three different pictures appeared. Sam couldn't speak. His mind was still trying to process what he was looking at—the place was a brothel. At first, he'd thought this place was a kind of private club, but never would he have imagined Vanessa working in a place like this.

"Take your time," the lady said to him as she kept leafing through her magazine. She didn't seem phased by his reaction at all. He probably wasn't the first man in here to be standing in place, speechless. The difference was that he couldn't speak because he was stunned, not because he couldn't choose which girl he wanted.

As the pictures above were cycling, Sam's jaw dropped. On the center monitor, he saw a picture of Vanessa, clear as day. The name next to the picture said "Alexa" and stated that she was nineteen, but Sam wasn't fooled.

Reacting on instinct, he said, "That one. In the middle. I want that one!"

The lady behind the counter told him it would cost a hundred dollars to access the room. As Sam was fishing for the money inside his belt, he asked the old lady how things worked, explaining that this was his first time, which was true.

She said that once he paid for the room, he was to go inside, get undressed, take a shower, and wait on the massage table for his hostess to join him. Once she was there, they could discuss her fees. She said that if he wanted to pay an extra twenty, he could have a room with a hot tub in it.

Sam's brain was going a mile a minute, and he was trying to think quickly on his feet. He told the lady he did wanted the hot tub and gave her the extra cash. She told him to head inside the last room at the end of the hallway on his left and wait—his hostess would be with him within twenty minutes. Sam thanked her and walked past the counter. When he got to the last door on his left, he went in. He was in no hurry for her to arrive. He had to use what little time he had to think about how he would handle things.

TWENTY-SIX

Downtown Philly
Chestnut Street, between 15th and 16th
Wednesday – May 15, 2013 – 4:08 p.m.

Sam walked inside the room and took in his surroundings—it was dimly lit and smelled of vanilla. There was a shower stall on one side of the room and a massage table on the opposite end. In the far corner, there was a bright red-hot tub, and Sam noticed that the jets were running, and steam was rising above the water. He spotted a folding chair close by the shower and sat down. While he was waiting for Vanessa to show up, he ran through his options. Finally, he settled on a strategy but didn't know if it was solid; he was running purely on instinct. He pulled out his phone and turned it on, running through everything he would need and double-checking that it was all working right.

About fifteen minutes later, he heard the door open. He kept his head down and pretended to stare at his screen. The young lady walking in said hello and came close to him. Sam kept his head down and could only see a pair of black stiletto heels, but he recognized the voice instantly. Before she got too close, he said without looking up, "If you don't mind getting in the tub, I'll be with you in a second. I just have to finish this."

"You can finish it later, honey—come join me now," she purred, as she ran her finger across his shoulder.

Sam shuddered at the feeling of her finger lazily tracing across his body. After all, he'd been through, it took all the restraint he could muster not to grab that finger and snap it right off her hand.

"No, I gotta finish this work thing first. It's important. I'll be with you in a minute; get in the tub, please."

"If you say so," she replied, sauntering across the room, swaying her hips.

When she got next to the tub, she started removing what little she was wearing. She unclasped her brassiere and let it fall to the floor. She started removing her thong, and when it got to the middle of her thighs, she bent down to pull it all the way to the floor. Sam couldn't help but peek, no matter how hard he tried. He jerked his head back down as fast as he could, but she'd seen him and let out a giggle. She removed her shoes and slipped into the Jacuzzi.

When Sam saw that she was seated at one end of the tub, he got up without raising his head, grabbed the chair, and walked over to her. He sat down and raised his head to meet her eyes.

"Hi, Vanessa. You and I are gonna have a talk now."

TWENTY-SEVEN

Downtown Philly
Chestnut Street, between 15th and 16th
Wednesday – May 15, 2013 – 4:18 p.m.

At first Sam noticed Vanessa looked puzzled. His voice must have sounded familiar to her and it looked like she was trying to figure out who it belonged to. When she finally realized who was standing in front of the hot tub, her facial expression turned from flirtatious to complete shock. She folded her arms across her chest in a futile attempt to hide her nudity.

"Mr. Brighton! W-What are you doing here?" she spluttered.

Sam got up, grabbed a towel from one of the hooks on the wall, and threw it at her.

"First thing's first—cover yourself up. I don't want to see any of that."

She grabbed the towel and pressed it against her chest, trying to cover the top of her body. The towel was soaked within a matter of seconds, but Vanessa didn't dare get up.

"Why are you here? What's going on? I thought you were in jail!"

"That's where I'm supposed to be right now, yes. Thanks to you, I might add. Problem is, you and I both know I didn't take that picture of you, so we're gonna have ourselves a little chat, and you're going to tell me everything I want to know. Understand?" Sam ordered calmly.

He'd noticed the two video cameras in each corner of the room. He didn't know if they were wired for sound, but he didn't want to take any chances. If he started shouting, it might complicate things.

"Oh God! Please don't hurt me! I'm sorry!" she said, her voice trembling. She probably never expected to see his face again.

"Vanessa, I have no intention of hurting you. If you tell me what I want to know, I'll leave you be, but if you don't, I can't promise anything… I'll do whatever I feel is necessary to get some answers out of you," he warned. Guilt twisted in the pit of his stomach as he saw the fear glimmering in her eyes, but he pushed it away and continued to hold her gaze.

"I'll scream if you touch me!"

"Trust me, the last thing I want to do is touch you. In fact, I'd like nothing more than to forget you ever existed. But you messed up my life big time, and you're going to help me put it back together whether you like it or not. If you scream, or if I find out you're lying to me, whatever happens next is on you. Answer my questions truthfully, and I'll be on my way. I promise you'll never see me again," he replied in a stoic tone.

"Please, leave me alone!" she begged. "I never wanted any of this to happen."

"Maybe you should have thought about that before you snapped a picture of yourself with my goddamn phone!" he hissed, his anger bleeding into his tone.

"I'm sorry!" was all she said.

"Are you?"

"Yes! I'm sorry! I never wanted to do this! I tried to warn you so many times, but you just wouldn't listen!" she cried. Tears had rolled down her cheeks. Even though she'd tried to appear older than she was when she first walked in the room, Sam was now looking at the face of a frightened child. She liked to act like a grown-up, but she wasn't one just yet.

"Well, you could've found another way to tell me or the cops for that matter. And what about your little performance in the courtroom? That was quite a number!" Sam added sarcastically. "To hear you talk up there, you're just an innocent little girl who got taken advantage of by an evil man. I guess you just forgot to tell everyone about *this* place," he said, motioning around the room.

"You don't understand..." she pleaded.

"Okay, so tell me why you did it then. Help me out here!" Sam's irritation was growing.

"I didn't have a choice!" she cried. "He made me do it!"

"Who's 'he'?"

After a few seconds of hesitation, she looked back at Sam, fear in her eyes. She looked terrified.

"I can't tell you. I'm sorry. He'll hurt me if I do."

"I'll freakin' hurt you right now if you don't!" Sam barked back. He reminded himself to keep his tone in check. "This isn't a game, Vanessa. My life is on the line, and I'll do whatever it takes to get out of this. Now, I'll only ask one more time, and you'd better answer me because I don't have a whole lot of patience these days. Who told you to take that picture?"

After a few seconds of silence, she stared back at Sam's stern expression.

"It was Principal Jackson."

Sam was momentarily speechless, not believing what he'd just heard.

"Jackson? Why?" was all he managed to say.

"I don't know. I swear!" Vanessa's voice was trembling; she was genuinely scared.

Sam took a deep breath and looked her in the eyes. After regaining his calm, he asked, "What happened? Why did Jackson ask you to do this?"

"I don't know why. I'm telling you the truth."

"Okay, let's say for now that I believe you. What I'm asking is why you agreed to do this for him."

"He was blackmailing me. He found out I worked here, and he threatened to expose me to the entire school. He promised me that if I did this, not only would he keep this a secret, but he could boost my grades and help me get into any college I want."

After a few moments, as Sam was trying to process this information as fast as his brain could muster, she added, "I never wanted to hurt you, Mr. Brighton. But I didn't have a choice. I'm sorry. You have to believe me!"

"It's okay. I do believe you. I just can't make sense out of any of this."

She went on. "He asked me to meet him after school in his office last week and told me what he wanted me to do. I didn't want to, but he said I didn't have a choice. He said that if I ever wanted to get into college, I had to do what he asked; otherwise, he would tip off the cops about this place, and I'd wind up in juvie'. He made me swear not to tell anyone! That's why I wanted to talk to you after class—I was trying to warn you. I thought you might be able to help me."

"Holy shit." Sam remained silent for a few seconds. "How did you do it? Did you hack my phone?"

"No. When I got to his office, he had your phone with him. He told me to get undressed, took the picture, then told me to leave. I tried to warn you afterward, but you blew me off. I even tried to look up your number online, but I couldn't find a way to reach you. By the time I got to school the next morning, it was too late."

"So why didn't you call the cops?"

"He said that they would never believe me. He told me he had the cops in his pocket and that, if I talked, he'd get rid of me. I'm not sure what he meant by it, but I didn't want to find out."

"This doesn't make any sense," Sam whispered, more to himself than to Vanessa.

"I told you everything I know! Now please leave!" she begged.

Sam looked at the young girl cowering in the hot tub, terrified of the man sitting in front of her. He suddenly felt bad for the kid.

"Vanessa, why are you doing this? What would your parents say if they knew?"

Vanessa snickered.

"My mom's a useless drunk, and my dad walked out on us when I was still a baby. I've been on my own since middle school," she said defiantly.

"But aren't you a minor? Isn't all this illegal?" Sam asked.

She snorted and laughed. "Yeah, I guess. What's your point?"

"What I mean is how did you end up here?"

"Please, Mr. Brighton. Don't act so surprised. You really think this kind of place checks for IDs? I can pass for eighteen anywhere I want! And guys are willing to pay extra for the younger girls," she answered with a bit of pride in her voice.

"But why are you doing *this*? Why not get a regular part-time job like all the other kids in your class?"

"Because I can make as much money working here in four hours than I would in a month working at minimum wage! I'm trying to save money for college so I can get the hell out of here!"

Her voice was shaking again, but Sam could tell the kid was doing her best to keep it together. He hadn't known that her life was such a disaster. On the outside, she'd always appeared to be the perfect American girl, but now, he understood it was a façade she'd put up to hide her reality.

"Thank you for your honesty, Vanessa. I won't bother you anymore."

"Will you tell anyone about this?" she asked.

"I'll try my best not to. I can't promise you anything, though. What you did got me convicted of a crime I didn't commit, and now, I'm a wanted criminal. I'll try to keep you out of this, but this was your doing, and you might have to live with the consequences. I'm sorry, but that's the way it has to be," Sam replied calmly, trying to reassure her. He would try to keep her out of it because, when it came down to it, she was just a child who had been roped into something against her will. But if it came down to him or her, he knew he would save himself first.

He got up from his chair and started walking to the door.

"Wait!" Vanessa shouted. "You still have to pay me. If I walk out of here without any money, it'll be suspicious!"

Sam was pretty sure that was a lie. They had cameras in the room, and if anyone had been watching, they'd know that what had happened here was far from the usual images they saw. But he didn't want to cause any more trouble, so he turned around and looked at Vanessa.

"How much?"

"A hundred should do it. If they ask what was going on, I'll just say that you wanted to talk and nothing else."

"And will they believe you?"

"Sure! You'd be surprised what kind of things some guys ask of us," she answered.

Sam didn't want to hear any of this, but just to be on the safe side, he took out a hundred-dollar bill from his money belt and approached the massage table. Before putting the money down, he looked back at Vanessa.

"Before I give you this, I just have a few more questions."

"Make it quick. Our time's almost up," she urged, pointing to a digital clock above the door.

"Okay. First question: Are you sure Jackson didn't say why he made you do this? Nothing at all?"

"No. Sorry."

"Fine. I guess I'll just have to go ask him myself," Sam grumbled. He then added, "One last question: How did Jackson find out you worked here?"

She sighed. "One Friday a couple of months ago, when it was a half-day, I cut class before lunch and came into work. Lunchtime on Fridays is one of our busiest times here. A girl can make a lot of dough in just a few hours. He walked in and recognized me from the pictures on the screens."

"That's one heck of a bad coincidence…" Sam reflected.

"Not really. I guess it was bound to happen," she replied with a sigh.

"What are you talking about? Why was it bound to happen?"

"Because he stops in every Friday before having lunch with his brother at City Hall."

"Holy hell!" Sam choked out. An instant later, he looked Vanessa in the eyes.

"Did he ever…?" he started, fearing he already knew the answer.

The girl didn't reply and simply looked down, ashamed.

"I'm sorry. I'll do my best to make things right. You have my word," Sam said. Then, he walked out the door.

TWENTY-EIGHT

Center City
Underneath the Chestnut Street Bridge
Thursday – May 16, 2013 – 5:41 p.m.

Sam was sitting in the dark, as he had been for the past day. The information he'd gotten out of Vanessa had shaken him to his very core. The man who had been his boss for more than a decade had betrayed him and destroyed his life. He'd walked back to his hideout, his mind adrift, and had been shaken out of his stupor only from pure hunger. He hadn't eaten much in the past few days.

After retrieving his backpack from the alley and putting his jacket and headgear back on, he'd headed back toward the river, stopping at the convenience store on the corner of 20th to buy a few items. He needed some time to think things through. Along the way, he'd eaten a bag of chips, two protein bars, and he'd downed a bottle of Gatorade. He kept the bottle aside in case nature called. Sam didn't want to expose himself unnecessarily, even if it only meant going to the restroom at a fast-food restaurant close by, so he had dug out a makeshift toilet at the far end of his cave. He'd used the restroom when he'd changed before and after his confrontation with Vanessa, but otherwise, he felt it more prudent to remain in the dark as much as possible. Sam hoped he wouldn't have to use it, as his cave already smelled terrible as it was. He pushed those thoughts out of his mind and focused on what he'd learned.

Although he now knew who was behind all this, he was still no closer to understanding the reason for his demise. His relationship with his former boss had always been one of mutual respect, or so he'd thought. Even though they sometimes had diametrically opposite views on the way the education system was supposed to operate, he respected the man for what he did daily and wouldn't have traded places with him for all the gold in the world. Sam had always felt that he belonged in a classroom, interacting with young minds eager to learn, not stuck behind a computer balancing budgets.

Vanessa had been nothing but a simple pawn in all of this, of that he was sure. The girl had been terrified when she'd seen him but had seemed even more scared of Jackson. He didn't blame her for what she'd done. Whereas before, he'd been outraged at her for ripping his life apart, now, he just felt pity. From what little he knew, her life wasn't an easy one, and she was doing all she could to leave it behind. Although Sam's mom had been loving and caring instead of an absent alcoholic like Vanessa's, he still knew how hard it was to grow up without a dad. He only hoped he could keep her out of trouble and that she would find her way to a happier life.

As the evening light was dimming outside his cave, Sam stared at the sky while he thought things over for the millionth time. As he gazed at a lone cloud lazily drifting above, he had a sudden epiphany. He remembered that there had been something about the picture he'd seen in the courtroom that bugged him, but he couldn't quite put his finger on it. He hadn't been able to get a good look at it back then, but now that he knew Jackson was behind all this, it would be a good idea to study the picture again.

The problem was that his phone was in an evidence box somewhere in a police station. As he looked up, he realized he was gazing at his answer: the cloud. His old cell phone was linked to two email accounts. The primary account functioned mostly as his own private email, but he'd also created a family account so he and Victoria could both access information about Sofia's school or mark events on a common calendar. Sam had linked his photo gallery with his family account because the only pictures he ever took were of his wife and child. He had set up Victoria's phone in the same fashion. That way, all the family photos were stored in a single, commonplace, and they could both access them without trouble.

Since everything nowadays was digital and he didn't want to lose anything in case they ever lost their phones or whenever they switched to new devices, all the pictures and videos they took were instantly backed up to the family account cloud for safekeeping.

He turned on his phone and went online, typed in his email provider's home address, and logged into his family account. He hadn't yet been locked out of that one; perhaps they'd never thought to look for it. He clicked on the link for his pictures, and after a few seconds of loading, all his photos came into view. The very first one on top of the list was the one that had started all of this.

Sam downloaded the file, sent it to his new account's cloud just in case, and logged out. He could study the photo at will now. After putting the phone in airplane mode to save battery life and limit transmissions, he opened the picture and stared at it. He recalled what Vanessa had said about meeting the principal in his office after school, and it hit him. He looked closer at the picture, past Vanessa's naked figure, then finally, he saw it.

Principal Donald Jackson had always been very proud of his athletic days in college. Not only did the man talk incessantly about it—he liked to show it off, too. He had framed his old basketball jersey, and it hung on the wall above his desk. When he looked with greater scrutiny at the upper left corner of the picture, he could clearly see a part of the jersey, with a few letters of his last name embroidered on the back.

This was it. At long last, he had something tangible to prove he was innocent. No one had the keys to the principal's office but the man himself. It would be hard for Jackson to claim that the photo had been taken inside his office without him being aware of it. It wasn't much to go on, but still, it was a start.

Sam then looked at the file name for the image he had just downloaded. Like most electronic devices, when his phone took a picture, it labeled the file using the date and time it had been taken. This picture was no different: when he looked at the file name, it marked the time of the photo as being taken on May 6 at 2:43 p.m. He had been in the mandatory staff meeting at that precise time, and the assistant principal had taken roll call. It proved that he hadn't been the one holding the phone that had taken that picture.

Still, Sam thought even though he finally had something, it was far from indisputable evidence. His adversaries could claim that the picture had been doctored or that the date stamp had been changed. He needed to find something a lot more concrete. Now that he had a thread, he could start pulling at it and see what would eventually unravel. He now knew how it had happened, but he wasn't even close to understanding why.

Late Thursday night, after many hours of meditation without getting any closer to understanding, Sam had to resign himself to the fact that he would need to be more proactive if he were to get to the truth.

He took the phone out of airplane mode, and after waiting for the device to come online, he sent a text message to Dean:

"Need help. Need you to hack school system and send me Principal Jackson's cell number. Hide your tracks. Thanks."

Sam got a reply an instant later before he even had a chance to turn his phone off. It wasn't surprising—Dean's daily workout regimen meant that he woke up every morning around 4:00 a.m.

"No problem. Give me a few hours. Keep safe."

Sam smiled upon seeing the speedy reply. He knew his friend would come through for him and that going inside the school system without being noticed would be child's play for Dean. He disassembled his phone and tried to rest while time passed.

Three hours later, Sam turned on his phone once more to see if he had a message.

He did. Dean had hacked into the school board's system and retrieved Donald Jackson's entire employee profile. He hadn't only sent Sam his cell number, but also his home number, address, license plate number, social security number, and even the bank account number where the man's paycheck was deposited. Sam hadn't asked for this much, but he knew it might eventually come in handy. He turned off his phone and saw the sunrise's reflection in the mirror windows of the large office tower across the river. He shut his eyes and attempted to get a few more hours of much-needed sleep.

TWENTY-NINE

South Philly
Corner of Broad and Snyder
Friday – May 17, 2013 – 10:46 a.m.

Sam was sitting on the large granite slab at the end of the subway's entrance on Broad Street, watching the school's parking
lot. Principal Jackson had his very own parking space, while the
rest of the teachers had to fight for a spot every morning. Sam
had always been happy to take public transit to work because if
you were driving in and got to work even a few minutes late,
you'd be out of a spot and would have to find a place to park
on the streets around the school, which was almost impossible.
The Philadelphia Parking Authority was very quick to hand out
fines, so when you showed up late, not only did you get your
paycheck docked—you had to pay off a parking ticket as well.

Donald Jackson never had to worry about such trivial matters. He had his own private space near the front entrance,
under the pretense that since he had to leave school often to
attend important meetings, the man couldn't afford to waste
time looking for his car in the lot. But everyone knew the matter
was related more to the man's ego than his schedule. Sam sat
down and watched the lot from across the street.

If what Vanessa had said was accurate, and he had no reason
to doubt that it wasn't, Principal Jackson would soon exit the
school on his way to City Hall, but not before stopping into the
massage parlor first.

At first, Sam had considered following him, but he decided
against it; he had already been aboard the subway twice from
this station and didn't want to become too familiar to the people working there. He still drew some stares, and his body odor
wasn't improving by sitting in a damp, dark cave. On the plus
side, this meant that folks who crossed his path gave him a

wider berth, so he felt he would be less likely to be scrutinized closely. Anyways, Jackson used his car to get around town, so it would be impossible to follow him using public transit. The only way he could tail him would be to use a cab, and Sam figured that would be akin to throwing money out the window.

As he waited for his target to appear, Sam reflected on his strategy. He had once read a biography written by the founder of the Navy's infamous Seal Team Six, and one of the most interesting things he'd learned from it was the way these elite soldiers reacted in the face of unexpected danger. When their enemies came out shooting, instead of retreating, these men went on the offensive. Sam found it fascinating that they could fight their natural instincts to flee and instead could fight back instantly. It threw their opponents off balance and gave them a good opportunity to win the fight.

He had applied the same logic to his situation. Sam would go on the offensive—he would try to shake the tree loose and see what fell. He wasn't ready to play his card about the picture just yet, but perhaps if he could disrupt Donald Jackson from his normal routine, the man would make a mistake that Sam could then exploit.

Eight minutes later, he saw Jackson's large figure exit the building. He was wearing sunglasses, and his bald head was shining in the sun as he walked with a confident stride to his car. Sam pulled out his cell phone, turned it on, and took out his Bluetooth earpiece, making sure it was connected to the phone. Right away he regretted not spending more money on a better model, because even though he had only been wearing it for a second, it was already very uncomfortable. Sam would just have to put up with it.

He brushed the long hair of his wig over the earpiece so it wouldn't be noticeable. Anyone walking by would just think he was some old weirdo talking to himself. He dialed Jackson's number and put the phone back in his pocket. As he heard the dial tone in his ear, he saw Jackson put his briefcase on top of his car and fumble to retrieve his phone. After a few rings, he heard the man's voice.

"Yeah?"

"Hello, Donald," Sam said simply.

"Who is this?" Jackson asked, putting his briefcase in the back of his car.

"You don't recognize my voice, Donald? I'll give you a hint—you set me up and tried to have me thrown in jail. Does that jog your memory?"

"Brighton? What the hell?" Jackson said as he looked at his phone's screen and tried to recognize the number. Sam had activated the privacy option on his end, so the only thing the man was seeing was *Unknown Number*.

"I know it was you who set me up, Donald. I'm just giving you a heads up to let you know that I'm coming for you. I'll make you pay for what you've done to me."

"What are you talking about, Sam? I've never done anything to you!" Jackson replied without much conviction.

"Cut the bullshit, Jackson!" Sam snapped. "I know it was you who set me up with that picture, and I'm going to take you down!"

"You will, huh? Jesus Christ, you're turning out to be as much of a pain in the ass as your old man was."

Sam was stung momentarily. Jackson had just made his first mistake; Sam never would have guessed this had anything to do with his father. The man had died from a robbery before he was born, and he'd never known him except for the few stories his mom had told him over the years. He now had a new lead to pursue.

"You still there, Brighton?" Jackson asked. Sam hadn't said a word in about twenty seconds while he was trying to process this new information. He stared at Jackson from a distance. The man wiped a bead of sweat from his forehead with the back of his hand then loosened his necktie.

"Yeah, I'm still here. I'm just thinking about what I'll do to you once I get my hands on you," Sam finally said.

Jackson laughed loudly enough that Sam was able to hear him from across the street.

"You think I'm scared of a scrawny little shit like you, Brighton? It takes a lot more than you to make me nervous," he boasted.

"You're sweating an awful lot for someone who says he's not nervous," Sam answered boldly.

Jackson whipped his head around in all directions, trying to catch sight of Sam. He finally understood that his enemy was close by, but he couldn't see him.

Sam got up and casually started walking down Snyder Avenue. He wanted to put some distance between himself and Jackson. He'd heard enough. Feeling bold, Sam said, "I'll see you around, Donald," then touched a button on his earpiece to end the call.

He took the phone apart as he was walking and stuffed everything in his pocket. When he was almost out of sight, Sam couldn't help but turn his head around one more time. He saw Jackson frozen in place, phone in his hand, still trying to figure out what had just happened.

THIRTY

Center City
Underneath the Chestnut Street Bridge
Friday – May 17, 2013 – 5:02 p.m.

Sam was back in his cave, trying to figure out what his next steps would be. He didn't know what his father had to do with all of this, but Donald Jackson had clearly said that he was involved in some way or other. The problem was, the man had been dead for almost fifty years now, so there was no easy way to figure it out. Sam's thoughts turned to his mother—would she have known what Jackson was talking about?

She'd spoken very little about her late husband, except to say he'd been a good man whose life was cut too short. Unfortunately, his mother was also gone, and even if she'd still been alive, her shattered memory might not have been able to provide him with answers.

He reflected on what to do. The only remaining link to his parents was a couple of boxes of random stuff that had been collected from his mother's apartment after her passing. It was his only lead—it seemed like a longshot, but it was worth a try. The problem now was how to get to those boxes; they were piled inside his hallway closet, and after what happened the last time he'd been inside his building, there was no way he could set foot in there again. Security was bound to have been strengthened after his last unwarranted visit there.

There was only one person who could help him retrieve those boxes, and he was reluctant to call. He had sworn to himself that he would keep Victoria out of this in the hopes of protecting his family from harm, but he didn't see any way around it. Sam took out his phone, turned it on, and dialed the hospital's number. He knew that, on Fridays, she ran her normal clinic with her residents and that she stayed late after her rounds to finish paperwork, rather than bring work home during the weekend.

The switchboard operator answered and asked how she might direct his call, and he asked to be transferred to the oncology department.

While he waited for the line to pick up, he tried to think of what to say to his wife when she finally heard his voice. Would she be relieved or pissed? Would she beg for him to come home to sort this mess out, or would she curse at him and tell him to go to hell?

The call was answered after a minute by the receptionist who ran the desk in the oncology department. Sam had talked to her on numerous occasions when he'd visited his wife at work, and he hoped she wouldn't recognize his voice. He talked in a lower tone and asked to be transferred to his wife's office. He knew that, at this hour, there was a possibility she wouldn't be in, but if she wasn't, he'd leave a voicemail. The receptionist transferred his call once more.

When his wife's voicemail kicked in, his heart skipped a beat. He hadn't heard her voice in a few days, but to him, it felt like centuries. He suddenly longed to be at her side—but becoming a free man had to take top priority. Still speaking in a low voice to mask his identity just in case, he asked that she call back a certain Dr. Henderson and gave the number of his burner cell.

Not knowing when she would call back, he had no choice but to keep his phone turned on; otherwise, he might miss her call. He lowered the screen's brightness to a minimum to maximize his battery life and went online. Sam searched his father's name but found very little, except for an electronic transcript of a newspaper article relating to his death. He made a few other searches with the Jackson name alongside his father's, but again, he came up empty. Sam searched his late father's newspaper website, too, but didn't find much. It wasn't easy to navigate on his phone's browser, so he gave up after only a few tries.

Twenty minutes later, he was startled by his phone's ringtone. He'd been lost in thought and hadn't noticed the time go by. He accepted the call and said nervously, "Hello?"

"Hi, I'm returning a call for Dr. Henderson."

As he heard his wife's voice again, his heart rate shot up, and he found it very hard to keep a cool head. There was no point in beating around the bush, so he went for the direct approach.

"Vicky, it's me," he said.

He heard a small gasp. "Sam? Is that really you?" He could hear the nervousness and relief lacing her voice. She hadn't seen or heard from him in days, and she must have been worried sick.

"Yeah, it is, sweetie. Listen, I need your help with something."

"What? Sam, where are you? Come home! You missed your sentencing hearing, and now, everyone is looking for you! The cops come by every night asking if we've seen you. Sofia's been crying for the past three days wondering where you are." Her words tumbled out in a rush, and he could hear her throat tightening as she fought back tears.

"I'm sorry, honey. I know how hard this must be on you and Sofia. Tell her I'm okay and that I'll see her real soon, alright? But honey, I need your help. This is all just a big mistake. I've been set up from the start, and I know who's behind this. I just need to figure out why."

"What are you talking about? Sam, you need to come home right now. We'll hire the best lawyer money can buy, and we'll figure out together how to settle this. Please come home!"

"I can't right now... I'm sorry. I'm doing everything I can to clear my name, and that's why I'm calling. I need to get something from our apartment, but I can't get inside the building again."

"What do you mean, 'again'?" she asked hesitantly. "Wait a second... Heather came over a little while ago and told me she'd seen a strange man on the 26th floor. Was that you?"

"Yeah, it was, but you can't tell anyone. I tried to get in and out without being seen, but I accidentally bumped into her. I just hope she didn't recognize me."

"I don't think she did, otherwise she would have told me, and everyone else for that matter. The entire building is talking about increasing security after a bum broke in. We've already been given new access cards, and they hired a security guard at the front door. I guess that's all because of you," her voice faltered.

"I know. Listen, it's critical that you don't tell anyone about this. You can't even tell anyone about this phone call. Not until I set things straight. Now, I need your help; otherwise, I'm dead in the water."

"Okay, but Sam, I'm not doing anything illegal. Sofia already thinks she's lost one parent—I'm not putting her through this again!"

"Don't worry, it'll be easy, you'll see. You remember the boxes of junk I brought back to our place after we cleared Mom's apartment? I need you to bring those over to me without people knowing."

"Boxes? Why?"

"It seems this whole thing has something to do with my father, and I need to find out if there's anything in there that can help me figure it out."

"Your dad? But you never knew him. He died before you were born! That doesn't make any sense!"

"I know it doesn't, but it's still the only lead I have right now. Now, are you going to help me or not?" Sam was getting nervous. He didn't want to spend too much time on the phone.

"Okay, tell me what you need," she said quickly.

"Thanks. It's pretty simple. Later tonight, at around 7:00 p.m., take both boxes and head over to the drugstore behind our building. Put all of Mom's succession files in there also. Throw the boxes inside the garbage container behind the drugstore on Walnut, like you're getting rid of old boxes of crap. I'll come by shortly after and retrieve them."

"Okay, that seems simple enough. I'll bring them and wait for you."

"No!" Sam all but shouted. "You can't be seen anywhere near me, you understand? If anything goes wrong, you need to be able to say you haven't seen or spoken to me since Monday, or they might consider you an accessory after the fact."

"But Sam, I need to see you! Sofia wants to see you!" Victoria begged, a small sob escaping.

Sam's heart broke. "I understand, and I'd like nothing more than to be with you guys, too, but you can't get involved in this. Promise me that after you drop off the boxes, you'll head straight back home!"

"Okay, I promise," she agreed hesitantly. "Can I at least tell Sofia that you're alive and well?"

"No. Make up something. Tell her the police think they've spotted me somewhere in New Jersey, or something like that, so she knows I'm still alive, but that's about it. We can't afford to have her say something that could jeopardize me."

"Alright, I'll think of something. I'll get the boxes and bring them tonight."

"Thank you, Vicky. You don't know how much this means to me. I'll see you real soon, okay?"

He heard her take a shaky breath. "Sam, I love you. Be careful, okay?"

"I will, I promise. I love you, too." After he said goodbye, Sam put the phone in airplane mode to cut off transmissions and set an alarm for 6:30 p.m. The fear of being tracked through his phone kept gnawing at the back of his mind but he couldn't afford to miss Victoria. He tried to push the thoughts away. For now, he would try to rest. He closed his eyes and fell asleep in an instant.

THIRTY-ONE

Center City
Corner of 24th and Walnut
Friday – May 17, 2013 – 6:54 p.m.

Sam was waiting for his wife to appear. After stopping at a nearby dog park to drink some water and top off his bottle, he sat down at a gas station across the street from the drugstore. He was sitting on the base of a streetlamp with his paper cup out but kept his eyes forward.

At precisely 7:00 p.m., he saw his wife walking into the drugstore's parking lot, carrying two banker's cardboard boxes piled up on top of each other. Victoria had gone out in sweats and sneakers, and her hair was tied in a loose bun. He hadn't told her to do any of it, but he found it perfect. She looked like someone who had spent an entire day doing some spring cleaning and was getting rid of unwanted knick-knacks. She deposited each box in the large garbage container in the far corner of the parking lot.

Once she was done, she just stood there, looking around. She was obviously trying to see if he was nearby. Sam doubted she could recognize him from this distance, especially with his disguise.

After a few minutes of searching for Sam, Victoria finally gave up and headed back to their apartment. Sam waited five minutes after she was out of sight and crossed the street to gather the boxes.

He pulled out both boxes from the bin and realized he couldn't carry both large items back to his hideout. Not only would it be very difficult to sneak into his makeshift home unnoticed while carrying them—it would look too suspicious to see a homeless man walk around with such items.

Sam fished out an old plastic bag from the bin, heaved out the first box, and started rifling through it. There were two old bowling trophies with his father's name on them, but Sam seriously doubted that his father's bowling abilities were the reason for all of this. Still erring on the cautious side, he took a few pictures of the trophies before tossing them back in the bin. He pulled out the folder in which all his mom's documents were placed and put it in the plastic bag. He also found a strange brass key with an inscription on it hanging at the end of a small chain. After photographing it from two different angles, he tossed it in the plastic bag. He took out the pictures from the frames and placed them in the folder at the bottom of the bag. Every time he pulled something out of the boxes, he took pictures to catalog them, just in case.

After about thirty minutes, he was done sorting through both boxes. He had gathered everything he thought could be relevant and had thrown everything else back in the boxes before hiding both behind the large trash containers. Hopefully, they wouldn't get thrown out immediately, and if needed, he could come back to get them. Still, he felt confident he'd been thorough in his search.

Sam put his backpack on and grabbed his plastic bag. Now, he could use the upcoming weekend to sift through everything and try to find something about his father that could help. He walked back to his hiding spot and settled in for the night.

THIRTY-TWO

Center City
Underneath the Chestnut Street Bridge
Saturday – May 18, 2013 – 5:58 a.m.

Sam was anxious to start perusing what he'd gathered from the boxes. When he'd made it back to his spot last night, it was already dark out, so there hadn't been any natural light for him to use. He had thought for a second of using his phone's light to get to work on his search but had decided against it—it would drain the battery too fast and wasn't worth it. So, he'd convinced himself to wait until morning and tried to rest, unsuccessfully.

Now, there was just enough light at the entrance of his alcove for him to read the documents and look at old photos. He started by looking at the few pictures he had, but there was nothing there that could help him; they were photos of himself as a kid or his mom in various stages of life.

There was one picture with his father in it, from their wedding. His mom looked happy and healthy. It struck Sam as he looked at the picture that he and his father looked very much the same. Sam had lived for a lot longer than his father unfortunately had, but when he examined the picture, it was almost like looking at himself in his late twenties. He took pictures of the photos with his phone to keep digital copies then put them back in the folder. He looked at the images of the bowling trophies he had taken, but they seemed irrelevant.

Sam retrieved the old brass key he'd found and looked at it from all angles. It was an odd shape, and one side had USB204 inscribed on it. Sam couldn't figure out what that meant, but he would try to find out later.

He then took out his mother's succession papers and went through them one more time. There were files about taxes that would need to be paid, her apartment's lease that needed settling, and an inventory of everything that had been registered with her name on it: credit cards, driver's license, bank accounts, various bills, and even her library card. So far, nothing seemed to be related to his situation.

Sam deactivated the airplane mode from his phone so he could access the internet. The first thing he did before opening the browser app was back up every picture he'd taken with his phone onto his new cloud storage drive. Now, if anything ever happened to the phone, he could always retrieve his stuff. While the files were uploading, Sam opened the default search engine installed on his phone; his gut told him there was just something about that brass key that could help unlock this mystery.

He typed *USB key*. As expected, there were millions of search results, but all of them looked to be related to buying or using digital storage devices.

He then tried *USB brass key*, but the results came up the same. Sam tried several other combinations and went through the first five pages of results on each search, but still only came up with links to buy or repair storage devices.

He then put in *USB Philadelphia* and started going through the many pages of results that appeared. As he scrolled down to the bottom of the fourth page, he was finally rewarded with something new. It was the link to the United Savings Bank in South Philly. Upon seeing this, Sam went back to his mother's files and took out the sheet of paper with the inventory of her late possessions. Near the bottom of the list, there was an item that caught his attention. It was noted that she'd been the co-owner, along with her late husband, of a safety deposit box at United Savings Bank, on Packer Avenue in South Philly.

Sam wasn't aware of such an account. He'd taken care of his mother's finances these last few years, but her social security checks were deposited in a different bank. That deposit box must have been dormant for quite a few years now.

Sam clicked on the link for the bank and searched for information about safety deposit boxes. He found information about how it all worked and navigated to the Frequently Asked Questions section, looking for information about successions. It stated that once a box owner passed away, his successors could retrieve the contents of the box after filling out the proper paperwork and paying the necessary fees.

Wanting to know more, Sam found the local branch's phone number and copied it into his phone. Lucky for him, this branch was open on Saturdays. Looking down at his phone he noticed that almost four hours had already gone by. He had not noticed the time fly as he searched online. The bank was now open. He decided to call right away.

Sam told the clerk who picked up his call about the safety deposit boxes and lied that his mother was in the late stages of cancer and that she would soon pass away. He wanted to know how he could retrieve the contents of her box once she was laid to rest. The clerk explained everything in clear detail and was very helpful. Sam then asked if someone besides the legal successor could access the box. Again, he lied and told her he lived overseas and might not be able to get to the bank in person. The young lady told him there was a form to fill out and that, once it was done, he could have someone open the box in his name.

Sam thanked her politely and hung up. He knew what he had to do—there was no way he could show up at the bank himself. He was a wanted criminal on the loose. As soon as he walked in and identified himself, security would be on top of him. He needed someone to get these things for him and pass them on. At first, he thought of asking his wife but then changed his mind. She'd already done enough for him as it was, and the bank was in South Philly, nowhere near where she worked or lived.

His next logical choice was to ask Dean for help again. He worked in South Philly, and it wouldn't be too long of a detour for him to swing by the bank after work. It would only take him about twenty minutes to walk down there, and he could hop on the subway a few blocks to the south right after.

Sam sent a text message to his friend, asking him if he was willing to help him again with something. He explained briefly that he needed him to run an errand for him in South Philly after work and asked what time would be best for them to talk on the phone; he would call him back then.

While he was waiting for his friend to reply, he needed to find a place where he could access a computer and printer. He would need to fill out the requisite forms before sending Dean over to the bank.

THIRTY-THREE

South Philly
Corner of 11th and Mifflin
Saturday – May 18, 2013 – 12:48 p.m.

After receiving a reply from Dean informing him of the best time to talk over the phone, Sam waited to call at the agreed-upon hour.

"Yo," Dean answered shortly when he picked up the call.

"Hey, it's me."

"So, what do you need?" Dean asked. He wasn't one to beat around the bush, and Sam appreciated his friend's direct approach.

"I need to retrieve something from a safety deposit box at a bank down on Packer Avenue. Do you know which one I'm talking about?"

"Yeah, I think I do. So, what's up?" Dean inquired.

"Well, since I'm a wanted criminal, I can't go inside. They'd call the cops as soon as they recognized my name. I was wondering if you would go in for me…"

"What's in the box?" Dean asked prudently.

"I don't know—that's the problem. But my gut tells me it has something to do with this whole mess I've found myself in," Sam explained. He had to tread carefully. He needed his friend's help, so he had to figure out a way to be convincing and reassuring at the same time.

"I ain't getting arrested for you Sam" his friend replied bluntly.

"The box belonged to my father… I seriously doubt there's anything illegal in there."

"Well then, I guess I don't see much of a problem," Dean replied.

Sam sighed in relief. "Okay. I'll be filling in all the required paperwork soon, and I'll send you a text letting you know where to pick it up. I'll be close by, keeping an eye out."

"Alright. So how do you want to proceed, exactly? You want to come to pick everything up at my house afterward?"

"No. Here's what I want you to do: after opening the box, just put everything inside a white plastic bag. You know, the kind you get at a drugstore."

"Yeah, okay. Then what?"

"Once you have everything in the bag, just step outside the bank and head back toward the subway station. I'll make contact," Sam instructed his friend.

"How?" Dean asked.

"I'd rather not say over the phone. I'm growing a little paranoid."

"I can see that," Dean chuckled.

Sam knew that his friend wouldn't ask all of this if he weren't truly worried about his safety. "Just trust me—I'll contact you. When I do, you'll know."

"Okay, I guess," Dean reluctantly agreed. "Can you at least tell me what's going on? I heard about your trial. That was unreal!" he exclaimed. "Then, a few days later, Vicky called me, asking if I'd seen you. She said you disappeared."

"Yeah, I kind of did. Listen, I can't say much since I don't have any concrete proof at the moment, but I'm a hundred percent sure I've been set up. Vanessa already confessed to me that she lied about the whole thing," Sam explained.

"Why would she make up something like that?" Dean asked incredulously.

"Listen, the only thing I can tell you so far is that Jackson's behind all of this for some reason."

"*Principal* Jackson?" Dean almost shouted into his phone.

"Shhhh!" Sam hissed. "Keep it to yourself. I don't know why he did it, but I know he's behind all of this. That's why I told you to hide your tracks. Be careful, buddy. Don't say a word to anyone, understand?"

"Will be," Dean agreed.

"Good. Text me right before heading to the bank. I'll be close by. And be careful," Sam insisted.

"Will do. Later," Dean said, before ending the call.

After hanging up with Dean, Sam spent the rest of his day going over everything he had one more time. He went online again and looked for a place where he could use a computer. After about an hour of searching for spots near where he was hiding, he came up empty. The only option that was remotely close by was the Free Library of Philadelphia, which he realized wasn't a viable option.

The issue wasn't how to get into the library itself—although the access was free for all citizens of the city, it didn't mean they would let anybody in and let them loose inside. You still had to have a member's card to enter and use the various services it provided. Sam couldn't very well walk up to the front desk in his present state and ask to be let in. They would ask for identification, and he didn't have any on him.

He tried to locate internet cafés close by, but while they'd been numerous only a few years ago, the proliferation of smartphones combined with readily accessible Wi-Fi connections in almost every place of business had rendered those cafés useless, and they had all progressively shut down.

He widened his search grid and after a short while found a place he could use—there was a community center in South Philly that had computers accessible for the residents who wished to enjoy modern technologies but didn't necessarily have the means or knowhow to do so. It was far from his hiding place and actually very close to the school, but he decided he would make the most of it. The bank with the safety deposit box was only about a dozen blocks away, so he could go scope out the bank before going over there to print his forms.

Sam spent some time walking around South Philly. He wandered around the bank to get a better feel for the area. After circling the block twice, he decided it was not a good idea to linger in one place for too long and headed back north towards

Passyunk Avenue. Once he got to the community center's front door, he walked in and was greeted by a friendly black man with a long, gray beard and receding hairline.

"Hi there!" the man said with a large smile. "Can I help you with something?"

"Uh, yeah…" Sam grumbled. "I want to write a résumé and print some copies. I'm looking for a job," he said, all the while looking down, feigning embarrassment while really just avoiding eye contact.

"Well, that's just great, friend. Congratulations!" the old man replied enthusiastically. "Do you need help using the computer? I can show you how it works and help you write your résumé if you want," he offered, pointing at the row of computers on the far wall.

"No thanks," Sam replied. "I know how to use computers. I used to be in logistics in the army," he lied, hoping it would be credible.

"Alright, then," the old man said. "Help yourself to any of our terminals. When you're done and you want to print out copies, let me know—it has to be sent to my printer. I'll let you get to work."

"Thank you," Sam mumbled. He walked over to the last computer on the right and settled in.

Sam went back to the bank's website and, after navigating through it for around ten minutes, found the requisite form that allowed someone else to access the contents of a safety deposit box. He downloaded the file and typed in all the relevant information, reviewing everything before saving it. Sam printed a copy and went to pick it up at the front desk. He borrowed a pen without asking and signed the form at the bottom of the page. Sam then folded the letter and placed it inside his jacket.

He walked back to his terminal and erased all the files he'd saved from the computer and shut it down. As he walked out, he nodded to the old man at the front desk.

"Good luck, friend!"

"Mmm-mm" Sam mumbled as the door closed behind him.

THIRTY-FOUR

South Philly
Corner of 15th and Packer Avenue
Monday – May 20, 2013 – 2:48 p.m.

After spending his entire Sunday holed up in his cave going over every part of his plan for retrieving whatever was inside the safety deposit box, Sam got a few hours of sleep. It was most likely due to severe exhaustion because it had been far from a comfortable setting. Nonetheless, he felt his energy level rise back up. As he traveled back to South Philly once more, his grumbling stomach let him know that he had to find some food; he figured he could grab something along the way.

As he was sitting underneath the overpass for the Schuylkill Expressway, Sam told himself that, while he waited for his friend and surveyed the bank, he should also look for new places to sleep. It had become quite tiresome for him to walk across the entire city so many times in the past few days. If he found a nice hiding place in South Philly, it would make things easier for him. On the other hand, it had become part of his routine to see his wife and child off every weekday morning, and he wasn't ready to give that up. He reminded himself that walking long distances was the least of his problems right now and that, as long as he remained mobile during the days, he was less likely to be spotted by the authorities.

Sam spied his friend walking down Packer Avenue from a distance; Dean's massive size made him hard to miss. Dean stopped next to a garbage can on the corner and bent down. He picked up the plastic bag containing the brass key and the signed form Sam had hidden underneath the trash can. Dean didn't have to look for long; it was right where Sam had told him in the detailed text he had sent an hour before.

He watched Dean walk inside the bank and could see him talking to someone through the large storefront windows but was unable to know what was really happening. At this point, he just had to put his entire trust in his long-time friend.

It took what seemed to Sam like an eternity but only half an hour for Dean to complete his task. Once Sam saw him exit the bank, he crossed the street and waited for him. Dean had been instructed to put the entire contents of the safety deposit box back into the plastic bag, and Sam hoped his friend had followed his instructions to the letter—but there was no reason to doubt him. It would most appear quite strange to the bank employees that someone would transport something thought so valuable in such a cheap way, but Sam didn't care. Once he had taken everything out, Dean was instructed to walk back toward Broad Street to grab the subway. Sam was ready to make contact.

As Dean approached the overpass, Sam began walking toward him, stooped over and still pretending to limp on his left leg. When they were both underneath the overpass, Sam bumped into Dean and mumbled, "Switch bags with me."

Dean was momentarily stunned to hear Sam's voice, but he regained his composure in a flash. He took Sam's plastic bag and gave his over while they were both still touching. It only took a fraction of a second for the brush pass to be completed. To anyone watching, it would only appear as if Dean had been bothered by a hobo. Both men resumed walking in opposite directions.

A few yards later, Sam's relief was cut short—he heard the squeal of tires behind him. He turned his head and saw a large black SUV stop on the curb just ahead of where his friend was walking. Two large black men, wearing bright red bandanas over their faces, leaped out of the vehicle and tried to grab Dean. Unfortunately for them, it appeared that no one had told them about the man they were supposed to attack—Dean fought back hard.

He pushed one man down to the ground and punched the second in the gut. His first assailant was getting back up, but Dean kicked him in the ribs to keep him down. The second man grabbed Dean from behind, but Sam's friend was simply too strong for him. He grabbed his opponent's arm, bent down and stepped back, and was behind the man before he could even realize what was happening.

Dean swept the man's legs with his left foot and fell on top of him to the ground, punching him in the back of the head several times. Dean didn't even look winded. As he was sitting on top of his aggressor, he glanced up to account for the other man who had tried to grab him. He hadn't noticed that the driver's side door of the SUV behind him had just been thrown open.

A third man raced around the back of the car and pulled out a large, chromed pistol. He walked up behind Dean, pressed the barrel of his gun to the back of his head and pulled the trigger.

Sam put his hand over his mouth as stifled a scream. He was powerless to do anything.

Dean's body went limp and he crumbled to the concrete. The man holding the gun waved his gun at his buddies and shouted a bunch of commands at them. He walked back to the front of the car and got behind the wheel as the other two other men slowly got up and searched Dean's body. They grabbed the plastic bag and his wallet.

The man at the wheel honked his horn and the two other men hobbled back inside the SUV. The car roared to life and, with tires screeching, swerved back into traffic.

Sam watched as the car turned a corner and disappeared. When he was sure that they were far enough away, he ran to Dean who was lying lifeless on the sidewalk. He kneeled and took his friend's head into his hands. There was a massive hole blown right above his right eyebrow. Dean's eyes were open as if he was still alive, but Sam knew that there was no coming back from such a wound. Tears began rolling down his cheeks.

"Why did you put up a fight?" he cried. "You should have let them take the bag. There was nothing in it!" he almost yelled out of frustration. His friend had been killed over a plastic bag full of discarded granola bar wrappings and blank sheets of paper.

He heard sirens coming from a distance. Looking down, he noticed that his hands were covered in Dean's blood. He couldn't hang around any longer. There was nothing he could do for Dean, except find the people behind all this and make them pay.

Sam put Dean's head back down delicately and shut his eyelids.

"I'm sorry buddy. I'll make this right I promise" he whispered to his deceased friend.

Sam got back up and looked around. It was time to get away. He wiped his bloody hands on his shirt and took off running.

THIRTY-FIVE

South Philly
Corner of 15th and Packer Avenue
Monday – May 20, 2013 – 5:42 p.m.

Sam had been sitting in a booth inside a nearby restaurant for about three hours, studying everything he had found. There was nothing else he could do about Dean, so he focused on finding out why all of this was happening.

The contents of the safety deposit box consisted of a single manila envelope. Inside, there was an old, undeveloped roll of film, a few large black-and-white pictures, and a notebook. Sam took his time studying everything.

It turned out the notebook had belonged to his late father, James Monroe, who had been investigating rumors of corrupt high-ranking police officers. There were a lot of scribbled notes in the first hundred pages, with various dates, names, and locations inscribed. After a few blank pages, he found the first draft of the last article his father had ever started to write. It read:

"For the past few years, there has been much unrest in the city of Philadelphia, particularly in the northern neighborhoods.

While the Civil Rights Movement is continuing its long march toward equality and social justice, people question the motivation behind the many acts of violence that have taken place throughout the city, but more often in the more predominantly black neighborhoods of North Philadelphia.

The shooting of twenty-four-year-old Willie Philyaw by police officers remains very controversial, as the official police report states that the young man attacked an officer with a knife, while residents of the area still claim he was unarmed and shot without reason.

Mayor Tate's efforts to better integrate black people to higher positions in the city's administration, along with the accepted proposal to place black NAACP lawyers in various neighborhood precincts, have been saluted by almost everyone, but it has failed to lower the tensions between the residents of these neighborhoods and the Philadelphia Police Department.

Many are still trying to understand the reason behind the Columbia Street riots that took place just a few weeks ago. There is still a lot of mystery behind the alleged attack suffered by officers Wells and Hoffs after they responded to a domestic dispute call early on August 28th, as there seems to be some contradictions between the two officers' statements.

The massive police response to the riots on the corner of 23rd and Columbia was unprecedented, as was the curfew imposed on the citizens of North Philadelphia. While the police commissioner's handling of the situation has been recognized as adequate by most and has given a lot of traction to his ever-rising political capital, the residents of the black neighborhoods of Philadelphia have not taken kindly to what the man known to some as 'The General' has stated to the press in the recent past, going as far as saying he would 'get their black asses.'

After weeks of investigating various rumors, it has become increasingly plausible that a few high-ranking police officers across the city have been inciting people to start riots. There is now documented proof of police officers bribing black residents of North Philadelphia in the hopes that a riot would ensue.

As you can see in the photos printed on the next page (have photo lab crop and enlarge for maximum effect), we have witnessed an exchange of what appears to be envelopes of money between the police and two unknown males on at least three different occasions in the last months. Each time, riots have erupted in these same areas only a few days later, the largest one being what we now call the Columbia Avenue Riots.

Not only have we been able to capture proof of officers trading favors with these assailants, but you can also see in picture X (make sure numbers match with photos before printing), those same two individuals throwing bricks at officers Wells and Hoffs at the beginning of the riots. It is still unclear who talked to Raymond Hall and encouraged him to spread the false rumor that a white patrolman beat and killed a pregnant black woman, but it is most likely the same two mystery men depicted in the photos.

The mobilization of over six hundred police officers in a matter of an hour is highly suspicious, almost as if someone in the administration had known ahead of time that riots would ensue in that sector.

While that remains, for the moment, impossible to prove, there is no denying the fact that the current police commissioner's popularity level has skyrocketed and that his quest for the mayor's chair is assured now more than ever. It is becoming apparent that there is a possible link between the man's rise to political power and the events happening in some parts of the city.

Still, many questions remain unanswered. If members of the city's police force have been purposely encouraging civil unrest in the hopes of furthering one of their own's political career, then these men have to answer for their actions.

As the city struggles to regain its composure, it is imperative that these allegations be looked into more profoundly. The Philadelphia Police Department must be more transparent and answer these questions if they ever hope to bring peace and stability back to our wonderful town."

THIRTY-SIX

South Philly
Corner of 15th and Packer Avenue
Monday – May 20, 2013 – 7:51 p.m.

Sam finished reading his father's article for the third time as he ordered another plate of appetizers and a refill of soda. He hadn't eaten anything in about twenty-four hours and very little in the past few days. Since he knew they wouldn't let him just sit in a booth for hours for free, he figured he would kill two birds with one stone and fill his belly as much as humanly possible while he sat there. He wasn't sure when his next meal would be, so he had to seize this opportunity. Sam looked at the menu and ordered the cheapest meal items he could find— now wasn't the time to be picky. He didn't have much of an appetite anyway but forced himself to eat.

Sam was getting a better understanding of what had happened to his father and why he'd chosen to keep these documents in a safe place.

During their brief telephone conversation, Donald Jackson had hinted to the fact that his father had been nosy and that what had happened to him wasn't an accident. It was a fatal mistake on Jackson's part, because if the man hadn't said anything, then Sam never would've thought to pick at that scab.

It was now clear that the investigation his father had been running for the few months preceding his death had irritated some powerful people. The problem was that Sam still had no clue how his own story fit into all this. He'd never even known his father, so he couldn't really consider himself a threat. The other main issue Sam was struggling with was that this all took place almost fifty years ago. All the major players in this story were either dead or on the verge of dying; the infamous police commissioner, who would go on to become mayor, had passed away more than twenty years ago, and as far as he could tell, all the high-ranking police officers the article talked about would most likely be dead, too. The improbable few who could still be alive probably weren't in any state to give him answers.

Sam put the notebook back in the manila envelope and took out the three enlarged black-and-white pictures. They depicted various stages of the Columbia Avenue Riots, the first capturing two kids in hoodies throwing objects at a police cruiser, the second picture showing kids breaking windows, and the third depicting the hundreds of police officers coming down on North Philly as they tried to contain the rioters. Sam remembered learning about those events in school but had forgotten most of it. Now, reading about it brought back some memories, but it wouldn't be enough—he would need to do some research to fill in the gaps.

He ordered a slice of chocolate cake along with a glass of milk as he analyzed the photos time and time again. His stomach felt full already, but he willed himself to stuff a bit of sweetness in before leaving. He put the pictures back inside the envelope, and as he did, he felt the roll of film at the bottom. He took it out and examined it.

It looked to be in pretty good shape, even though it had been in storage for decades. He took out his phone and turned on the Wi-Fi so he could use the restaurant's network; he'd already used almost half his data and was trying to conserve as much as possible. The connection was far slower than the network he was used to, and it only added to his irritation as his thought kept returning to Dean. The waitress must have sensed this because she left Sam alone for the most part. Luckily for him, it was a slow Monday night and there were no major sporting events that he could see on the big screens, so the place was quiet, and he wasn't bothered by anyone. If he ordered items periodically, the staff paid him no mind.

He remembered that there was a photo studio around 19th Street, close to his apartment, but he wasn't sure if they could work with film. Now that pretty much everything was digital, there were very few places left that had the equipment and knowhow to work with it. If that place couldn't get it done, he would keep looking until he found something more suitable.

He searched a map until he found the studio in question and clicked on the link for their web page. Sam was relieved to see they proclaimed to work with all types of media support, including film. He found their business hours and made a mental note to be there as they opened first thing tomorrow morning.

As Sam was finishing his last bite of cake and stuffing everything back inside the envelope then his backpack, he motioned for the waitress to bring him the bill. Sam wanted to leave a generous tip but decided against it—although he felt crummy about short-changing the poor girl who had brought him food and drink all evening.

He had another long walk ahead of him but now he didn't mind as much. Sam got up and strode out quickly, hoping to avoid the waitress's reaction when she saw that he had not left anything for her on the table.

As he headed north, his thoughts turned back to his best friend. Sam promised himself to do right by him by the time this was all over.

THIRTY-SEVEN

Center City
Underneath the Chestnut Street Bridge
Tuesday – May 21, 2013 – 8:49 a.m.

The sun was shining brightly over the city and glimmered in the ripples over the water of the Schuylkill River. It was going to be another hot day—Sam dreaded having to step out of the shade, but he decided he wouldn't be able to stay inside his cave for much longer. The ever-increasing smell of refuse that assaulted his nostrils was becoming intolerable, and the heat and humidity that was about to roll over the city wouldn't help matters at all. He told himself that he might as well make the most of his day while remaining watchful.

He climbed through the fence and wandered back to his usual observation post to see his family off, as he did every morning. Once they were out of sight, he headed east down the street. The photo studio was only a few blocks away.

When the young woman in charge of opening the store for the start of another business day went to unlock the doors, she was met with a strange man in rags waiting for her to open. She opened the doors and stepped back as Sam approached.

"Hi," she started warily as Sam pushed his way inside.

"Hello," Sam said, after looking around to see if anyone else was near the store. "I need some film developed right away."

"Sure, we can do that," the girl replied in a curious tone. She looked Sam up and down but didn't say a word about his appearance. "Let's see what you got," she continued after a few seconds. Although she seemed happy to help, she kept a safe distance from him.

Sam pulled out the roll of film from the manila envelope and handed it over.

"Please be careful. It's very old," he told her, watching attentively as she manipulated the roll in her hands.

"I'll say!" she answered as she looked at the item from all angles. "I've never even heard of this company. How old is this anyway?"

"About fifty years old. It belonged to my uncle. I found it in his stuff after he passed away. Guess they're old family pictures or something," Sam lied.

"I'm so sorry to hear that. My deepest condolences," she replied. "It'll be a challenge, but it shouldn't take more than a day. It looks to be in pretty good shape, so we should be able to pull everything from it. I can't guarantee anything, though. You understand, right?"

"Just do your best," Sam told her. "I would appreciate getting it as soon as possible, though."

"Well, I guess I might get it done by six this evening…"

"Is there any way we can make it even faster?" Sam asked politely, trying to keep his anxiety at bay.

"I'm sorry… I've already got a bunch of commands ahead of yours."

"What if I paid a little extra?" Sam inquired. "Would that compensate for the time you lost on your other jobs?"

The girl raised her eyebrows, surprised to hear Sam's offer— Sam was sure he didn't look like someone who could spend a lot of money, let alone pay extra fees. She looked at the roll again and sighed.

"I suppose I can make an exception. But I'll have to charge you a twenty-five percent surcharge. And I'll need the payment in advance," she said, looking at Sam suspiciously. Clearly, the strange man with his old roll of film was an unusual sight for her, and she obviously didn't feel too comfortable with what he was asking.

"Deal," Sam agreed. "Ring it up on the register. I'll pay you now, and I'll be back after lunch to pick up my order. Oh, and while you're at it, can you enlarge each picture, say to about letter size?"

"Sure thing. It'll just cost a little more."

"No problem."

The girl went behind the counter and rang up the price on the register. She looked up at Sam and asked, "Is there a number where I can reach you once it's done?"

"No," he replied politely. "I'll just swing back at one this afternoon to pick everything up." Sam paid her the exact amount she asked for and headed out the door.

He walked for another few blocks and entered a Staples office supply store. He made his way to the back, ignoring the stares of the other patrons milling about. When he got to the copy center at the very far end of the first floor, he checked out the photocopiers and asked for help. The clerk explained that to work the machine, he had to insert a credit or debit card and that whatever work he did would be automatically charged to it. Sam thanked him and waited for the young man to attend to another customer.

He pulled out one of the prepaid credit cards he'd purchased what seemed to him to be ages ago but, in fact, had only been a week. He inserted it in the slot and waited for the copier to recognize it. Once everything was in order, he took out his father's notebook and copied every single page.

It took Sam over thirty minutes to go through the entire notebook, but he was rewarded with a fresh pile of papers with all his father's notes on them.

He took the pile and placed it in the machine's feeder to make another round of copies. Once the second set was done, he stacked the pile back in the feeder, and this time, selected the option to scan the papers. He typed in his new email address and pressed the Start button.

While waiting for the machine to complete its job, he took out his phone. After powering it on, he opened his mail app and checked to see if he'd received the file with the scanned pages. He refreshed his page a few times until the message appeared and opened the file to make sure everything had been done right. Once he'd verified it, he sent it to his personal cloud storage drive and shut off his phone.

Checking the clock on the wall, he noticed that it had been a little over two hours since he'd dropped off the roll of film. He gathered all his belongings and walked back out onto Chestnut. He decided that by the time he arrived back at the photo studio, the work would most likely be done, and if not, he could wait for it in the cool, air-conditioned store.

As he arrived at the studio, the spunky brunette who had greeted him earlier saw him through the plate glass window and waved at him with a huge smile. She gave him the thumbs up, and Sam responded in kind.

He walked to the counter, and she handed him a thin, letter-sized envelope. He thanked her, saying he couldn't wait to see what was inside.

"Do you mind if I stay here for a while to look these over?" he asked politely.

"Sure!" she replied with a smile. "Help yourself. And if there's anything else you need, just let me know."

"Well, now that you mention it..." Sam started, "is there a magnifying glass I could borrow?"

"Of course." She disappeared behind the counter and brought back a large magnifying glass, handing it over to Sam. "It was a lot of fun working on such an old piece! We don't see many of those nowadays—I'm glad I got the chance."

"Glad to hear it," said Sam. "Thank you."

He sat down and opened the envelope eagerly. There were a dozen pictures, and all of them showed a car parked on the side of the street, with a police officer and two other men talking. They looked like the other three he'd seen in the envelope from the safety deposit box. He started flipping through them. A few frames later, he could see the officer pass something to the other men.

As Sam reached the last frame, he suddenly lost his breath. The picture showed all three men staring in the camera's direction. The police officer looked shocked, but it was the other participants who caught Sam's attention.

Even though the man was now much heavier and had a lot less hair, there was no mistaking it—Sam was looking at a picture of Donald Jackson, or rather, *two* Donald Jacksons.

THIRTY-EIGHT

Downtown Philly
Corner of Chestnut and 19th
Tuesday – May 21, 2013 – 12:18 p.m.

"Got you, you bastard!" Sam whispered. The girl behind the register raised her head but didn't say a word. Sam apologized and thanked her for the good work, put the pictures back inside the envelope, and stormed out.

He had to restrain from running as he marched back to Staples. He had to make copies of these pictures, just to be cautious. When he showed up for the second time that day at the copy center, the young man who had helped him earlier gave him a quizzical look but didn't say a thing.

Sam inserted his prepaid card again and encouraged the machine to move along faster. Once everything was ready, he scanned every picture he'd just received. Once it was done, he checked everything on his phone and stored the files, just as he had earlier. Before shutting down the machine, he made three sets of paper copies. He would need them for his next step.

After finishing, he sat at the large work counter and organized everything. He took one pile of the copies he'd made earlier and included a copy of every picture he had in his file on top. He put it all in a large mailing envelope and repeated the process again.

Sam put one envelope back into his backpack and went to the service counter. Getting the young man's attention, he asked him to help him send the envelope by courier to be delivered next Monday. He didn't want the package to arrive at its destination before then, as it was his fallback strategy. It was an ace in the hole, in case what he planned to accomplish didn't work or if he got caught before that. They filled out the paperwork together, and Sam thanked the young man before walking out.

As he ambled back toward the river and a bit of shade, something caught his attention. There was a newsstand on the corner of 19th, and out of the corner of his eye, Sam glimpsed a picture on the front page of the *Philadelphia Inquirer* that froze him in his steps. He was looking at a picture of himself, his old self, and right next to his image was one of Dean. Above the photos, the headline read, "*South Philly High teacher shot to death by former colleague.*"

Sam felt like someone had just punched him in the stomach. He swallowed the bile that rose in his throat, and the world around him started spinning. Desperately trying to regain his composure, he purchased a copy of the paper. His brain was no longer able to focus on maintaining a low profile, so he sprinted back to his hideout, not caring how it would appear to the people around him.

Once he got back inside his alcove, he stumbled in just far enough to still have a bit of light and sat down. He opened the paper and started reading, while tears rolled down his face.

Center City
Underneath the Chestnut Street Bridge
Wednesday – May 22, 2013 – 11:17 p.m.

Sam had been sitting in the dark for more than twenty-four hours. He kept reading the article over and over:

"An investigation is underway as the body of a man shot to death was found in South Philly late yesterday afternoon. Police found Dean Ashton, 42, unresponsive of the sidewalk on the corner of Packer and 15th. Investigators say the victim was shot once to the head with a large caliber pistol. The man was pronounced dead at the scene by the EMTs.

Police say that the main suspect in this shooting is Samuel Brighton, age 44, a former colleague of Ashton. Brighton has already made the headlines earlier this year. He was charged and convicted of possession of child pornography after nude photos of his students were found on his phone. Brighton has since skipped bail and has a warrant out for his arrest.

Philadelphia Police are actively searching for the whereabouts of Samuel Brighton and are asking the public for help in locating him. If anyone suspects having seen Samuel Brighton, police suggest calling the PPD tip line. Officials strongly recommend that you do not attempt to approach Brighton by any means, as he is considered armed and extremely dangerous."

Sam couldn't believe it. This was all complete and utter fabrication. He knew down in his very core that Dean's death was related to his feud with Jackson. He had seen the goons grab Dean after their exchange under the overpass, but he never would've thought the man capable of such cold-blooded murder. Dean had only tried to help and had paid with his life. As he stared at the picture of his late friend, Sam swore to himself that he would bring those bastards down, no matter the cost. If they wanted a fight, they were going to get one.

Center City
Underneath the Chestnut Street Bridge
Wednesday – May 22, 2013 – 11:52 p.m.

Sleep had been impossible so far. Memories of his best friend were haunting Sam, and whenever he wasn't thinking of the good times they'd shared, he was laying out a plan to bring Donald Jackson down once and for all.

The plan was to stay holed up in his cave until Friday morning and take his time planning for every contingency. He ignored his stomach growling—he hadn't eaten anything since Monday night, and even though he had filled up at the restaurant, that was now more than forty-eight hours ago. But food would have to wait. He knew the human body could go on for an extended period without food, but not without water. He'd kept his old bottle of Gatorade and, after rinsing it, had filled it up at a nearby park to make sure he stayed hydrated.

After triple-checking that all his gear was properly stored in his backpack and all his digital files were still on his cloud, he closed his eyes and tried to get some sleep. Sam knew it would be difficult with all the thoughts swimming around in his head, but he still had to try.

As he reminisced about the last time he'd seen his best friend, being bored senseless by a long and pointless presentation, Sam was shaken out of his reveries by the high-pitched shrieks of a woman. He tried to ignore it and told himself that it was an old woman who had seen a raccoon on the river trail, or something similar.

But two seconds later, he heard the same screams again and again. Finally, the woman began calling for help.

Sam crept closer to see what was going on, all the while remaining in the shadows. He saw an imposing young man with a shaved head and long beard, his arms covered in tattoos, grabbing a young woman by the waist. She was wearing a tight blue dress and high heels and was trying her best to free herself from his grip, but the man was almost twice her size and too strong for her.

Sam told himself this wasn't his fight and that someone was bound to come along to help. But as the seconds went by, not a soul walked down the river trail, which wasn't unusual at this late hour. The woman kept screaming for anyone to help and tried to fight back as best she could, but she was no match for the monster who had her in his grasp.

Sam tried to ignore the screams, but as he watched the man pin the young lady down to the ground and try to get on top of her, his brain screamed at him that he just couldn't stand by and do nothing. He was already in a world of trouble, but even if he somehow got out of this mess, he would never be able to look at himself in the mirror if he did nothing about this.

He retrieved his backpack and undid the flap in an instant. After taking out what he needed, he closed it and hid it underneath some rubble at the far end of the cave.

He stepped out of his hideout and ran across the train tracks, jumping over the fence.

As he came closer to the struggle, he shouted, "Hey! Get the hell off her right now!"

The man looked up, and as he saw the slim, disheveled figure standing in front of him, he chuckled and replied, "Stay out of this, old man. This doesn't concern you."

The young woman pinned underneath his massive legs looked back and saw the homeless man standing just a few feet away.

"Please help me!" she screamed as she kept trying to break free.

"I said get the hell off her! Right now!" Sam growled.

"Move along, pops, or I just might have to hurt *you* too!" the assailant said, clearly not intimidated.

Knowing he would never physically match this beast, Sam had only one card left to play. He undid his jacket's button and shouted again as he walked closer, "This is your last warning. Let her go!"

As the large man raised his head once more, his expression turned from a scowl to surprise and, finally, to fear as he realized he was gazing down the barrel of a pistol.

After staring at the gun pointed at him for a few seconds, the man stood up slowly and backed away from the young woman. She was lying on the grass, weeping.

"What's your name?" Sam asked the young lady in a calm voice, as she struggled to pull her dress back down over her underwear.

"What?" she asked wildly, looking for one of her high heels.

"What's your name?"

"Mary," she gasped out.

"Okay, Mary. I want you to get as far from here as you can, as quick as you can. Get to the train station. There's a bunch of cops over there," Sam instructed her, all the while keeping his eyes on her assailant.

For a moment, she remained still, a look of disbelief clouding her eyes.

"Go on, get!" Sam barked.

"Thank you! Thank you!" she cried out as she wiped the tears from her cheeks. Then, she started running up the stairway that led to Market Street.

When she was all the way up to street level, she turned around once more to look back down at her savior then resumed running toward the train station.

When Sam turned back to the large man who had attempted to rape the young woman just a few seconds earlier, he noticed that he was smiling and approaching Sam slowly.

"Get back. I'll shoot!" Sam shouted.

"I don't think you will, old man," he sneered, still approaching one careful step at a time. "It doesn't even look like you know how to use that thing."

Sam backed away. It wasn't in his nature to use violence. This man, on the other end, seemed very at ease with using brute force to get what he wanted. Sam guessed that his adversary could tell he was bluffing. He kept advancing toward him, slowly but surely, a menacing grin spreading across his face.

As he got within a few feet from Sam, they could hear the faint sound of police sirens approaching from the east and he caught the reflection of blue and red lights reflecting on the windows of the buildings above. He noticed the lights were getting brighter by the second. The police were very close by, and Sam had to move.

The large man had come to the same conclusion and ran away, sprinting northbound along the river path.

"Shit! Shit! Shit!" Sam cursed in a harsh whisper. He placed the pistol in the small of his back and started barrelling south along the river.

As he was fleeing, Sam realized the impact of what he'd just done. Even though he knew it was the right thing to do, he'd come out of hiding and exposed himself. There was no way he could get back inside his hideout now. His backpack containing all the intel he'd gathered so far was still there, but it was now impossible to head back and retrieve it before the cops showed up. If he was seen anywhere near there, they might go looking and find his gear.

Still cursing, Sam ran down the river path as fast as he could. He would have to figure out a way to get back in once the heat died down.

FORTY-ONE

Center City
Corner of Market and 23rd
Thursday – May 23, 2013 – 7:12 a.m.

The skies were overcast with menacing clouds, and the rain was pouring down, as it had been for the past three hours, with no end in sight.

Sam had been walking aimlessly around the city since his encounter on the river path. Everything he'd been planning for the last couple of days was unraveling. Not only had his best friend died because he'd sent him to do something he should have done himself; but now, he'd come out of hiding and had nowhere else to find shelter.

After running to the nearest stairway to get off the river path, Sam had walked at a brisk pace for a few hours around the neighborhood, hopelessly trying to find a place to hide. At this very moment, the police had to be interviewing the victim he had rescued, and after explaining how she had been saved by a helpful homeless man, she had surely given a long and detailed description of him. Sam couldn't blame the woman—he would have done the same in her situation.

Sam's number one priority had been to change his appearance. If he stayed in his army clothes for too long, it would be easy for the cops to spot him. He had kept in the shadows and walked through the alleyways to avoid being seen as much as possible, but this late at night, the streets were deserted, so he stood out like a sore thumb in his desert camouflage outfit. Sam found refuge in an alleyway and sat behind a garbage bin. He decided to wait for daybreak and for the foot traffic around town to pick up before heading out again.

The sun was up now, but no one could tell; the sky had turned to dark gray overnight. It was still raining and what had started as a slight sprinkle had grown in intensity as the hours passed. Sam was keeping an eye on the street at the end of the alley, counting the number of pedestrians per minute in his head.

Even though the number of people walking by had gone up significantly, Sam couldn't muster the courage to get up. He was terrified of being seen. Sam was soaking wet from the rain but didn't even notice it anymore, except when he shivered from the cold. He was running through every option he could think of, but he just couldn't see a way out anymore.

The police had been searching for him ever since he'd skipped bail, but probably without much effort. Now, they were looking for him as the prime suspect in Dean's murder, and he was sure Jackson had a hand in that also. If that wasn't bad enough, he had come out of hiding at the worst time. He knew that the cops would be on the lookout for Mary's aggressor, but she surely had been asked about the man who had helped her. So, the cops now had Sam's description, although there was no way for them to know it had been him. Even though they wouldn't be actively looking for the man Mary had described, it still made him easier to spot by the authorities, especially down by the river.

Things were not going well for him. A thorough investigation of Dean's murder would prove that he wasn't responsible for it, but then again, after the way his case had been handled, he didn't know how thorough they would be on this one either. Now, the police were on the lookout for persons of interest on three separate cases, each one implicating Sam. Still, he reminded himself that whatever the outcome, he had at least done one thing right in helping that poor young woman on the river path. Maybe if he was caught, it would help mitigate his sentence.

Sam was trying to keep warm as best he could when he heard the squeaking sound of his salvation. As he looked up, he saw an old man hunched over and pushing a rusty shopping cart up the street. The cart was filled to the brim with what the old man would most likely deem his most precious possessions—plastic bags full of discarded aluminum cans. He stopped next to a garbage can and rifled through it, hoping to find another piece of treasure.

Sam kept his eyes on the man. He was shorter than Sam but seemed to have a similar build. It was hard to tell because he was wearing a staggering amount of layered clothing. The man must have had at least a dozen shirts worn one over the other, a hoodie vest and a black raincoat on top of everything. He was wearing an old black beanie hat, and his faded blue jeans were ripped at both knees. As the old man was elbow deep inside the garbage can, Sam made his move.

He walked toward him and coughed to get his attention. The old man looked up and eyed him suspiciously. He must have thought Sam was also after the contents of the garbage can, so Sam held both palms up in a gesture of peaceful approach. He asked the old man, "Hi there. How are you doing, fella'?"

"I found this first! Get away from here!" the man snarled, confirming what Sam thought.

"Easy, friend. I'm not after your stuff. I just want to ask you something."

"Whatchoo want?" the man asked as he bent back down over the trash can to resume his search.

"I'm wondering… Are you hungry? How would you like to make a bit of money so you can buy a nice warm meal?" Sam asked.

The man looked back at Sam and said nothing for a few seconds.

"Whatchoo mean?" he asked Sam.

"I mean that if you want to, you could do something for me, and in return, I'll give you some money and let you be on your way."

"I ain't interested in doin' any sexual stuff with you, mister, so you best be on your way!" the old man replied harshly.

Sam chuckled at his answer. He hadn't thought about it, but maybe there were some sick folks around town who craved some weird sexual favors, and the homeless were probably a good target for them, as they would be more motivated to put their pride aside in order to make some quick cash.

"Relax, old man. It's not about sex, I assure you. I'm talking about you and me doing a bit of trading," Sam said, as he kept approaching him. There was no need for everyone around to hear this conversation, so he got closer to avoid making too much noise.

"A trade?" the man asked. "What kind of trade?"

"It's pretty simple, and it's a good deal for you. How about you come find me down that alley when you're done searching?" Sam asked, pointing down to the spot where he'd been sitting.

"Uh-huh," the man grunted.

Sam went back to wait, and five minutes later, the old man sidled his way, struggling to push his cart. When he got to Sam, he asked, "So, what'choo wanna trade?"

"It's simple. You give me your coat, your sweater vest, and your hat. In return, I'll give you this jacket—which is in much better condition than yours—my hat, and I'll even throw in twenty bucks for your trouble."

At the sound of money, the old man's eyes lit up.

"Show me the money first," he demanded.

Sam understood the man's suspicions, so he fished inside his pocket for the money he'd taken out of his money belt earlier and showed him a twenty-dollar bill. Sam was just hoping the man wouldn't try to stick him up, but from the looks of him, he wouldn't be able to do much harm even if he tried.

"Make it forty, and you got yourself a deal, mister," the man said.

"Thirty," Sam replied. "Sorry, that's all I have left," he lied.

"Deal!" the old man agreed with a toothless smile.

Sam took off his hat and jacket and handed them over. They were wet through and through, but the rain would stop at some point, and he was sure the old man would be happy.

The man grabbed Sam's clothing and threw them inside his cart.

"Now it's your turn, friend," Sam said.

The old man removed his hat, jacket, and hoodie and gave them to Sam. Sam handed him the money he'd promised and thanked him. As Sam put his new clothes on, his nostrils were assaulted by the pungent smell. It wasn't surprising. These clothes hadn't been washed in a long time, if ever, and the man was dressed as if he were in Antarctica when, in fact, the weather was closer to a hundred degrees. Sam smelled like he was wearing an old gym bag. Whether he wound up a free man or sent to jail, the first thing he would do was take a shower when this was all over. They both turned away from each other without a word and headed off in different directions.

FORTY-TWO

Center City
Corner of Market and 23rd
Thursday – May 23, 2013 – 1:25 p.m.

The rain had stopped, and the sun was peeking through the clouds. It promised to be another balmy day, but Sam was just happy to be out of the rain for now. As his new rags were drying, their odor began fading, but not nearly enough. Sam had difficulty breathing at first, but he eventually got used to it.

The good news was that if the police were indeed looking for a bum in old army clothes, they would find one, but it would be a dead end. Even if the old man he had traded with was interrogated by the police, Sam was sure he was in no condition to help them much. It had been dark and raining, and from the way he'd held the money so close to his eyes, Sam was sure the man could barely see a few feet in front of him.

He felt safer in his new appearance, even if he reeked from a mile away, so he allowed himself to relax a bit. He had a lot to do and not much time to do it. Tomorrow would be a big day, and he needed to be ready.

He crossed the river over Market Street and looked to the river path on the other side of the water. There was a lone police officer stopping people and asking them questions. No doubt he was stationed there in the hopes that someone would remember seeing Mary's assailant, where he'd come from or where he'd gone.

Sam didn't waste another second hanging around. His hideout was compromised, and he wouldn't be able to use it for a while. But he still had to retrieve his backpack from there, if it hadn't already been found. He would have to wait until nightfall and try to sneak in undetected. Until then, he would move on to another part of his planning. Sam was tired, he smelled horrible, and he was almost out of money. Still, he could *not* give up. He was so close to his goal, so he pushed all the negative thoughts from his mind and focused on what would happen in the next twenty-four hours.

He started ambling downtown, keeping his fake limp as he walked and hunching his back to conceal his appearance to a maximum. As he trudged along, he kept looking around to find a new place to hide, but so far, he was coming up empty.

When he reached his destination on the corner of Chestnut and 15th, he slowed down even more. His senses became heightened, and his brain registered every sight and sound around him. His nose was useless since it was still fighting a losing battle with the clothes on his back, but Sam kept a watchful eye for any security cameras and police officers.

He walked around the massive, white, stone building of City Hall. As he looked up and saw the statue of William Penn standing atop the clock tower, he wondered what the founding father of Pennsylvania would think of the two men who were attempting to take control of the state at that very instant. He doubted Penn would approve.

Sam surveyed the interior courtyard through the large stone arches and tried to register as much information as possible without entering or staying in one place for too long. He walked around the outside of the building and repeated the process each time on the three other sides.

The courtyard was an open area with an entrance to the subway station in the middle. There were small tables with wrought iron chairs for people to sit at and eat. A few vendors on the perimeter of the building had set up shop, and there was a lone coffee cart inside the courtyard.

Sam kept exploring around City Hall, noting every entrance and exit and mapping the locations of the police officers he saw. He didn't know if they were stationed there or if they walked around, but at first glance, they all seemed to have a sector to patrol.

After a few minutes, he went back to the alley from earlier in the week, when he'd wanted to ambush Vanessa. As he neared it, his thoughts shifted to the young girl. He didn't know if she was alive and well or if she had suffered the same fate as Dean. He now knew that there wasn't much Donald Jackson was unwilling to do to get what he wanted, but he prayed that Vanessa was alright.

The two large garbage containers he'd sat between were still in place and would prove a valuable spot to hide his backpack when he made his move. The only problem now was to figure out a way to get his gear back without getting caught.

After two hours of scouting, he moved away from City Hall. There was no need to hang around anymore, and the longer he stayed, the higher his chances of being recognized were. He'd seen what he needed to see, and it was time to leave before he attracted too much attention.

As he was limping back toward Center City, he stopped on the corner of 17th and saw another tiny alley behind the street. He found a spot to sit down for a few minutes. Sam needed to rest, if only for a short while. He'd barely slept in the past three days and hadn't eaten anything since the restaurant. Sam was having trouble focusing when it mattered most, but he just told himself to suck it up for the hundredth time and pushed himself back up. There was a pressing matter at hand—he had to figure out a way to get his gear back; otherwise, tomorrow would be a no-go.

Sam cut across 17th Street and turned left a few blocks later. He crossed over the Market Street Bridge and walked two hundred feet to get a good view of his former hideout from across the river.

For now, there weren't any police present as far as he could tell, but still, he reminded himself that he had to be careful. The policeman he'd seen earlier might have left for a few minutes for his lunch break, or he might be somewhere else that Sam just couldn't see from so far away. He tried to decide how he would manage to get in and out without being noticed. After analyzing the scene, he thought he might have an idea, but he wasn't sure if it was safe or if he even had the physical abilities to pull it off, but right now he couldn't think of anything else. He would just have to try.

With at least another twelve hours to go until it was late enough to pull his little stunt, Sam had to find a way to stay away from the public eye and maybe find a bit of food. If he didn't get any of his strength back up soon, he wouldn't even be able to walk to City Hall tomorrow, let alone be in any shape to be efficient.

He roamed westbound and entered University City. The neighborhood had been entering a renaissance for the past few years, and what had been an ugly, yet functional part of town was turning into a glitzy place filled with trendy restaurants, bars, brand-new apartment buildings, and business towers. He didn't fit the décor at all, but he had confidence that his looks and personal hygiene would keep most people at bay.

Right across the river was a large multi-level public parking structure. There were a few shops down on the first level, and Sam would stop by from time to time whenever he visited his wife at the hospital or at her research center. Nestled on the first level were a large convenience store and a small sandwich shop.

He walked into the convenience store, and just as he entered, everyone inside seemed to freeze. Sam didn't look like the regular clientele, comprised mostly of students and hipsters. He ignored the stares and made a beeline for the refrigerator in the back.

Sam picked up two large bottles of Gatorade then hobbled over to the row of granola and power bars. He picked up five power bars, choosing the sweetest variety he could find, paid for his items without saying a single word, and left. Sam was tempted to go next door to the sandwich place but decided against it; there was no need to draw any more unwanted attention.

He knew there was a small park called Highline Field just a few blocks away, behind the old post office building somewhere around 31st and Chestnut. The park was underneath an elevated train track and next to a parking lot, so it was always pretty much deserted. Sam remembered walking by the park a hundred times and wondering each time whose brilliant idea it had been to put a park there. Now, he was thanking whoever had thought of it.

Sam found a spot to sit on the ground behind one of the massive pillars that supported the train track a hundred feet above and drank both bottles as he ate three of his power bars. He kept the last two inside his jacket, saving them for later when the hunger would return. He knew he couldn't sleep here, but he felt a lot better with food in his belly for the moment; a surge of energy washed through him.

Sam figured he would stay put if no one bothered him. If someone got curious, he would act like the old lunatic people assumed he was and scurry out of sight.

FORTY-THREE

Center City
Corner of Chestnut and 24th
Thursday – May 23, 2013 – 11:35 p.m.

Night had fallen on the city, and the streets were deserted. There was a powerful storm gathering, and the distant rumble of thunder was becoming more and more frequent.

Sam thanked whichever god was responsible for the weather these days, as it would make his job that much easier—people would remain indoors, and the police would stay in their cruisers. But for now, he could still see the occasional pedestrian or cyclist going by, so he would avoid entering from the river path as he did before and try to sneak in.

As a slight drizzle started coming down, Sam made his way onto Chestnut Street, right above the train track. The large apartment building on the north side of the street had an underground parking garage right next to the alcove he'd been using for shelter. There was a massive block of electrical equipment right outside the parking structure to power the entire building. The equipment was completely secured by a chain-link fence that ran on all sides, and even on top, to prevent anyone from playing with it or getting electrocuted.

Sam calculated that the drop from the bridge to the top of the fence box was about ten feet. If he did it right, he could land on top of the box then climb down the fence to his former hideout without setting foot on the river path. If he did it wrong, he might go right through the fence upon landing and would die by a massive electrical shock. His life wasn't worth much these days, so he figured it was worth a shot.

Taking a few deep breaths, Sam climbed over the railing and went down as much as possible without letting go to minimize the force of his landing. Looking down to make sure he was right above the strongest spot on the fence, he let go and landed softly. The chain-link cage rattled a bit, but it held up Sam's weight. Not wanting to stay there any longer than necessary, he started climbing down and was soon on ground level.

Panting with relief, he turned on his phone with shaking hands and activated the flashlight. Although he knew where his backpack was hidden—in the deepest and darkest recess of the cave—there was nowhere near enough light outside to navigate without his phone.

As soon as he turned toward the entrance, he was suddenly faced with a young man who had chosen this spot to shelter himself from the elements. Although there had been some signs of previous use when he had first started using this place as a hideout, this was the first person he had come across.

"What the fuck you doing here?" the young man yelled with a fierce scowl on his face.

Sam was still trying to process what he was seeing. The kid looked like a nightmare. Although he couldn't have been any older than twenty, years of living a drug-fueled life had taken its toll on him. He was wearing unlaced sneakers and dirty basket-ball shorts. His chest was bare and covered in bruises. The blond hair on his head was matted, he had scabs all over his face, and as he hissed at Sam like a stray cat, Sam saw that he had only two teeth left in his mouth. When Sam looked down, his worst fear was confirmed—the kid was holding some sort of shiv he'd manufactured out of an old screwdriver.

Sam hadn't been inside in a short while, so the kid must have thought he'd vacated the place and claimed it as his own. Now, someone was invading his territory, and he wasn't prepared to concede any ground.

"Easy, kid. I just need to get something I left in here. I don't mean you any harm," Sam said, forcing a calm tone. He held his hands at shoulder level with his palms open to try and appease him.

"Get out of here. This is my crib! Everything here is mine!" the young man jeered, still holding his shiv in front of him, attempting to keep Sam at bay.

Sam was at a standstill, he needed his bag back—everything he needed was in there, and what he had planned for tomorrow would never work unless he had all his equipment. He tried to reason with the kid once more.

"Listen, kid. I only need a few seconds to grab something I left here a while ago. Let me pass. I'll go in there and get it, then I'll be on my way. No harm, no foul. Trust me."

"Bitch, didn't you hear me? I said this is my house! Everything here's mine! And if you forgot something in here, well, now that's mine, too. Now, leave before I gut you!"

Sam steeled himself. "Can't do it. Sorry. I need what's in there. What if I gave you some money in exchange for passage?" Sam asked. He was bluffing of course—he barely had any money left on him.

"Oh, so you got money? Well then, fork it over!" the kid said, approaching slowly.

Sam cursed himself. This was not going well, and they were both standing at the entrance of the hideout, completely exposed. He was still trying to figure out a way to convince the kid to let him pass when the young man lunged forward.

Sam jumped back, but he was a second too late. The kid managed to slice open the back of his hand. As Sam stared at his wound, the junkie attacked once more, but this time, Sam saw him coming and stepped sideways to avoid the attack. He grabbed the boy's arm and tried to neutralize his weapon.

The kid was like a rabid animal, hissing and screeching as he tried to kill the intruder. Both men wrestled for the weapon, but the junkie was twenty years younger than Sam, and his body was overstimulated by whatever drug he had just taken. They both fell, and the kid climbed on top of Sam.

They struggled and grunted as they each attempted to over-power the other. Sam tried as best he could to tug away the shiv, but the kid gripped it with both hands and tried to use his own body's weight to press down on Sam. Sam grabbed his opponent's hands in his own and shoved back as hard as he could to keep the sharp object away from his body. He tried to wiggle free, but it was impossible without releasing the grip he had on the kid's hands.

Sam struggled away from the attacker, but the kid slowly plunged his weapon into Sam's lower abdomen. Sam screamed as he felt the pain of the sharp metal object penetrate his skin deeper and deeper. If he didn't do something soon, he would never see the sunrise, and his legacy would be of a wanted pe-dophile and murderer who had died alone under a bridge. This was not how he would go out.

Sam gathered all the energy he could muster, ignoring the pain in his abdomen. Jerking his body sideways, he managed to get a bit of room to move. He kneed the young man in the groin several times until he rolled away, writhing in pain. His grip had loosened as Sam was kneeing him, so Sam got a hold on the shiv and wrenched it away from his opponent's hands.

The kid was now lying on his back right next to Sam, clutch-ing his lower parts and trying to catch his breath.

With a fury unbeknownst to him, Sam turned on his side and, as he screamed with rage, stabbed the kid in the leg with his own weapon. All the frustrations he had accumulated over the past weeks were finally allowed an output, and he stabbed the young man with a tremendous amount of force. The junkie howled in pain, and as Sam was winding up for a second round, the boy rolled away and fled.

Sam took a few seconds once he was sure that the kid was gone for good to catch his breath, then he touched his wound. When he pulled his hand away, it was covered in blood.

He struggled up and tried to find his phone. Sam spotted a tiny sliver of light coming from the flashlight. He had dropped the phone when the fight first started, and as he looked closer, he saw that the screen was now cracked. Sam went through the apps quickly to make sure everything was still running. Apart from physical damage, everything was intact. He used the flashlight to find the backpack he had hidden.

The pain in his side was growing in intensity. He needed help. There was no way he could show up in an emergency room, though, since the medical staff would immediately report the suspicious wound to the police. There was only one thing he could do—he dialed the number of the only person who could save him.

FORTY-FOUR

Center City
Corner of Chestnut and 24th
Friday – May 24, 2013 – 12:09 a.m.

The phone started vibrating on the nightstand, and it took a few seconds for Victoria to understand where the noise was coming from. After three rings, she picked up.

"Hello?" she said in a groggy voice, still not entirely awake.

"Vicky, it's me. Pretend it's the hospital calling," Sam said.

"Uh…" Flustered, she rose and sat at the edge of the bed, trying to shake the cobwebs out of her head.

"Pretend it's the hospital calling! I don't want Sofia to know it's me. Please, I need your help."

"Hi, Doctor. What can I do for you?" Victoria said in a confused voice.

Sam heard the faint sound of Sofia calling her mom from a distance. It almost sounded like they were in the same room.

"Is Sofia in our room?" Sam asked abruptly.

"Yes… Hang on a second, Doctor," Victoria said in hushed tones, keeping up with the charade.

Sam heard her whisper, "It's just the hospital calling, sweetie; go back to sleep."

"Why is she in our room?" Sam asked.

"She's been having terrible nightmares, Sam," his wife whispered into the phone. "She's been sleeping with me for the past few nights. Why are you calling? What's wrong?"

"I need your help, Vicky. I'm badly injured, and if I don't get help soon, I won't last until morning."

"What happened?"

"I'll explain everything later, but right now, I need you to grab your emergency kit and get to me," Sam instructed.

"Where are you?"

"You know the place where you dropped off the stuff earlier this week? Meet me there as soon as possible. I'll find you." Sam didn't know if anyone could listen in on their conversation, but with everything that had gone wrong in the past few days, he didn't want to take any chances, so he kept it as vague as possible.

"Okay, I'll be there in about ten minutes. What do you need?"

"I need you to stitch me up and dress a wound. And if you can, I could sure use some—"

The line dropped, and the call ended.

"Hello? Hello, Vic?" Sam said. When he turned his phone over, he saw the phone was dead. The flashlight had been left on for the duration of his fight, and it had drained the battery. He cursed at the junkie who had made everything unnecessarily complicated. If he had just let him pass in peace, he would have been in and out in under a minute, and the kid could have shot himself up with whatever crap he was using for the rest of the night. Now, Sam was injured and pissed.

He walked to the entrance of the alcove and looked up at the chain link fence box. Even if he could climb back on top, which he seriously doubted he could in his current condition, there was no way he could jump high enough to catch the railing and shimmy back up, even on his best day.

So, he walked out onto the train track, slipped through the fence, and emerged onto the river path. The only thing that had turned out well so far was that the rain had become heavier, so the path was now deserted. He stumbled to the stairway that led to the bridge and made his way up, clutching his abdomen. Once he was back at street level, he headed over to his rendezvous with Victoria.

FORTY-FIVE

Center City
Corner of Chestnut and 24th
Friday – May 24, 2013 – 12:50 a.m.

Sam was hiding behind a car across the parking lot, pressing a hand against his wound to stem the blood pouring out of him as he waited for his wife. He'd plugged his phone into one of the charging sticks he'd purchased; he would need his phone to be up and running tomorrow, so after making sure it was charging, he put it back inside his bag to shield it from the rain.

Sam saw a tall, slim figure in dark clothing appear, holding an umbrella in one hand and a leather bag in the other. His felt a pang in his heart at the sight of Victoria. She walked up to the garbage bins where she'd dropped off the boxes a few days earlier and looked around, searching for Sam.

Sam got up and walked toward her. When she saw the dark figure approaching, she immediately clutched her bag close to her chest. Sam realized that he didn't look anything like she was used to and that she was most likely afraid of getting mugged.

"Vicky, it's me," he said in a low voice as he got close. When he was five feet away, he stopped and allowed her the chance to look at him so she could recognize him.

Her eyes opened wide. "Sam? What the hell? What happened to you? You look like crap!"

"Feel like it, too," he responded.

"I'm sorry, that's not what I meant. It's just…" Victoria paused for a moment, as her analytical mind processed his appearance.

"Don't worry, honey. I know I don't look my best right now, but I have my reasons. Now, I need you to help me fix this."

He pointed to the dark spot on his abdomen—there was a large bloodstain on his shirt around the area where he'd been stabbed.

"Holy crap!" she breathed.

Sam took her hand and led her behind the garbage container. He sat down and grimaced from the pain as he lifted the shirt and showed Victoria his wound. She kneeled and started examining him.

"How did this happen?" she asked, pulling out her medical gear.

"Junkie tried to kill me with a screwdriver or something because he thought I wanted to rob him."

"Oh, my lord!" she gasped. She knew Sam was in trouble and was up to something, but Sam was sure she never could have pictured her husband fighting with a junkie in a million years.

She looked closer and pulled out everything she would need to fix him up and began rubbing at the wound with a disinfectant swab. Sam winced in pain.

"This might hurt a bit," she said to him, as she was threading a needle.

"It already hurts like hell. Can't imagine it'll get any worse," he replied, chuckling darkly. Nevertheless, he took the shoulder strap of his backpack and bit down on it as she started inserting the needle into his skin. He grunted in pain, causing Victoria to stop, but Sam motioned for her to keep going.

"How exactly did this happen?" his wife asked without looking up, as she stitched up his wound.

"I'd found a little spot where I could hide out and work in peace for the last couple of days, but when I went back there earlier tonight, some kid had taken it," Sam explained. "When I tried to walk past him to get to some stuff I had hidden there, he jumped me."

"And you said he was a junkie?"

"Can't say for sure, but it looked like it. He looked like hell and the way he was acting… He looked like his brain was pretty fried."

"Do you know what he was using? Intravenous drugs, maybe?" she asked, her medical brain working at full capacity, going through every possible injury he could have sustained or disease he could have contracted.

"I wouldn't know. He seemed erratic. If I had to guess, I'd say crack or meth, something along those lines. He looked pretty wound up."

"That sounds about right. You'll need a tetanus shot at the very least, and more than likely, a hepatitis test. He might have been infected or been in contact with infected blood and passed it on to you when he stabbed you," she said as she was finishing up.

"That'll just have to wait, I guess. I'm sure you heard the news, so you know I can't show my face at a hospital right now."

"You're talking about Dean?" she asked quietly. Her tone had been comforting, but she looked nervous.

Sam was amazed at how she worked. There was only a little bit of light coming from a streetlamp across the street, and rain was pouring down. Yet, Victoria worked with speedy yet precise gestures and didn't seem phased at all by her poor operating conditions. Sam remembered that she'd spent two years volunteering in Central America before she met him, so he figured she must have seen her share of less-than-optimal working stations.

"Honey, you know I never would have hurt him… It's all a big setup."

"I couldn't believe what I was reading when someone showed it to me," she whispered. "Even Paul called and asked me about it. He couldn't make any sense of it either."

She paused for a second and looked Sam in the eyes.

"I had a hard time believing you when this whole thing started, especially after the trial. But after everything they're saying about you, I understand that it just *can't* be true. The man they're describing isn't the man I married. I'm sorry I ever doubted you," she said firmly, even as her eyes started brimming with tears. She was finding it hard to look Sam in the eyes any longer, so she glanced back down at what she was doing and finished her work without saying another word.

When she was done stitching, she cut the filament and put a dressing on top of his wound.

Sam laid his palm softly on his wife's cheek and raised her head to meet his gaze. In a reassuring tone, he said, "Vicky, I know why all this is happening. It all started with Principal Jackson."

"Jackson? But why? What does he have to do with any of this?" she asked.

"I can't get into the details right now. It's for your own safety."

They both sat in silence for a minute and after a moment, she looked up at him.

Her eyes lit up as she remembered the end of their conversation on the phone earlier. "What was the other thing you wanted? The line got disconnected before you could finish. I tried calling back, but the number was blocked."

"Oh, it's not important. It's just that I haven't eaten in a few days and I'm almost out of money. I wanted to ask you to bring me a little bit of grub and some spare cash, but don't worry about it… I'll manage."

Victoria dug through her medical bag and pulled out a roll of LifeSavers—she kept them there in case she ever needed to treat someone with hypoglycemia—and handed it to Sam.

"It's not much, but it's all I have on me. Sorry," she told him, pressing the pack into his hands.

"That's fine, sweetie. Don't worry about it. Thanks."

"Do you want me to go get something from the fridge and bring it back?"

"No," he replied curtly. "Sorry, I don't mean to be rude, but the less time you spend around me, the better. You've already done more than I could ever thank you for. You need to head back home and look after our little girl."

"Okay, I guess…"

"You need to get out of here now, Vicky. Go home. This'll all be over in a few days, I promise you. I'm almost done," he said, holding his wife's hand.

"Sam, I'm worried about you," she whispered, looking into his eyes.

"Don't worry. It's almost over. And if it gets dangerous, I'll turn myself in, I promise," he reassured her.

"Be safe, honey…" She began leaning in for a kiss but stopped halfway. For a second, she hesitated. Sam couldn't blame her. He looked scruffy and smelled like a dumpster.

Sam took a long look at his wife's face. Her hair was wet and strewn across her forehead, and she wasn't wearing any makeup. Still, Sam thought she was the most beautiful woman he'd ever seen, and his love for her grew even deeper. It reignited the flame that was consuming him, and his desire to get his freedom back was as strong as it had ever been. As he was gazing at her, he knew Victoria felt his love, a love stronger than words. She resumed leaning in and kissed him softly.

She then got up, gave him one last longing look, and walked briskly back to their apartment.

Sam remained where he was sitting. He ate all the candy she'd given him and downed the water bottle he kept in his backpack. Sugar and water would help him minimize the impact of his wound. He watched his wife walk away, and even though he had difficulty believing in His existence, he still thanked God for putting her in his life.

FORTY-SIX

Downtown Philly
Corner of 15th and Chestnut
Friday – May 24, 2013 – 10:23 a.m.

The walk toward City Hall seemed a lot longer than what Sam was now used to. Although his wife had done a terrific job patching him up, he still had lost a lot of blood, and he had nothing to numb the pain, so every step he took sent a sharp throb all the way up his thigh and through his torso.

The rain had stopped in the early hours of the morning, and now, the sun was in full display. The sky was bright blue, and only a few puffy white clouds could be seen slowly rolling by. Today would be a beautiful day, but Sam couldn't enjoy the weather right now—he was on a mission. Today was his big day.

He had kept to the alleys that ran alongside Chestnut Street as much as he could to avoid being seen and only rejoined the foot traffic when the alleys came to a dead end. When he got downtown, he stopped inside the burger place next to City Hall and went in the restroom.

There, he organized everything in the order he would need them, placing his most important things on top for quicker access. Before changing, he checked his wound. Aside from a tiny speck of blood on the bandage, the stitching Victoria had done was holding up well. He pulled out his clean clothes and undressed. After changing into his jeans and dress shirt, he put his many dirty shirts back over his clean clothes. That way, if he needed to change fast, he could just remove the shirts or put them back on without having to find a bathroom to hide in. He took the opportunity to answer nature's call, too, and used the time to double-check that everything he needed was working properly. Once he was done, he repacked all his stuff.

After exiting the restroom, he entered the street and headed to the alley behind the massage parlor he'd used before. He stuffed everything he would need in his pockets, holstered the pistol in the small of his back, then set out to wait for his prey.

Sam crossed Chestnut and sat down on the sidewalk, right across the street from the entrance to Shikoku. If what Vanessa had said was accurate, Donald Jackson would arrive soon for his weekly "stress therapy."

About an hour into his stakeout, Sam caught sight of Jackson's impressive figure out of the corner of his eye. The man was stumping up the staircase that led out from the underground parking lot underneath City Hall. He marched with a purpose. There was a strut in his step as he approached the metal door that led customers into Shikoku's sinful business place.

He jerked open the door and strode in without ever looking back, as if he were untouchable, even though Sam knew that what he was about to do was a criminal offense.

Knowing he had at least thirty minutes to wait until Jackson came back, Sam took the time to discreetly check his equipment. Even though he'd already checked it twice in the restroom, he couldn't afford any slip-ups, so he went through everything once more.

He pulled out his phone just enough to see the top of the screen—the battery life was over seventy percent. It was more than enough for what he had to do. He made sure all the connections were stable and that all the applications he would need ran smoothly. Once he was certain everything was fine, he put it all back in his pockets and made his way across the street and into the alley's entrance.

Vanessa had told Sam that Jackson stopped by every Friday before having lunch with his brother at City Hall. Being the mayor, Davis Jackson's office was in the old building. Sam reasoned that since it had been raining for a few days and that today was a mild and sunny day, they would most likely enjoy the spring weather and eat outside.

Sam planned to tail Donald until he found a place to ambush him. If they stayed inside or went to a restaurant, he would wait until Jackson ventured down to retrieve his car and surprise him there. Sam knew it was a ballsy move, but time was working against him. The longer he stayed outside, the higher his chances of getting caught. Add to the fact that his injury was barely tolerable, and Sam wasn't sure how many more days he would last if he failed today.

As he stood in the alley, looking out at the corner of 15th and Chestnut, Sam saw Donald Jackson use the crosswalk to head toward City Hall. Sam followed from afar but remained outside the courtyard. He saw, in the distance, Jackson sit a table in the far corner, waiting for someone. It was time for Sam to make his move.

He ran back to the dumpster, removed his smelly old jacket and beanie hat, and put them inside the bag. He put on his Phillies cap and placed the gray sweater vest he had bargained from the old hobo over his forearm, hiding his right hand. Checking himself out to make sure everything was in place; he walked with a quick pace back across the street and entered the courtyard. He looked halfway normal in his present attire, like an aging tourist, so no one paid any attention to him. As he watched the table at the far end of the courtyard, Sam smiled— he had finally caught a break.

Both Jackson brothers were seated at a round table across from each other, focused entirely on their discussion. Even though they were identical twins, you could hardly tell. Donald Jackson had a huge gut that protruded underneath his cheap white shirt and generic black tie, he shaved his head and wore reading spectacles. Although Davis Jackson was the older brother by a few minutes, he looked at least fifteen years younger. His hair was neatly trimmed. He was a few inches shorter than Donald, but he still retained an athletic figure. He wore an expensive Italian silk suit with a bright red tie.

Sam couldn't have asked for anything better. He would confront both men and take them down in a single swing.

Sam grabbed a chair from a nearby empty table and took a seat at the Jackson table without asking permission.

"What the fuck?" Donald asked, shocked to see an old geezer sit down with them without so much as a hello.

"Hi, Donald. Nice to see you again. And you, Davis. It's a pleasure to finally meet you," Sam said calmly.

It took a second for Donald to register Sam's voice and see through his new appearance. He started to open his mouth, but Sam held up his hand, instructing the man to stop talking.

"Before either of you say anything, you should know that right now, underneath this table, there's a pistol pointed at both of you. If you make a sound or any sudden move, you won't make it to the end of your lunch. Now, both of you put your hands on the table so I can see them at all times. Davis, feel free to peek under the tablecloth to confirm what I'm saying," Sam said, still keeping calm, acting as if he were talking to two old friends. He used his left hand to adjust his thick glasses, pinching the left leg of his frames between his index and thumb.

Davis bent sideways and looked underneath the white linen tablecloth. He immediately saw the pistol and sat upright again. He looked at his brother.

"What's this about, Donald? You want to tell me why some weirdo's sitting at my table pointing a gun at me?"

Before Donald could answer, Sam cut him off.

"Where are my manners? Allow me to introduce myself properly. My name is Samuel Brighton. Your brother here tried to have me sent to jail for a crime I didn't commit." Sam kept an eye on both brothers, but as he finished talking, he saw in Davis's eyes that he recognized the name and wasn't expecting to ever be sitting face to face with him.

"Damn, Brighton, you look like shit! And you smell like you swam in the sewer. What happened to you?" Sam's former boss asked with a chuckle.

"Yeah, it's been a rough couple of weeks, Donald. Thanks to you, I might add."

"What do you want, Sam? Are you here to kill me? To kill us? You'll never walk out of here alive!" Donald sneered defiantly.

"Donald, if I wanted you dead, I would have shot you the last time we spoke on the phone, in the school's parking lot. I was a hundred feet away from you."

Donald's expression said it all. The man knew that Sam had been watching him the last time they'd spoken, but he never would have guessed that he'd been so close.

"So now, Donald, you and your brother are going to tell me exactly why you decided to fuck up my life, and you're going to come clean... even if it's the last thing you do." Sam spoke in a low, threatening voice. There were many people around, and the last thing he needed was to draw attention to himself.

"And why would we do that?"

"Because if you don't, I'll shoot you and watch you bleed to death in the middle of City Hall, you prick!" Sam snapped.

Davis finally stepped into the conversation.

"Let's everybody calm down. Okay, what do you want to know? There's no need to get violent here."

"Oh, I got a bunch of questions for you both, but we'll start with an easy one." Sam looked over at Donald. "How did you put that picture on my phone? Did you hack it?"

Principal Jackson couldn't help himself—he chuckled malevolently.

"No, you fool. I took it from your desk while all of you were at the staff meeting. It was almost too easy. As principal, I have the keys to every lock in the school. But honestly, what kind of idiot doesn't put a lock on his phone these days? You made it almost too easy," he snickered with a sly grin.

"So, that entire pointless meeting was just to get me away from my desk and steal my phone?"

"I really did have to give that presentation, but knowing that everyone would be there, I passed the ball to my vice-principal.

I knew the teachers' lounge would be empty, and I could take your phone and put it back without being seen. I went back to my office and made that little slut get undressed. I snapped the picture and told her to get lost. Once she was gone, I put your cell back inside your desk, and everything was set. All I had to do after that was nudge the cops in the right direction. No one could possibly have any idea that I was involved, except Vanessa, but I made sure she knew her place."

"That's where you made your first mistake." Sam pushed copies of Vanessa's picture to both men. Davis looked at it for a second and turned it over, but Donald took his time, gazing at it with hungry eyes.

"Look in the upper left corner, Donald. You can clearly see part of your precious basketball jersey hanging on the wall. It would have been impossible for me to take that picture without you knowing," Sam pointed out with his index finger.

Donald looked at the picture more greater care, while Davis turned his copy over once more and inspected it.

"Fuck!" Donald whispered; while his twin brother simply sighed.

"From your reaction, Davis, I gather that you knew about this, but you didn't expect your little brother to screw up like that," Sam said.

"This proves nothing," Donald blustered out. His brother had stopped looking at the photo and seemed lost in thought.

"Maybe not, but I'm betting it's enough for me to appeal and ask for a new trial. Things unraveled so fast; I didn't even have time to notice it before." Sam's eyes flicked to Davis. "I suppose the speedy trial and harsh sentence was all part of the plan, Mr. Mayor?"

Davis didn't respond, but his facial expression betrayed him.

"Did you also have a hand in my attorney's shitty performance at trial?"

Davis Jackson seemed to be considering his answer when Donald chimed in.

"We told him he'd be next in line for District Attorney if he didn't put up a fight in court. You'd be surprised what some folks are willing to do to move up in the world."

Again, Davis Jackson sighed, unhappy that his brother had divulged information so recklessly.

Sam could see that what was supposed to have been a bulletproof plan was crumbling before their eyes.

FORTY-SEVEN

Downtown Philly
Corner of 15th and Chestnut
Friday – May 24, 2013 – 11:57 a.m.

While both brothers were seated in front of Sam, trying to think of a way to handle the situation, Sam pressed on. He didn't want to give them an opportunity to think of a way out. If he kept them unbalanced, he could use it to his advantage.

"Okay, now that I understand the 'how,' let's move on to the 'why'." Sam pulled out the files and pictures he'd copied a few days earlier.

"I found some interesting documents a little while ago, stashed away inside a safety deposit box in South Philly. There was an intriguing article about the race riots of '69 and how, apparently, some people might have poured gasoline on the fire to keep the riots going. Does that ring a bell, gentlemen?" He looked at both, trying to gauge their reactions. Davis remained calm, but Sam could see a large vein protruding out of Donald's bald head.

"I don't know what you're talking about, Mr. Brighton," Davis said.

"I thought you might say that, which is why I'd like you to look at this." Sam pushed both sets of pictures toward each brother. "If you look at the first few photos, you see a pair of tall kids throwing rocks at cops during the Columbia Avenue riots. But keep flipping through them."

When he saw the brothers arrive at the second-to-last picture, Sam added, "That one sure looks like pictures of a dirty cop giving an envelope full of cash to two boys in exchange for a favor. Now, if only we could see who those two interesting young men are…" Sam lingered.

They both flipped to the last picture and froze, silent as they stared in disbelief.

"Now, I know a lot of time has passed, but that sure as hell looks like a set of twins talking with the officer, and there's just something about them that looks *very* familiar. Don't you agree?"

After a minute of silence, Donald scoffed. "Bullshit. You have nothing here."

"Oh, but I beg to differ, Donald," Sam answered, turning his head toward the mayor. "I bet a lot of people would be interested in seeing these pictures, don't you, Mr. Senator?" he added sarcastically.

"How did you get these?" Davis asked. The man was most likely running a plausible legal defense in his mind as they were talking.

"That's the funny part!" Sam said. "If your little brother here had kept his mouth shut, I never would have found them in the first place. But he told me I was as troublesome as my father, so he basically steered me in the right direction."

Upon hearing Sam's explanation, Davis turned to look at his brother with the shadow of a glare—his brother's impulsiveness had screwed up their plans. Sam guessed from his reaction that it wasn't the first time Donald's rash decision making had led them into trouble.

"Which leads me to my next question: how did you know about my father? He died before I was born—I never knew him. How could you have known we were even related?"

"It's just a strange coincidence, really," Donald answered. "I didn't know that you were James Monroe's kid until your old lady died. As the principal, I'm forced to attend wakes and funerals for my employees. I hate going to those damn things, but it comes with the job, I guess. Anyway, when I got to the old bat's wake, I saw that she'd been the wife of the late James Monroe. It took me a while to remember where I'd heard that name, but once it came back to me, I put two and two together. I never would've known otherwise."

Hearing Donald talk so slanderously about his mother made Sam furious, but he realized that he was baiting him, trying to destabilize Sam so he would make a mistake he could exploit. Sam kept his emotions in check and continued.

"So, you see, Davis, if Donald hadn't said a thing, I never would have found these documents. At worst, for me at least, I would have probably thrown them away. But your little brother screwed up again..."

"It's a shame we weren't able to catch you when you got them. You chose to send Ashton in your place, and he paid with his *life*. Some friend you are!" Donald spat, still attempting to incite a reaction from Sam.

"Yeah, about that," Sam continued. "You want to tell me why you had my best friend killed? He was innocent in all of this! All he did was grab something for me at the bank." A slight tremor slipped into his voice. The thought of his friend brought back so many emotions, but he tried his best to remain calm.

"That's where you made a mistake, Brighton. After your arrest, I called the IT folks at the school board, and they put a flag on Vanessa's file so I would be notified as soon as someone accessed it. I had a feeling that little piece of ass would cause me some trouble, but I just couldn't get rid of something so tasty," Donald Jackson said, smiling widely.

"Please, Donald... let's stay on topic," Davis said. The older sibling looked disgusted when he heard his brother talking about a young girl in such a way. Sam figured that Davis had always known about his brother's tastes but had never been an actual witness to it.

Donald brushed his brother off and continued. "So, when your pal accessed Vanessa's file, I had a couple of boys from the old neighborhood tail him to see where he went and who he met, feeling it might lead me to you. When they called me and told me he'd stepped inside the bank on Packer, I put all the pieces together and figured he was after your father's files. I couldn't afford to let you look at them."

"Wait a second. How did you know my father had stashed something in that bank?" Sam asked instantly, but after a few seconds, it dawned on him. He let loose a breath. "You killed my father? Why?"

"Because when your old man took that last picture there," Donald said, as he pointed to the picture of the brothers receiving the money, "the officer had the presence of mind to note his license plate as he sped away from us. He put a BOLO on it, and when he tracked him down outside the bank, he asked us to get rid of him. He said there was another five grand in it for us if we wasted him," Donald answered with a bit of pride in his voice.

Sam tried to process everything while remaining calm, but he found it almost impossible. *That asshole killed my father, killed my best friend, had me arrested… just to cover up his own sins,* he thought venomously. He felt an almost insurmountable urge to jump over the table and grab Donald's throat, to just end everything here and now. It took all his effort to resist that urge, but he reminded himself that if he hurt either one of them, prison would be unavoidable, no matter what the Jackson brothers had done.

Death would be too easy for them, he told himself. *Let them both rot in jail.* He'd been silent for a few seconds, but he needed to press on with his interrogation.

"So, you killed him?" he asked. "Were you in on it, too?" He turned toward Davis, who had fallen silent.

"Who do you think was driving the getaway car, stupid?" Donald guffawed.

Again, his older brother sighed. Donald had just confessed to murder and had implicated his brother. Sam's plan was working. Although Davis remained calm and looked in control, Donald was becoming brash and reckless.

"So, when you heard that Dean was inside the bank, you knew he was after whatever was hidden there," Sam went on, mostly for his own understanding.

"Yep. We knew your old man had stashed something in that bank, but we didn't know what. I asked the boys to waste him and steal whatever he had, hoping I could recover whatever was in there, but all he had on him was a plastic bag full of useless crap. I guess he'd somehow already passed it on to you. Your buddy made the mistake of trying to help you and he paid a huge price for that mistake."

Sam stared at Davis. The man was silent, but he kept looking at his brother and shaking his head. Sam turned again to Donald. The man was so arrogant, he talked about his criminal actions as if he didn't have a care in the world. As hard as it was to listen to, Sam needed to exploit that arrogance as much as possible.

"But he was innocent! He didn't know anything!"

Donald Jackson snorted.

"I don't give a rat's ass! That idiot got in my way and I got rid of him. Plain and simple."

"So, you had him killed. Just like that?" Sam asked roughly, all the while keeping his voice low and his demeanor calm. Donald was still trying to rattle him, and it took every ounce of willpower Sam had not to jump over the table and try to end the man's life right then and there. But Sam's strategy was working so far, so he tried to put his emotions aside and remain cool.

"Yeah, well I couldn't let him go, could I? I wasn't sure what you had told him. So, I figured I might as well kill two birds with one stone if you catch my drift. Calling in another anonymous tip and framing you for his murder was just icing on the cake." Donald didn't even seem bothered as he recounted the gruesome murders he'd orchestrated and even taken part in. Sam had always found him a bit narcissistic, but clearly, the man was a sociopath.

Sam sucked in a deep breath to ground himself. "I have to hand it to you, Donald. That was a bold move. It limited my movements around town, always having to look over my shoulder. But you and I both know the murder charge won't stick."

"Who cares, Sam? What I wanted was to give the cops a little extra incentive to find you and put you down for good. If they couldn't do it, we would have gotten to you inside the jail. Davis has sent a lot of unsavory characters there during his stint as District Attorney—we could have easily found one who could be…" he paused for a moment, "*motivated* to take you out in exchange for a little leniency."

"You motherfucker!" Sam gasped out. "You'll pay for this, I swear!"

Donald chuckled. "That's what you think, Sam. Like I said, we own the cops, and my brother here can pull the entire resources of his office to make sure you wind up in jail for a long time."

FORTY-EIGHT

Downtown Philly
Corner of 15th and Chestnut
Friday – May 24, 2013 – 12:28 p.m.

Sam glared at both brothers and pointed at the files and pictures laid out in front of them.

"So, let me get this straight. All of this started way before I was even born, and the bottom line is that it's all because of money?"

Davis propped his elbows on the table and laid his chin on top of his fists.

"It's not that simple, Mr. Brighton. You can't possibly imagine what it was like growing up as a black kid in North Philly. There was no hope, no future for us. But when that cop approached us and offered us more money than we had ever seen in our entire lives, we saw an opening—an opportunity for change."

"What change?" Sam asked.

"We used that money to get into college. I wanted to practice law and make the city a better and safer place. Donald wanted to be an educator so he could influence kids and steer them toward a better life."

Sam snorted at Davis's justification.

"And killing a man is just a means to an end for you?"

"I didn't approve of the way Mr. Monroe's situation was handled, but we weren't given a choice. That cop had us by the balls and could do away with us in a flash if we walked away. I'm not sure if you'll believe me when I say that not a day goes by that I don't regret the way things turned out."

"You're right. I don't believe you. You could have come clean anytime you wanted in the last forty years!" Sam couldn't believe the man's arrogance. There he was, pretending to be sorry for what he had done when he'd had decades to make things right.

"That's true. But as I climbed the ladder in the justice system, I learned that I could make a difference for this city. There was a lot I could accomplish for the betterment of the people of Philadelphia, maybe who knows eventually for this country, but I wouldn't be able to do any of it if I turned myself in."

Sam sighed upon hearing the man wind up his little political speech. The lunatic believed that what he had done was *justified* in the larger scheme of things, and Sam wanted to call him on it.

"So, committing murder, sorry *murders*, for you two bastards, is justifiable because it will help save more lives in the long run?"

"That's a bit of an oversimplification on your part, but yes, I suppose so," Davis answered. The man's ambition apparently had no limit.

"We know what this country needs, Brighton. Davis and I grew up in the 'hood, and we understand how things work. We know better than anyone how to fix this country," Donald intervened.

"So, all of this was just a big plot to make sure this information never saw the light of day, right?" he asked them.

"Unfortunately for you, Mr. Brighton, you had to be sacrificed," Davis said calmly. "James Monroe was the only person in this world who knew what we had done as kids. That kind of information would have killed our careers. For a long time, we thought we were protected, the evidence lost inside the bank. We even figured that after years of being inactive, the bank would close James Monroe's account and throw away whatever was in that box," Davis explained. "We kept tabs on your mother with the help of the police force for a while, but when we learned about her mental health problems, we were certain we were safe. When Donald learned that you were James Monroe's son, we decided we needed to act fast. We couldn't know what your father might have left behind for you." Davis paused to catch his breath.

"We have big plans for this nation, Mr. Brighton. The United States will become a beacon of modern greatness, but not if we're not allowed to achieve our destiny," Davis replied serenely.

Sam couldn't help but chuckle as he heard them talk as if they were prophets sent down from heaven to salvage the country. It was time to bring them back down to earth. Sam again pointed at the stacks of files and pictures he'd laid out.

"This is where you messed up big time, Donald. If you hadn't tried to get rid of me in the first place, none of this would've happened. But now, I got you."

"Bullshit!" Donald replied. "You've got nothing here. Tell him, Davis!"

Sam turned toward him.

"There's nothing concrete here, Mr. Brighton. None of this will make any sort of impact."

"What do you mean?" Sam probed.

"I mean that the copy of your father's draft can be refuted as the rantings of a lunatic. The man's dead, along with everyone who would have been able to attest to any of this. The former police commissioner, your father's editor, the officers he alleged were implicated—they're all dead. The only people who are still alive are me and Donald, and we'll deny any involvement."

"I still have pictures of the both of you rioting," Sam interjected.

"Everyone was rioting on that day, Mr. Brighton. We'll just say we were swept up by the crowd and threw a few rocks. If we spin this right, it might even come out favorable for us, you know?" Davis reflected, his political mind working to reshape the events and give them a favorable light. "We were teens stuck in a dead-end life in the ghetto, and we were sick of the way things were; but after seeing that violence didn't accomplish anything, we bettered ourselves through education and hard work, and now, we want to give back to our country… or something along those lines." Davis was already thinking of ways to turn Sam's allegations to his advantage; meanwhile, Donald was just grinning like a madman.

"I still have the picture of you taking a bribe from a cop. There's nothing you can do about that one—it's clear as day!"

"We can easily say these pictures were doctored by a crazy man on the run from the law. We'll say that you've lost all control and are trying to blame others for your problems."

"No one will believe you, Sam. You're wanted for murder, remember?" Donald added with a grin.

"A murder *you* committed, asshole!" Sam hissed, as the anger seeped into his voice.

"But you can't prove it, and that's what matters in the end," Davis said.

"See, we're holding all the cards here, Sam," Donald interjected with an exaggerated sigh. "By next Monday, Davis will be a US Senator, and I'll be sitting right alongside him. You can't win this one, Sam. It's over."

"Maybe you're right, Donald. Maybe I can't win. But it doesn't mean I can't try," Sam said fiercely.

"Give yourself up, Mr. Brighton," Davis advised in a calm demeanor. "You're already in a lot of trouble and kicking the hornet's nest won't do you any good. You think you have evidence on us, but you really don't—you have nothing."

Sam pinched his glasses between his index and thumb. "Actually, I have everything I need," he replied, as the tiny pinhole light inside his left eye frame turned from green to red.

Sam laid the gun on the table underneath a napkin and got up.

"It's been a pleasure, boys." With that, he turned and started running toward the subway's entrance inside the courtyard.

Donald jumped up and grabbed the gun from underneath the napkin, but as he raised it to fire, the gun felt light. When he looked at the magazine, he realized it was empty.

"Motherfucker!" he screamed. He spun around, searching for Sam, but he was already gone.

FORTY-NINE

Downtown Philly
Corner of 15th and Chestnut
Friday – May 24, 2013 – 1:09 p.m.

Sam ran into the stairway that led down to the subway for City Hall Station inside the courtyard. By now, he was sure the Jackson twins had figured out the pistol wasn't loaded, and that Sam was now in possession of a very damaging video. It was time to get as far away as possible.

As he took the steps two by two, sprinting down the stairs, he heard Donald's scream and felt a ping of pleasure from knowing he had finally stuck it to him.

Once he was at the bottom of the stairs, Sam pulled out his Septa card and crashed through the turnstile. He resumed walking but kept a fast pace, like someone who was late for work. While he walked, he threw on his gray sweater vest and removed his hat and glasses. He stowed the glasses away in his pocket but kept his hand on top of them. They were his most prized possession at the moment, and he knew the Jackson twins would do anything to recover them.

When he got close to the track for the Orange Line, Sam slowed down to blend in with the crowd. He kept his head down and walked the entire length of the track.

Once he got to the end, he walked up a flight of stairs and crossed the main hall toward the stairway that led to the Blue Line. As he moved, he saw two police officers standing next to each other. One of them seemed to be searching the crowd, while the other was talking in the microphone pinned to his shoulder strap. Sam figured that the word had already gotten out and the police had been given a description of a suspect to apprehend. Sam was sure that Davis Jackson knew just the right people to call to get the alert out as quickly as possible.

He arrived at the Blue Line entrance and went down the long corridor that led to 15th and Market Station. He needed to get back to the surface as soon as possible, but he couldn't do it at City Hall. By now, the police had most likely blocked all exits and were scanning the crowds, looking for him.

Sam had picked out the location of his ambush well. City Hall Station was a nexus of various trains, trolleys, and subway lines. Even if the police were posted outside every entrance to the station, it was impossible for them to shut it down completely.

The place was a virtual maze of corridors and stairways that allowed travelers to get from one public transit system to the next without having to step foot outside—Sam counted on using that to his advantage.

As he got to the end of the corridor, he saw a merchant selling the usual Philadelphia paraphernalia to the tourists who bustled around one of the main attractions to the city. Sam walked up to him and checked out the merchandise. Without bargaining, he bought a bright green sweatshirt with the famous Love logo on it and a red Sixers baseball cap. He took his purchase and immediately took off his gray sweater vest, put on the sweatshirt and cap, and resumed walking.

He'd just changed his appearance once more. The Jacksons had to have given a description of him as he left, so that meant that the police were currently searching for a man with a gray Phillies cap and a light blue dress shirt. There wasn't much he could do about the pants and shoes, but at least it would throw off the cops, if only for a fraction of time. Police officers were trained to identify people through changes in facial hair or clothing, but Sam figured there was no point in making it easy for them.

After throwing away his old cap and sweater vest in the nearest garbage can, he took the steps three at a time.

When he got to the top of the stairway, Sam was going so fast that he wasn't paying attention to the people around him. As he took the last step, he ran right into a police officer who was heading down. No doubt, he'd been called away from another posting to help with the manhunt. Sam's weight was no match for the patrolman's bulk, and he fell on his rear. He managed to grab the handrail before tumbling all the way down.

"Hey!" the man bellowed at Sam as he tried to stand back up.

Sam bowed and kept his head down to shield his face as much as he could.

"Sorry, officer. I'm late for work. Didn't see you there. Sorry," he pleaded.

"Watch it next time," the grumpy officer grunted. He turned away and started going down the stairs. Sam heard the cop mumble "*asshole*" as he left.

After taking a few steps, the officer stopped and turned around, looking for the man he'd just bumped into. He saw the figure in the green sweatshirt resume running and turn the corner.

Sam raced down 15th Street, and at the next corner, he turned into an alley. He scampered behind the garbage bin and retrieved his backpack, taking out his coat and beanie hat while tossing the baseball cap inside the nearest trash container. There was no time for him to change right now. He would have to find a suitable place for it later. After donning the coat and hat, he shouldered his backpack and went back onto Chestnut, walking with his back hunched over and his ever-present fake limp.

As he walked, he felt a jolt of pain in his abdomen. He reached underneath his shirt, touched his injury, and as he removed his hand, he noticed there was a bit of blood on it. Sam had most likely torn a few stitches while running or when he fell down the stairs, but for now, he would just have to deal with it. He figured that the adrenaline from his getaway must have blocked his brain from registering pain, but now that it was safer and things were getting back to normal, it had returned in full force. The bleeding didn't seem too bad, and Sam thought the wound would most likely heal again once he found a place to rest.

He resumed walking and tried to think of a place to go. His mission had been a complete success—he had captured a full confession from Donald and Davis Jackson without their knowing. Now, all he had to do was survive until tomorrow.

FIFTY

Center City
Rittenhouse Square
Friday – May 24, 2013 – 4:49 p.m.

At first, Sam thought about going back to his original hideout. He had chased away rather forcefully the only person he'd seen in there thus far, and for a while, he felt that it would be a good place to lay low.

But as he walked up toward the Schuylkill River, he changed his mind. The first issue he had with going back was that there might be the occasional police patrol roving around. The place had seen its share of action in the last few days. A young woman had narrowly escaped being raped when a homeless man had held back her assailant at gunpoint. A young drug addict had been stabbed fighting for shelter. Add to the fact that Sam was already wanted for eluding his sentence, murdering his best friend, and threatening the life of the mayor—the area was simply too hot right now. Although he felt confident that the authorities had no idea that two of the three individuals they were searching for were actually one and the same, there was no reason to take any chances.

Another problem was what to do if he went inside and was confronted yet again with people who had moved in since the place had been vacated. Were they going to be just as aggressive and territorial, or would they leave him be? His experience so far was that half the homeless folks he'd come across were peaceful and quiet, while the other half were rabid dogs who would kill him for a few dollars or a scrap of food.

The final issue was what to do if he hung around there for too long and the kid he'd attacked came back for revenge. It had taken all Sam had to get rid of that junkie the first time around, and he'd been in rather good shape. Now, he was even more exhausted, famished, and grimacing in pain. Sam might have gotten the better of the kid once, but he doubted he could do it again. So, he shuffled around the area searching for an idea.

When he approached his apartment building, he thought about sneaking back in but dismissed that idea as well. The access cards had been changed, and Victoria had told him they'd stepped up security, so there was no way he could get inside without being noticed. If he could survive the next twenty-four hours, he would be back in the comfort of his home soon enough, but for now, the place was off-limits.

As he limped away, his ears focused on the loud noises coming from a few blocks away. He could hear what sounded like music, but it was hard to tell from a distance. As he kept walking south on 22nd, the music became louder, and he could make out the sounds of people shouting over the usual clamor of cars honking and people bustling about. He went to check it out.

When he reached the corner of 22nd and Walnut, Sam looked around and turned to walk toward the noise. Two blocks later, he understood what it was. The Spring Festival on Rittenhouse Row took place every weekend during the month of May. Sam's family enjoyed going to Rittenhouse Square, as it offered large, open spaces for Sofia to run around in the grass. They could toss a football around or have a picnic. It was the closest thing to nature from where they lived. The park was also lined with shops and restaurants. Sam had more than once stopped there to go get a coffee and browse the bookshop across the street before enjoying his brew on a park bench.

Throughout May, the park was surrounded by tents where various merchants sold their wares to passersby. There were farmers displaying fruits and vegetables, as well as independent artists attempting to sell their crafts. The festival took place from Thursday to Sunday every weekend. Analyzing the entire setup, Sam had an idea. He walked around the park, trying to find what he was looking for.

As he reached the opposite side of the park, Sam spotted what he wanted. The world kept advancing through the computer age, and that meant that everything was turning digital, even money. Fewer people carried cash around, as most places of business now accepted credit and debit cards.

But technology needed juice to run, and that's what Sam was looking for right now—it took a lot of electricity to power all these gadgets. Most merchants around the park had registers with all the equipment necessary for their customers to pay without cash. There were generators in each corner of the park, and all the neighboring tents were plugged into them with extension cords.

Sam located a tent that had a power bar, allowing its owner to plug in multiple items simultaneously. Once he was certain nobody was looking, Sam plugged in his phone and covered it with some litter. He then strolled around the area, always keeping an eye on where he'd left his phone. Although he had backed up everything in his cloud drive and could always retrieve the information with another device, that would take up a lot of time he didn't have. The most important item in his life right now was his glasses, and to avoid losing them, he had resumed wearing them on his face.

After waiting for about thirty minutes, Sam walked back behind the tent and changed the outlet from his phone to the charging stick he'd used already once. He would need a lot of juice to do what he had to during the night, and he had no idea where he would find a place to refill his batteries should he run out of power. It was best to be at one hundred percent before beginning the task at hand. After another twenty minutes of nervous pacing in the vicinity of the tent, Sam went back to unplug his charging stick.

As he bent down to retrieve it, he felt a hand press down on his shoulder.

"What do you think you're doing?"

Sam grabbed his charging stick, put it in his pocket, and turned around. A young man in his late teens, face full of pimples and wearing a yellow jacket and utility belt, was standing over him. His jacket identified him as a member of public security employed during the festival to help manage the crowds. Sam knew they spent most of their days pointing parents to the nearest public restrooms so their little ones could avoid soiling their pants. He held his radio in his left hand, while the other one was still grabbing Sam's jacket.

Sam got up and faced the young man. He was under six feet tall and couldn't have weighed more than a hundred and fifty pounds. When he saw Sam get up, his right hand moved away from Sam's jacket and went to his utility belt, where he held his right hand over his retracted billy-club.

The young man started talking on his radio, "This is Aaron. I'm at the corner of 21st and Walnut. I have a suspicious individual attempting to steal property from one of the vendors. Requesting backup."

Sam couldn't believe his bad luck. He tried to explain, "I wasn't stealing anything—this is mine. I was just using the outlet to charge something."

"Sure looked like you were stealing something to me," the kid replied.

Sam sighed with exasperation. He didn't need the hassle right now. He started to move away, but the kid holstered his radio and grabbed Sam's jacket again.

"You're going to wait here with me until we sort this out, sir."

"Let go of me right now!"

The young man tightened his grip.

Sam couldn't afford for the police to get him, not when he was so close. His instincts took over.

He spun around, releasing his backpack from his shoulder as he removed his jacket. The security guard stumbled back as he lost his grip and Sam threw a vicious left hook, putting all his weight behind it. The shot hit the kid right on the jaw, and he fell like a bag of rocks, clutching his face as he lay down on the concrete sidewalk.

Sam couldn't afford to give the kid the opportunity to get back up. He also realized that a bunch of bystanders had just witnessed the assault; help would arrive in a matter of seconds, so there wasn't any time to hang around. He grabbed his backpack, threw it over his shoulders, and started running. He heard a few folks yell out for him to stop, but no one attempted to get in his way.

Sam pushed through the crowds as fast as he could and ran across Walnut Street without stopping to look first. He was almost run over by a cab, but the car stopped just before it hit him. The driver honked furiously and started screaming obscenities in Sam's direction, but Sam paid him no attention and kept sprinting down the sidewalk, looking for a place to hide.

FIFTY-ONE

Center City
Rittenhouse Square
Friday – May 24, 2013 – 6:51 p.m.

Sam was rushing back in the direction of the Schuylkill River out of pure habit. He had done it so many times now that it only felt natural to head in that direction when he didn't know where to go.

As he hit the corner of 22nd and Walnut, he noticed a string of abandoned apartment buildings on his right. The thought of hiding out in one of them while the heat died down and laying low for the night crept into his mind. Unfortunately, the site was fenced so the construction crew that was in the process of renovating the buildings wouldn't be bothered by squatters. Sam couldn't afford to stand still while he thought about his options, so he resumed running.

Sam turned right on 22nd and then again on the next corner. He wound up in the alley behind the abandoned buildings, searching for a way in. There was a barb-wired fence in the back of the lot as well to keep people out.

He didn't have to time to lollygag around, looking for a way across the fence, and he could hear the voices of the security team behind him, only a few hundred feet away. They were asking people if they'd seen him, giving passersby a brief description of Sam. It wouldn't take long for them to learn he'd fled down this alley.

Just as he was about to take off again, his eyes caught sight of a large yellow trash container. The container was made of tough steel and stood at about eight feet tall; it was located just outside the fence, under a long trash chute that ran alongside one of the buildings. The construction workers could toss whatever materials they didn't keep down the chute into the trash container without much effort. Sam figured that the company renovating the site didn't feel the need to secure trash, so they kept it outside the perimeter, allowing the trucks charged with hauling away the container to take it away with ease.

Sam took off in its direction. As he was approaching, he removed his backpack and tossed it in. He climbed the container's wall and jumped into the pile of trash. When he fell, he stifled a scream of pain as he felt another one of his suture points give out. He landed roughly in a pile of discarded drywall panels and wooden studs.

Thinking fast, he grabbed a pair of large drywall pieces and placed them on top of his body, concealing himself. Then, he laid there motionless, praying that nobody had seen him jump in.

He heard a small group of security guards scrambling down the alley, looking for the man who had punched one of their own. The crackle of radios could be heard over their voices. One of them sounded like he was on the phone, presumably with the police, coordinating the search as the rest of his team scoured the area.

Sam could only guess at what they were doing and where they were looking. He sat still and attempted to slow his breathing, but it wasn't easy as the pain from his wound kept shooting up his side. He closed his eyes and waited for the danger to pass.

FIFTY-TWO

Center City
Rittenhouse Square
Friday – May 24, 2013 – 10:21 p.m.

After more than three hours of lying motionless inside the garbage container, Sam decided it was safe to move around a bit. He hadn't heard a sound in a long while. Even the faraway sounds of the Spring Festival had disappeared, as citizens had returned home when the sun had gone down.

Sam didn't dare come out of the garbage container yet. He moved some trash around to make a bit of room in one of its corners, retrieved his backpack, and took out all the items he would need for the night. He figured that since he was sitting at the bottom of a tall steel container, he wouldn't be visible from the outside unless someone climbed up and looked inside. His only worry was the faint glow of his phone's screen as he turned it on—it might be visible to someone who walked down the alley, no matter how unlikely at this late hour.

Sam took some of the drywall panels and propped them up to build a makeshift tent. The drywall was covered in mold and smelled terrible, but there was nothing he could do about that. A part of him began to worry about breathing moldy air, but he figured that a single night of exposure wouldn't do much harm. *I have a lot more pressing health issues to deal with right now anyway*, he thought. His focus was to remain free and alive through the night and finish what he'd set out to do.

Once he saw that his phone was turned on and fully functional, he opened the phone's settings menu and turned down the screen's brightness to a minimum. It was very dark, as the panels he'd set up kept the light from his phone from escaping and also kept the lights from the city from entering his hiding place, so he saw very well. It would also help maximize the phone's battery life.

Sam needed to get to work. He had about seven hours to get everything done. Even though it was Friday, Sam decided he would need to leave at the crack of dawn, just in case some construction workers showed up for the weekend shift. He would cut it close, but if he worked through the night, he might just be able to pull this off.

FIFTY-THREE

Center City
Rittenhouse Square
Friday – May 24, 2013 – 11:02 p.m.

The faint glow of the phone's screen lit up Sam's face as he worked tirelessly. He had started by plugging his glasses into his phone using the cables and adapters he'd bought when he first set out on his mission. He downloaded the entire video file of the Jacksons' confession, which took over twenty minutes to transfer. Once the transfer was complete, Sam took out his Bluetooth earpiece and opened the video file. He had to first make sure that the image and video were working; otherwise, this would be a complete waste of time.

Sam watched the entire video and gritted his teeth every time Donald and Davis spoke. His anger toward them hadn't diminished, but now, instead of rage, he was filled with a sense of purpose. He could see the finish line now—all he had to do was work on this last step and live through the night.

After viewing the entire video to ensure that everything was clear and audible from start to finish, he opened the video file from his encounter with Vanessa at the massage parlor and did the same. Once he was sure that everything was good on the second file, he turned on the data for his phone. The files were massive, so he pulled out all his prepaid credit cards and filled up his data plan to a maximum. He then uploaded the files onto his cloud drive. It took over forty-five minutes for the transfer to complete, and now that he had secure copies of both videos stored away, he could get to work.

The videos were too long for him to send to anyone in a single piece, so he downloaded a free video editor. After installing the program, he put the phone back in airplane mode so as not to use any data when he didn't absolutely need to.

He plugged in one of his charging sticks and got to work breaking down the videos into smaller individual files that could be sent by email or social media. Sam worked nonstop throughout the night and burned through his first charging stick and half of the second one. He was glad he'd thought of refilling them in the afternoon, or he never would have been able to finish his task.

Sam watched every single video file once more to be certain that the audio and video worked perfectly; once he was satisfied, he turned off airplane mode and sent them all up to his cloud drive. Everything he'd gathered since he set out to find the truth was safely stored away. He was almost done now. After wiping off all his digital tracks on his phone, he powered down and tried to rest.

He saw the faint glow of the sunrise creeping on the horizon. Workers might return to the site soon, so after tossing his bag over the edge, he jumped over the wall of the container and landed on the concrete. He grunted as pain shot up his side, but he shrugged it off and focused on his next destination.

FIFTY-FOUR

Center City
Rittenhouse Square
Saturday – May 25, 2013 – 8:38 a.m.

After exiting at the first sign of daylight, Sam moved around the block to stretch his legs and went back to the park.

It was getting crowded, even though it was still very early in the morning. The Rittenhouse Spring Festival attracted folks from all around the city, so the area filled up fast. Sam remembered coming here every spring and worrying the entire day about losing Sofia in the crowd, but the kid loved it, which was all that mattered.

Now, he was using the same crowd as cover. His appearance had again changed slightly—he'd left his black jacket behind when he'd fled the park the day before, so it would be hard for law enforcement to spot him through the hundreds of people present.

Sam put in his earpiece and made a phone call. It was hard to hear the dial tone, as the noise was becoming increasingly loud, so he moved to the opposite side of the park, far away from the large speakers blasting pop music. After the fourth ring, the line picked up.

"This is Fox29 Philadelphia. How can I direct your call, please?" a soft female voice answered.

Sam's plan was to expose what he'd found out publicly through the media. He was pretty sure none of it would be admissible in court, as the brothers had been filmed without their knowledge. They also had seemed confident that they could refute all the other evidence he had, mainly his father's work, so going through the justice system felt like a dead end to him.

But what politicians feared more than anything else was bad press. Even if Sam couldn't stop Donald and Davis Jackson by going to the police, he could at least do a lot of damage to their political careers. The election was only two days away, and Sam doubted that they would be able to recover before Monday after the story broke out.

He had chosen Fox because Davis was running as a Democrat despite having a rather tough stance on crime. Fox and Democrats were natural enemies, and Sam thought they would be the most motivated outlet to go after this story.

"Hi. I'd like to be transferred to your newsroom, specifically a person in charge of covering the upcoming election," he asked the friendly receptionist.

"Certainly. Hold, please," she said as she transferred his call.

After a minute of listening to soft music, the call was picked up, and a male voice said, "Mat Linden."

"Hello, Mr. Linden. You don't know me, but I have something that I think would interest you," Sam said. He made a conscious effort to remain calm, but he felt butterflies in his stomach. *This is it, the end of the line*, he said to himself. If he could pass everything he had on to the media, Sam was sure they would pick up the ball and run with it.

"Who's this?" Linden asked.

"I'd rather not say, but I have something you might want to look at."

"Is this a joke? Who is this?"

"This is no joke, I assure you," Sam replied. "I have video evidence that implicates Davis Jackson in some very nasty business."

"Yeah, right," Linden scoffed. He sounded annoyed.

Sam figured that the accusation was so severe that it would be very hard for someone to believe it upon hearing it for the first time. Davis Jackson had always projected the image of the unflappable attorney who had worked to put bad guys away, a dedicated mayor, and a man above any reproach. He needed to tread carefully and make sure he kept the reporter on the line. He could always call another outlet, but he felt that this was his best bet.

"Okay, how about this? Can you give me your email address, please? I'll send you an excerpt of the video right now if you want."

"Shit, you're not kidding, are you? You really have something on Jackson? What is it?" Mat Linden asked with a sudden surge of excitement in his voice.

"Give me your address, and you'll see for yourself in a minute."

"Okay, it's MLinden@fox29philly.com." He spelled it out for Sam's benefit. "And who are you exactly? Do you work for his campaign?"

"No, I do not. I'd rather not say over the phone," Sam said in his earpiece as he sent the most damaging clip to the reporter. "Okay, the file is on its way. Check your inbox—you should have it by now. Look at the video. I'll hold the line."

Sam heard a desk chair rolling and keys being tapped on a keyboard.

"Okay, got it. Hang on, it has to be scanned for viruses before I can open it,"

Linden said.

After about a minute, Sam could hear the faint audio of the video he'd sent being played on the man's computer.

"You killed my father? Why?"

"Because when your old man took that last picture there, the officer had the presence of mind to note his license plate as he sped away from us. He put a BOLO on it, and when he finally tracked him down outside the bank, he asked us to get rid of him. He said there was another five grand in it for us if we wasted him."

"So, you killed him? Were you in on it, too?"

"Who do you think was driving the getaway car, stupid?"

Sam knew the video had ended from having watched it over and over. He waited for the reporter on the other end of the line to speak.

It took a few seconds, but Mat Linden came back on the line.

"This is incredible. How did you get this?"

"Never mind how I got it," Sam replied hastily. "You want the rest of it or not? This is only a fraction of what I'm holding. I'm not just talking about Donald and Davis Jackson being implicated in a murder. I'm also talking about police corruption, extortion, the works!" Sam finished enthusiastically.

"Yes, of course, I want the rest. Can you send it now?"

Mat Linden sounded like a giddy schoolboy, and for good reason—he had just been handed the story of the year on a silver platter.

"I can't, the files are too massive. I want to meet face to face, and I'll hand you everything I have. But I'll need a few things from you in return."

"What? You mean money? I'm sorry, we don't pay for information here."

"Bullshit. I'm sure you'd pay for all of this, as would all your competitors. But no, Mr. Linden, I'm not asking for money."

"What do you want, then?"

"I need your help," Sam said point-blank.

"My help? What for? And you still haven't told me who you are," Linden replied.

"Okay, then, let's start with that." Sam took a deep breath and said, "My name is Samuel Brighton. I've been set up by the Jackson brothers for having a naked photo of one of my students. Does that ring a bell?"

"Brighton… Yes, I remember now. Aren't you wanted for skipping bail?"

"Among other things, yes. Donald Jackson has also tried to frame me for the murder of my best friend, Dean Ashton."

"Yes, I remember… The guy shot in the back of the head in South Philly. Wait a minute… You're saying all this was set up by Davis Jackson? Why?"

"It was mostly set up by his brother Donald, but Davis was implicated also to a degree. I'll explain everything once we meet. But I need your word that once I pass everything on to you, you'll help me out in return."

"Sure thing. Tell me what you need, and I'll see if I can make it happen."

"I need your help getting safe passage," was all Sam said.

"Safe passage? What do you mean? You want me to help you get across the border? I can't do that!" Linden replied frantically.

"Not across the border—across the *river*. I'll explain when I see you. Be at the front entrance of your building in exactly one hour." Then, Sam hung up and turned off his phone.

FIFTY-FIVE

Old Philadelphia
Corner of Market and 4th
Saturday – May 25, 2013 – 10:21 a.m.

Sam had checked the various news outlets on his phone the night before and read the headlines pertaining to the election so he could keep informed. It had drained the last remnants of his battery life, but he felt it was necessary. Reading the different ways the same story was covered was the reason he had chosen Fox as his prime candidate. Their coverage of the Jackson campaign was more aggressive, and they pointed out flaws whenever they could find one, while the other networks seemed to only praise the mayor. He'd bet that Fox would be very interested in what he had to show, and they had indeed jumped at the chance. It was almost over.

As Sam got out of Rittenhouse Square after navigating through the throngs of people crowding the sidewalks, he walked a few blocks north before turning toward Old Philadelphia. He'd read online that the Jackson clan was holding a major political rally in Independence Park to gather support for the final push of the election. The election was all but won for Jackson, so the rally was more of a fundraiser than anything else. Sam's normal route would have taken him straight through the park, but he had no desire to go anywhere near it.

Not only did he want to avoid the hundreds of cops that would be stationed around the park for crowd control—he wanted to make sure there wasn't even the slightest chance he could bump into one of his enemies or be spotted in the crowd.

What should have taken only a half-hour to travel took twice the time, since Sam had to circle around Independence Park to get to his destination.

As he arrived close to the building, he walked by once before showing himself. He went across the street from the studio and resumed his limp as he checked out his surroundings. At first glance, there was no sign of danger. He waited for a few minutes and passed in front of the building a second time.

On his second pass, he saw a young man in his late twenties, dressed in chinos and wearing brown leather shoes and a light blue Polo shirt with the Fox29 logo stitched on the left breast pocket. He had thin glasses and a trendy, short haircut. Sam recognized Mat Linden from his profile photo on Facebook and turned in his direction. Before Sam could say anything, Linden waved him off and said sternly, "I don't have any change, buddy. Beat it."

"Mr. Linden, I believe you've been waiting for me," Sam replied in a low voice.

Linden was speechless. He hadn't anticipated Sam's appearance and had looked right through the man approaching him, never suspecting that it was, in fact, the man he had been waiting for.

"Samuel Brighton? Is that you?"

"Yes, it is. Sorry if my hair's a little out of place," Sam said with a coy smile, trying to lighten the mood and put the young man at ease. "Mind if we go inside now. I don't like being this exposed."

"Sure. Sorry. Right this way," Linden said, pointing at the front entrance.

As they walked in, Sam noticed the employees of the station stare at him as he passed by. They were probably wondering who this bum was and what he was doing inside their nice shiny offices. They walked through the bullpen, and when they got to Linden's cubicle, Sam took the man's chair before he could even offer it. He sat down with a low grunt and sighed in relief. Compared to his living conditions for the past two weeks, the chair felt like heaven.

"Take a seat, I guess," Linden said, mildly objecting to the dirty old man sitting in his desk chair. He would have to throw it away once they were done. "Can I get you a glass of water or something?" he asked politely.

"A glass would be nice, yes. Make it five glasses. And some food would be great, too. I'm sort of hungry," Sam said, as he took out his phone and cables from his backpack.

Linden picked up his phone and called the receptionist at the front desk. He asked her to bring five bottles of water and whatever food she could find. After exchanging a few arguments, he told her he would reimburse her for what she bought from the vending machines. When he turned around, he saw that Sam was already busy plugging his phone into his desktop computer.

"I'll upload everything to your computer. It might take a while—there's a lot of it. Once it's all set, I'll explain everything and answer any questions you might have."

Sam created a folder on the man's desktop and transferred everything he had on his phone. The young lady manning the front desk arrived with the water bottles, two bags of chips, and a chocolate bar from the vending machines. Sam thanked her, but she seemed put off by his shaggy appearance and quickly walked away without saying a word.

Sam drank an entire bottle in under ten seconds and tore open the bags of chips. He gulped everything down as fast as he could stuff it in his mouth while he kept his eyes on the monitor to check the transfer's progress.

The transfer was almost complete just as he finished his candy bar. He drank another bottle and stuffed the other three in his backpack. While they waited for the task to be over, Sam asked Linden where the restrooms were, and the young reporter told him to go to the end of the hallway on his right.

He picked up his pack and headed for the bathroom. Once he was there, he took care of his natural ablutions then washed his face as best he could over the sink. While he was far from looking his best, he still felt a lot better than earlier. He felt that he was nearing the end and could almost taste freedom on the tip of his tongue.

When he got back to Linden's desk, he noticed that he had brought in a second chair, and the young man was looking at the monitor. The transfer had just finished, and he was waiting for Sam to show him everything he had. Sam took out the documents in his bag and laid them across the desk.

They took over three hours going over every single item of information Sam had gathered in the past twelve days. They watched the video of Vanessa twice and the Jacksons' four times, while Linden jotted down some notes on a pad as the video played.

Mat questioned Sam over and over, going through his story and trying to find any discrepancies or flaws. Sam answered every question as best he could but left out the parts where his wife had helped him recover the boxes or heal his wounds. Until this was over, there was no good reason to implicate his family. He recounted Dean's involvement in retrieving the contents of the safety deposit box and how he had been killed by thugs in broad daylight. Linden had replayed Donald Jackson's video to see if both stories matched.

After the third hour of viewing and questioning, it appeared that Mat Linden had run out of things to ask. He told Sam that he would have to go over all the material with his boss before running the story, but that everything looked solid.

The young reporter asked Sam if he would like to rest while he went over everything with his boss once more, and Sam agreed instantly. Linden told him there was a leather chair in the breakroom down the hall; he could use it to rest while they worked.

Sam left his stuff next to the desk and shuffled over to the breakroom. As he walked inside, he didn't say a single word to the other people present and just crashed in the large leather chair, pulling the lever and putting his feet up. He noticed that all the other occupants had discreetly left the room, but he just didn't care anymore. It only took a second for him to fall into a deep sleep.

FIFTY-SIX

Old Philadelphia
Corner of Market and 4th
Saturday – May 25, 2013 – 3:16 p.m.

Sam was sound asleep, sunk deep in the soft cushions of the leather chair in the employee breakroom, his eyes closed and a slight grin on his face.

He was dreaming of the beach, the souvenirs of lazy days spent near the ocean with his family floating around in his head. They had spent at least three weekends every summer driving down to the shores in southern New Jersey to enjoy the water. It was a much-needed getaway for them since they lived in such a large metropolitan area.

They always left early on Saturday morning in a rented car and drove down to enjoy the sun's rays and the sounds of waves crashing. It was a healthy change of pace from the pollution and noise of the city. Ultimately, they'd found two very quaint little towns right next to each other, Strathmere and Avalon. Strathmere offered miles of pristine sand and clear water, while Avalon was the typical seaside village, lined with restaurants and shops. For a while, they had even considered buying a place in the area but had decided against it. If they were free to travel wherever they pleased, they could always discover the next little diamond in the rough.

As images of his daughter playing in the sand and his wife lying on a beach towel reading a book drifted across his mind, Sam started hearing male voices piercing through his thoughts.

He began opening his eyes. Before he could remember where he was or how long he had been sleeping, his mind registered the shock of the sight in front of him. Two police officers were standing in the doorway of the breakroom, hands on their holsters. It was the same two cops who had arrested him in the first place, over two weeks ago. The old sergeant still had a look of perpetual anger on his face, and his younger colleague stayed a step behind with a stoic yet professional expression.

"Nice to see you again, asshole," the sergeant said.

"Samuel Brighton. You're under arrest," the younger cop said as his colleague approached Sam with his hand on his holster.

Sam couldn't believe it. How had they found him? It didn't make any sense. No one knew he was inside the offices of the television studio—no one except Mat Linden.

The older policeman grabbed Sam by the collar and threw him to the ground. He put a knee in the middle of his back and grasped one of his arms, pulling it hard behind him. Sam tried to fight back, but his body had still not yet recovered from his injury, and he was no match for the man pinning him to the ground. He gave up his struggle and offered his second arm, as the officer finished cuffing him.

Sam was hauled to his feet, and as he was escorted out of the room, the young officer began citing him his Miranda Rights once more.

When they got to the front entrance, he saw people frozen in place, staring at the scene and not saying a word. He looked at the young receptionist, but as soon as her eyes met Sam's, she glanced down at her desk.

He was led out to where a patrol car was waiting. It was parked on the sidewalk, and the lights were flashing. It drew unwanted attention from the people nearby, gawking at the sight of a homeless man being taken away. He even saw a few flashes as he was led down the front steps.

When he got to the car, Sam turned around, and he spotted Mat Linden. The young man was standing on the front steps of the building, watching the police as they took Sam away. His facial expression offered no clue as to what he was thinking or why he was standing there, but the mere fact that he was standing there told Sam he was the one who had called the cops on him.

"Linden! You sold me out! Why would you do this?" Sam yelled out as the officer opened the door to the back seat of the patrol car.

The young man did not utter a single word in response.

"Asshole! I gave you *everything*, and this is how you repay me? I'll get you for this! I swear!" Sam screamed at the top of his lungs as he tried to kick his way free.

The older officer turned Sam around toward the open door. He put his hand on top of Sam's head to help him stoop down and enter the car, but at the last second, he rammed Sam's skull into the doorframe with all his might.

Sam's body went limp, and he fell on the back seat.

FIFTY-SEVEN

Philadelphia Police Department
Corner of Race and 8th
Saturday – May 25, 2013 – 7:01 p.m.

Sam's original plan was to ask Linden for a ride across the Delaware River so he could get to Camden, New Jersey. The Benjamin Franklin Bridge that allowed such passage was too long and had too much traffic for Sam to cross it on foot.

If he got across the river into Camden, Sam had intended to instruct Linden to drive down Cooper Street for a few blocks. There, he would get out of the vehicle, reaching his final destination.

He had no intention of living as a fugitive for the rest of his life. He had made Victoria a solemn promise that he would turn himself in if he ever got into trouble—that was his plan if he ever managed to get across the river.

The U.S. Marshals had offices in Camden, on the corner of Cooper and 3rd. Sam didn't trust the local Philly police force, for good reason. His father had uncovered a conspiracy almost fifty years ago, and Sam doubted that the PPD would enjoy the truth being exposed any more than the Jacksons did. Donald Jackson's boasting of how they had a lot of influence inside the police department only cemented Sam's decision not to go to the local authorities.

If he crossed the state line between Pennsylvania and New Jersey, Sam would become a target for the Marshals. He planned on making their manhunt the easiest one in history by walking right up to their front door. They could keep him out of reach of the Philadelphia Police as everything was sorted out. The only thing Sam had ever wanted to do was find the truth and clear his name, even if that meant he would stay locked up, kept from his family and the outside world for years and years.

Now, he was lying down on the concrete floor of the holding cell inside the Philadelphia Police Department's station.

When he woke up, it took him some time to understand where he was. He saw the gray metal bars of the holding cell, and memories of his arrest came flooding back.

Sam got up slowly and tried to shake the cobwebs out of his brain, but the blow he'd suffered was severe. His head was pounding, and his eyes had trouble focusing.

As he stood up, he asked the desk sergeant where he was, but the man ignored him. He asked if he could make his mandatory phone call, but again, the pudgy man kept on reading the sports section of his newspaper as if he hadn't heard him. Sam kept trying for a few minutes, but to no avail—he eventually gave up.

He looked around and saw six other men stranded in the same holding cell as he was. They all looked mean and eyeballed Sam with menacing glares. Sam spotted a concrete bench in the corner and went to take a seat. He kept his head down and avoided eye contact as he tried to gather his thoughts and figure out what would happen next.

The most likely scenario was that he would be taken before the court once more so his sentence could be prolonged by a few decades then immediately sent to jail. His murder accusation would be tried in his absence, and he would be informed of the verdict via videoconference in his cell.

The fact that he was right back where he'd started was weighing down on Sam's shoulders like hundred-pound dumbbells. But he just couldn't give up. He had an ace in the hole— all he could do was trust it would be used. The only silver lining he could think of at that particular instant, was that after so many days spent outside living as a vagrant, a cell with a mattress, three square meals a day, and a daily shower almost sounded nice.

He heard footsteps coming from the end of the hallway and turned his head toward the noise like everyone else in his cage. The revolting taste of vomit rose in his throat as he saw Donald Jackson approaching the holding area.

He was wearing his standard white linen shirt and cheap black tie, but what caught Sam's attention the most was the way he was walking.

The man had a spring in his step, almost skipping down the long corridor and smiling from ear to ear like the damn Cheshire Cat. In his left hand, he was holding a pair of thick eyeglasses. Sam's hand shot up to his face, and he realized that he had left them at the television station; his biggest asset was now in his enemy's hands.

Donald Jackson entered the holding room and, in a low voice, politely asked the desk sergeant, "Would you mind giving us the room for a few minutes?"

This time, the old man's hearing appeared to have healed as if by a miracle. He folded his paper under his arm and walked out of the room. When he turned the corner at the end of the hall and was out of sight, Donald Jackson approached the cell.

"Hello, Sam. Nice to see you again so soon."

Sam got up and walked to the edge of his cell. He gripped the iron bars with both hands, and his knuckles turned white.

"You piece of shit! What do you want now? You came here to gloat, is that it?"

"Not at all, Sam. I actually came here to thank you."

"Thank me for what?"

Jackson's right hand fished inside his pocket, and he pulled out a cell phone.

"For handing over every shred of evidence you had against us to our friend Mr. Linden. That made things a hell of a lot easier for us."

Sam attempted to grab Jackson through the bars, but he was in such bad shape that the man dodged out of the way with ease. Jackson laughed heartily.

"Nice try, Sam."

"I swear, if I ever get out of here, I'll find you and make you pay. You can count on it!" Sam growled.

"You're not about to get out of here any time soon, my friend."

"I'm not your goddamn friend, you lying sack of shit!"

"Be that as it may, I just felt like coming over and saying one last goodbye. It's been fun, Sam, but in a few days, we'll be on our way to Washington." Jackson turned around and started to leave.

"This isn't over Jackson. You hear me? This isn't over!" Sam screamed in fury.

Jackson stopped and turned toward Sam. He looked at him, and his smile almost turned into a grimace.

"You remember how I told you we had some friends in high places, Sam?"

"What about it?" Sam asked. He didn't understand where this conversation was going.

"Well, we also got a lot of friends in *low* places. Get some, boys!" Jackson shouted.

Sam barely had time to understand that his former boss was talking to the other men in his cell. He was still staring at Jackson when the first punch landed on the back of his head.

Sam was dazed, and his legs gave out. He fell to the floor as more punches landed on his head and chest.

He tried to protect himself as best he could, but he was in no condition to fight back. Even if he had been, he was simply outnumbered. Punches and kicks kept raining down on him, and Sam rolled himself into a ball and prayed someone would come soon.

He felt one last blow to his head before the lights went out.

FIFTY-EIGHT

**Thomas Jefferson University Hospital
Corner of Chestnut and 11th
Monday – May 27, 2013 – 4:39 p.m.**

As light filtered through his right eyelid, Sam slowly began to open it. The first thing he realized was that his left eye refused to open. The images sent to his brain were still blurry, and as he gazed around, he tried to understand where he was.

From the bright, fluorescent lights and constant beeping emanating from the machine next to him, Sam concluded that he was lying in a hospital bed. His left arm was in a cast and hung from a contraption attached to the ceiling. He had trouble breathing, and every time he inhaled, it felt like someone was swinging a sledgehammer to his chest.

Sam attempted to raise his right arm, but as he did, he heard metal clanging on metal. He tried to focus and through the haze, he saw that he was handcuffed to the bed's railing.

Sam laid his head back on the pillow and attempted to recollect how he had ended up here—his mind drew a blank.

Looking at the door to his room, he saw a uniformed officer standing guard outside. He called out to him, and the man turned to look at him but immediately resumed his position. Sam called out again but was only met with silence.

His head was pounding like a jackhammer, and he felt nauseated. He found the red button next to his head and called for a nurse.

A few minutes later, a petite lady in her fifties with short, gray hair and a soft smile entered the room after asking the policeman standing guard to let her through. She walked up to Sam and said, "I see you're awake. That's good. How are you feeling?"

"My head hurts like hell," Sam answered in a coarse voice.

"That's normal. It seems you took quite a beating."

"Where am I?" Sam asked.

"You're at Thomas Jefferson Hospital. We're going to take great care of you. Now that you're up, can you answer a few questions? Can you tell me your name, for starters?"

Sam opened his mouth to answer then stopped. His head was a maze, and he tried as hard as he could to drag the information from the back of his mind to no avail. He was stuck, and he racked his brain, trying to find the answer. His breath quickened as panic started to sink in. "I… I don't know," he mumbled shakily.

"Okay, that's not a problem. We'll try again later." She nodded at him then looked down at Sam's file and asked, "Can you tell me anything about what happened to you?"

"No. I'm sorry."

"That's okay. Don't worry about that for now. You didn't have any identification on you when the cops brought you in here. Your file just says, 'John Doe.' Do you know someone we can call as a contact? I see a tan line on your ring finger. Were you married? Maybe we can call your ex-wife? Can you remember her name? Or anybody else we could call?"

Sam was trying to dredge up the answers to all her questions, but his brain just couldn't seem to process the information.

"I can't remember a thing. Sorry. My head really hurts."

"I'll have the doctor come look at you. And don't worry about anything—we can try to find out who you are later when you're feeling better."

Looking past the nurse and into the hallway, Sam could see a large television screen above the waiting area. As his vision began to focus, he saw the images of two black men, holding hands high above their heads, smiling and waving to the crowd.

"I know them…" Sam whispered, his heart suddenly beating a lot faster. A bead of sweat started rolling down his forehead. His breathing accelerated, and he became agitated.

"Are you alright?" the nurse asked, as she turned toward the television screen. When she turned back to look at Sam, he was convulsing in his bed. Frantically, she rang the emergency button and called for help.

FIFTY-NINE

Thomas Jefferson University Hospital
Corner of Chestnut and 11th
Friday – May 31, 2013 – 10:23 a.m.

Sam woke up and opened his eyes. His left eyelid was opening just a bit now, and he could see more clearly. He looked around the room and remembered where he was.

Sam tried to speak, but he couldn't make a sound. His mouth was dry, and he felt a large plastic tube that had been shoved down his throat. It took him a while to fumble around and find the red button attached to his bed, but when he did, he pounded on the buzzer.

As the buzzer sounded above his bed, the officer outside the door turned around, caught sight of Sam, and shouted, "Nurse! He's awake!"

The nurse rushed in and, with a beaming smile, said, "Good! You're awake!"

As he regained awareness, everything he'd struggled to remember flooded back into his mind. He tried to speak again, but the nurse stopped him immediately.

"Hold on a second. Let's get rid of all this first. Then a drink of water, and then you can try to speak."

She removed the apparatus with great care, but the plastic tube being dragged out of his throat felt like sandpaper. When it was out, Sam coughed repeatedly and motioned the nurse for a glass of water. She handed him a small paper cup, and he tried to drink it down. The first few attempts at swallowing failed miserably, but eventually, he was able to drink the small amount of water left in the cup. He made a hand gesture at the nurse, asking for more, and she refilled his cup. This time, he drank every drop.

"Where am I? What's going on?" Sam asked in a coarse whisper.

"You're in the hospital at Thomas Jefferson's. Do you remember your name?"

"Sam. Sam Brighton," he answered with a strange look on his face. Why wouldn't he know his own name?

"That's good. Let's keep going," she said and asked questions about his date of birth, place of birth, and current address. She wrote down everything Sam said on his medical chart.

"Why are you asking me this? What's going on?"

"Well, Mr. Brighton, when you were first brought here, you were in bad shape. Someone had beaten you severely, and you had temporary amnesia. You took a turn for the worse, and we had to chemically induce a coma to relieve the swelling inside your cranium. We were worried about you for a while. It's good to see you're making a quick recovery."

"Coma? What do you mean? How long was I out? What day is it?" Sam asked in a panic, remembering that the last time he had been conscious was inside a holding cell at the police station. He recalled his encounter with Donald Jackson, with that smug grin on his face, and the upcoming election he was trying to stop.

"Relax, Mr. Brighton. Don't work yourself up too much! You still need to rest. You were out for about four days. It's Friday, May 31st, today."

"Friday? Oh, shit!"

"What's wrong?" she asked.

"My phone! Where's my cell phone?" Sam asked frantically.

"I don't know anything about a cell phone, sorry."

Sam remembered that the last time he had seen his phone, it had been in Donald Jackson's hand.

"The election. I've got to stop them!" he shouted.

"The election? Oh my God, what a mess that thing!" she said with a chuckle.

"What do you mean?"

"Relax, Mr. Brighton… There'll be plenty of time to chat. For now, you need to rest. I'm glad to hear that you finally recovered your memory, but you're not out of the woods just yet. Now, is there someone you want us to call for you?"

Sam's head was still hurting like crazy, but he was putting the pieces back together.

"My wife. Victoria," he whispered, his throat still chafed from the breathing apparatus that had been lodged in his trachea only a few minutes earlier.

The nurse handed him a sip of water and a pen and notepad.

"Here. Write her name and a number where we can reach her if you can remember. Your throat will feel better in a little while, but for now, let's try to avoid any unnecessary discomfort."

Sam wrote down Victoria's name and cell phone number before passing the notepad back to the nurse.

"Alrighty. We'll try to get a hold of her today and tell her to come down here. Until then, get some rest. You'll be back on your feet soon enough."

The nurse was barely able to finish uttering her last word before Sam fell back asleep.

SIXTY

Thomas Jefferson University Hospital
Corner of Chestnut and 11th
Saturday – June 1, 2013 – 9:17 a.m.

Sam woke up to the gentle feeling of a hand stroking his fore-arm. When he opened his eyes, he saw Victoria sitting beside the bed, reading a stack of papers in one hand while she kept touch on her husband.

He turned his head and saw Sofia sitting in an old, green, plastic chair, watching television. Victoria noticed Sam stirring and raised her head. "Rise and shine, sleepyhead."

"Daddy! You're up!" Sofia shouted happily.

"Hey, guys," Sam said, smiling. He hadn't seen his daughter in weeks and was elated to see she was in good spirits. His eyes shifted to his wife sitting at his bedside, holding his hand. He had missed them so much. No matter how things would turn out, he was just glad to be reunited with his family.

"How are you feeling, honey?" his wife asked.

"Pretty good, I guess. What time is it?"

"It's around 9 a.m. on Saturday morning."

"Okay, thanks… I'm just still trying to figure out what's go-ing on here…" he mumbled.

"Yeah, I suppose you have a lot of questions. Sofia, why don't you go downstairs to the cafeteria and grab us some food, okay?" she asked their daughter as she handed her some money.

"I'm starving," Sam said to his little girl.

"I'm on it, Dad!" Sofia said enthusiastically, and she bolted out of the room.

"Okay, now we can talk," Victoria continued. "What do you want to know?"

"God, I have about a hundred questions for you right now…" Sam sighed.

"Start with one, and we'll work our way down the list," she replied.

"Fair enough. How did I end up here?"

"You got attacked while you were in holding. Seems the sergeant on duty had left his post to go to the bathroom, and the other prisoners jumped you while there was no one around to intervene."

Sam recalled that Jackson had asked the desk sergeant to leave the room. It brought up his next question in a flash.

"When did you learn about this?"

"Only yesterday. Someone very high up in the police department gave orders to keep a lid on this. The officer that called it in told the paramedics they hadn't yet identified you, so they tagged you with 'John Doe.'" She grimaced, her eyes flashing angrily.

"Jackson! I know it was him. He must have called in a favor!" Sam said, realizing why the nurse had no information on him and why his family hadn't been notified of his transfer to the hospital. "What happened with the election? Did they win? Did you get my package?" he asked frantically.

"Yes, I did, and thank God I did," Victoria said. "The election... That's quite a story. Are you sure you're up for it?"

"Up for what? Tell me!" Sam couldn't wait any longer. He needed to know what had happened.

"Okay, then. The election on Monday was a landslide. Davis Jackson was pronounced Senator-Elect in the middle of the afternoon, even before all the ballots had been counted. His opponent conceded victory right around lunchtime."

"Shit!" Sam cursed.

"Hold on, Sam. Let me finish."

Sam gave her a small nod.

"When I got to my office on Monday, I had received a package. I opened it and saw that it contained a bunch of photos and copies of documents. In the beginning, I couldn't make sense of any of it. Then, I saw the letter you had written. You gave me very precise instructions about how to access your remote drive and what to do with everything it contained.

"I tried doing much of it myself, but I got overwhelmed—so I called Paul. He was still trying to process Dean's death, but when I told him I had some proof that you weren't the one responsible, he agreed to help.

"We met at our apartment around supper time. I tried to send Sofia out, but she wouldn't have it, so she helped us out, too." She shook her head and laughed.

"We all saw the videos you'd filmed and the pictures you'd saved. I called the police department to see if they had any news, but they told me they were still searching for you. Guess that was a lie. Someone wanted to keep you hidden.

"So, Paul took both videos and uploaded them to YouTube and a few other online platforms. He sent the links to all the local radio and TV stations from an anonymous email account he'd created, too.

"We then both went on our Facebook accounts and told people to check out the links to the video. It went viral within a few hours, and soon enough, everyone in town had seen it. The news networks picked up the story, too, and it ran continuously on all stations," she continued breathlessly.

"The next morning, reporters from all networks were asking for an interview with Davis Jackson, but he refused to go on camera. By the end of the day, a judge had declared that the results of the election were suspended pending an investigation and the city council voted to suspend Davis Jackson indefinitely."

"So, Jackson's not the mayor anymore?" Sam asked, relief washing over him.

"Not anymore, no. By Wednesday morning, City Hall was overwhelmed by protesters calling for his resignation. Jackson tried to downplay the allegations against him and his brother, but the damage had been done. There was no way he could deny being in that video you shot. He then panicked and tried to put all the blame on Donald, claiming he had no idea what his brother had done, but by then, all his supporters had deserted him. Nobody believed him. He resigned Wednesday evening."

"What about Donald Jackson?" Sam asked eagerly. "What happened to him?"

"That's a good question, Sam. Short answer is we don't know. No one's seen or heard from him since Tuesday. Reporters have been looking for him, and police say they're searching for him. Rumors are he skipped town."

"Shit. Well, at least we stopped those two assholes from taking office. Guess that's a win," Sam said, his expression downcast.

"Smile, you fool!" Victoria said, giggling. "You haven't even heard the best part yet!"

"What is it?"

"The morning after we released the videos, I got a bunch of calls from lawyers who wanted to represent you in your appeal. Some of them even offered to work pro bono! I hired the best and most expensive one I could find, and he got to work immediately."

"And?" Sam couldn't wait to learn more. He was hanging on to Victoria's every word.

"And a judge called for your trial to be reopened and also ordered the police to investigate the allegations regarding Dean and your father's murders."

"That's wonderful!" Sam was in shock.

"Our lawyer says your new trial should start by the middle of next week, but he says that with all the evidence you've uncovered and the public outcry regarding the Jacksons' actions, your case is a slam dunk. He even managed to negotiate with the judge for you to be on home arrest while you await your trial, once you're out of the hospital of course."

Sam couldn't believe what he was hearing. Victoria had been his ace in the hole, and she had come through even more brilliantly than he could have ever expected. He could finally see the light at the end of this long, dark tunnel.

SIXTY-ONE

United States Court of Appeals
Corner of Market and 6th
Thursday – June 27, 2013 – 3:49 p.m.

Victoria and Sam were walking out of the courthouse holding hands, with Sofia following a few paces behind—they had allowed her to skip school for this very special day. About a dozen reporters and photographers ran up to them, bombarding Sam with questions and taking pictures, but the Brighton family ignored them and walked away.

Sam was released from the hospital three days after his and Victoria's conversation. Victoria had argued with Sam's doctor and had convinced him to let her take the reins of her husband's recovery. The hospital didn't put up much of a fight—they were glad to free up a bed for someone else.

Sam was put on home arrest; he wore an ankle monitor and was confined to his house until his trial was over. The judge had determined that even though he didn't think he posed an immediate threat to anyone's life, his actions in the previous weeks, combined with the fact that Donald Jackson was still on the loose, convinced him it was safer for everyone if he remained home for the time being.

Victoria had resumed working, taking time off when Sam had to meet with his legal team or appear in court. It had become a bit of a burden, as her husband wasn't allowed to leave their condo, not even to do the groceries or run errands, but she soldiered on without complaining.

Sam, on the other hand, was growing impatient, what with being confined to such a small space twenty-four hours a day. There had been some restricting conditions to his liberation—mainly that he wasn't allowed to use the internet for the duration of his appeal. Victoria bought him a PlayStation3, and Sam had taken up gaming to pass the time. Some of his colleagues had called to offer their congratulations, but he let the voicemail pick up and never returned their calls. Those pricks had shunned him when they'd thought he was guilty, and now, they were all sympathetic. *They can all go to hell*, Sam thought.

They'd been allowed to visit Dean's grave, but with a police escort. Victoria and Sam had tried to comfort Paul as best they could, but he was still struggling with his loss. Sam reflected on how difficult it had been on Vicky to be without him for only a few weeks and couldn't fathom what Paul was feeling, knowing that the man he loved and shared his life with would never come back.

When the bailiff removed Sam's ankle monitor a few days later, after he was cleared of all charges, Sam felt a huge weight fall off his shoulders. He was finally free. Mostly, he was elated that he'd been able to surmount all obstacles and get to the truth, but another part of him was still nervous. Donald Jackson hadn't been seen or heard of in weeks, and the police were still actively searching for him. They had offered Sam protection, but he'd declined. They would go away for a long while on a family vacation, and besides, Sam didn't trust the police any-more. He knew that most of them were good cops, but the recent events had made him reluctant to put his life in their hands.

When they walked out of the courthouse, Victoria asked Sam if he wanted to go home.

"No," he replied. "I've been locked inside our place for the better part of a month now. You go on ahead with Sofia. There's one last thing I have to do. I'll catch up a little later."

Victoria gave Sam a nervous look, but he assured her that he wouldn't do anything risky. There was just one last person he had to see. After that, they would book a flight for tomorrow morning and get away from all this for a while.

His wife took their daughter's hand, and Sam kissed them both, telling them to wait for him at home.

SIXTY-TWO

Old Philadelphia
Corner of Market and 4th
Thursday – June 27, 2013 – 4:21 p.m.

Sam walked up the front steps of the large brick building and headed for the front desk. The friendly receptionist smiled at him and asked how she could help. She didn't even come close to recognizing him from the last time she'd seen him—Sam now looked quite respectable.

Sam asked to meet with the station manager, and the receptionist called his office. After a short discussion, she informed Sam that the man was in a meeting and wasn't available today. She asked if he wanted to make an appointment.

"Tell him Sam Brighton wants to see him," he told her.

She immediately recognized his name. Sam's story had made headlines in the city for weeks and had even made the national headlines for a few days. Philly was the sixth largest town in the country, and it had shocked the American public that something like this could happen in such an important metropolitan area. As a result, Sam had become a minor celebrity. His house arrest had kept him out of the public eye for the most part, and he had declined all requests for interviews, so while his name was now famous, his face was still somewhat forgettable.

The receptionist told the manager what Sam had said and hung up the phone.

"He says he'll be down in a minute," she told Sam with a smile and googly eyes.

Sam thanked her and took a seat while he waited.

Five minutes later, a man in his early sixties with a huge belly and bushy beard walked up to him. He had short, cropped hair on the sides of his head and was completely bald on top, wearing wire-framed glasses that accentuated the glimmer in his eyes.

"Hi, there! You must be Sam Brighton. It's an honor to meet you. I'm Roy Parker, the station manager here. What can I do for you?"

"Nice to see you, Mr. Parker. I'm here because I'd like to file a complaint against one of your employees," Sam said politely.

"Okay…" the man uttered with a quizzical look. "I thought you had reconsidered our offer for an exclusive interview…?" he asked hopefully.

"No. I'm sorry, but no interviews. Can we talk in your office?"

"Sure thing. Follow me," Parker said, leading the way.

They went up the elevator to the top floor and walked across the building until they reached the manager's office. He had a large corner office with huge windows that offered a gorgeous view of Old Philadelphia and the Delaware River not far away.

He offered Sam a seat and asked if he wanted something to drink, which Sam declined.

"I'd like to file a complaint against one of your reporters," he repeated.

"So you said. May I ask what for?"

Sam took a deep breath. "I showed up here a while ago, a few days before the videos were released on YouTube, and talked to one of your young reporters. I showed him everything I had on the Jackson twins. He promised he would help me, but instead of breaking the story, he called the cops on me while I was asleep and got rid of all the evidence I had on them."

"What?" the manager barked, looking furious.

"You heard me. He turned me in and informed Donald and Davis Jackson that he had found me. He handed my phone and spyglasses over to them and tried to get rid of the evidence I had. Luckily for me, I'm a paranoid little bastard—I had stored digital copies of everything before walking in your studio."

"I can't believe this!"

"Now, I'd like for us to go meet this young man so you and I can talk to him. His name his Mat Linden."

Roy Parker sighed upon hearing the name, and Sam figured this wasn't the first time the kid had screwed up but that this one took the cake.

"Follow me," Parker grunted as he got up from his chair.

They went down to the second floor and entered the news-room. There was a hush as the manager walked across the room, and everyone became a lot busier. They walked up to Linden's desk. He was facing his computer and didn't hear them coming. Parker coughed, startling Linden, and he spun around. First, he saw his boss, but then, his eyes met Sam's. Even though Sam's appearance had been drastically cleaned up, Linden still recognized the man standing in front of him. The reporter's face turned white, and he tried to back away in his chair, but he was confined to his cubicle and had nowhere to go.

"Mat," Parker began roughly. "I think you recognize Mr. Brighton here. He says that he came to you with the story of Mayor Jackson, but that, instead of helping him, you stabbed him in the back. Is that true?"

It took a few seconds for Linden to respond, but he finally stammered, "N-No, it's not, boss. I don't have a clue as to what he's talking about."

"Excuse me," interjected Sam. He pushed Linden aside and opened the folder on the screen's desktop. Linden had kept all the files on his computer. "What about this?" Sam asked as he pointed to the screen.

"What, this?" Linden replied nervously. "I downloaded them a couple of days ago. I thought I would work on the story and see if we'd missed anything. I'm just trying to help, Mr. Parker."

Sam looked over at the station manager. The look on his face said that he thought it was all a bunch of lies but that it was credible. Sam sighed and went back to the computer. He opened the internet browser and logged into the account he had created on his phone. The inbox was empty, as he had never received any messages at that address, but he clicked on the folder containing the messages that had been sent. There was only one—Sam double-clicked on the email and opened it.

"There," Sam said triumphantly. "This is an email I sent you on Saturday, May 25th, three days before the videos were released online. There's a file attached to it. You want me to play it for your boss, Mat?" he threatened.

Mat bowed his head. There was no point in denying anymore.

"I'm sorry," Linden whispered.

"Why the hell would you do such a thing, Mat?" Roy Parker asked. "You're supposed to protect your sources, not screw them over. We could've broken the story first and made huge headlines!"

"I'm sorry, Roy," was all Linden said.

"You mind telling me why you called the cops on me and handed my phone to Donald Jackson, Mat?" Sam snarled.

"He told me that if I helped him out, I would get all the exclusives from City Hall until Davis was sworn in as Senator and then he'd name me as his press secretary" Linden muttered with a shameful look.

"Well, that was a big mistake, Mat. The last person in the world you should trust as a reporter is a politician. I thought you knew better!"

"I'm sorry, boss," the young man repeated, keeping his head down and staring at his shoes.

"Not as sorry as I am, Mat. Clear out your desk, son. You're done. I want you gone within an hour," Parker said firmly.

Linden raised his head and tried to protest, but Parker put up his palm and motioned for the kid to shut up. There was no place for debate. Linden sighed and started gathering his things.

After leaving Linden's cubicle, Parker walked Sam back to the front entrance. As they got to the front door, he said, "I'm sorry about all of this, Mr. Brighton. This never should have happened. This station prides itself on ethics and betraying a source is unacceptable. I'll make sure that all my employees know about it. And you can bet that Mat Linden will never get a job as a reporter anywhere on the east coast, I can guarantee you that."

Sam shook the man's hand. "Thank you. That's all I wanted to hear."

Parker opened the door for his guest, and Sam walked out and took three deep breaths. Maybe he was imagining things, but the air felt better now. He had accomplished everything he had wanted to do. It was time to go home.

While he walked up Chestnut on the way back to his condo, where he couldn't wait to be with his family, Sam reflected on what he had been through. His first thoughts went to Dean. He would never forget the sacrifice his best friend had made, and he told himself that he needed to go check in on Paul to see how he was doing.

The city had a different vibe now. For the past weeks, every sight, sound, or smell had meant danger for him. He had been under continuous stress. Now, he was able to walk the streets again, as a free man, and those sights and sounds now made him feel alive. Even the air seemed to taste a bit sweeter.

EPILOGUE

Encinitas, 26 miles north of San Diego
Corner of Encinitas Boulevard and Balour Drive
Wednesday – August 21, 2013 – 8:41 a.m.

When Sam had returned home on the night of June 27th, the family had eaten a large pizza Sam had picked up along the way and watched movies. Sofia's school was over, so she was allowed to stay up for as long as she wanted.

After the movie was done, they had turned on their laptop and gone online; they bought plane tickets set to leave the very next morning and went off to bed.

They splurged for first-class seats as they flew from Philly to Copenhagen.

After spending three weeks traveling throughout northern Europe, they flew home—it was time for a new adventure.

While they'd traveled, Sam and Victoria kept in contact with their life in Philadelphia.

Sam had learned that Donald Jackson had been found stabbed to death near his childhood home in North Philly. The prime suspect was Davis Jackson, who was caught a few days later by the Canadian Border Patrol, trying to cross into Ontario with a group of migrant workers from Central America. His trial took place a few weeks later, and he was quickly convicted and handed a life sentence.

The authorities had decided not to pursue the case on Donald Jackson after he had been found dead and felt it was better for everyone to just forget he'd ever existed. The FBI had found a high-ranking police officer who had been in service at the time of James Monroe's investigation, but since the man was in his late nineties, the court decided it wasn't worth the time and effort to pursue criminal charges against him and that it would be easier to leave the old man to live out his last days in peace.

Sam had tasked his attorney with suing the pants off the school board. They had dragged his name through the mud when this all began and let a sociopath like Donald Jackson in charge of their biggest establishment for decades. Sam's lawyer got a huge amount of money since the school board desperately wanted to settle out of court and keep out of the press. They settled for three-and-a-half million dollars. Sam agreed not to divulge any details in exchange for the large sum that covered all the years of salary he would lose for the rest of his workable career and the damages suffered by his family. He could have kept it all and chosen not to work another day in his life, but it wasn't in Sam's character to just sit idle. Upon his return to the city, Sam took care of his legal fees then started spreading the money around.

He gave Paul Gardner five hundred thousand dollars, as he felt that, without Dean's help, he never could have made it out alive. The money would never bring Dean back, but it would help Paul move on so he could eventually heal his emotional wounds.

Sam gave over a million dollars to a series of homeless shelters all across the city. After having lived for only a few weeks as they did, he felt a tremendous amount of respect for those poor souls who had to eke out a living, not knowing when their next meal would be or if they would find a place to lay their heads at night.

He then wrote a check for fifty thousand dollars to the East Passyunk Community Recreation Center to thank them for allowing him to use their computers when he'd needed to fill out forms to access his parents' safety deposit box. At first, they didn't understand what Sam was talking about and thought it was a prank call, but after getting through to the gentle old soul who had helped Sam, the clerk recalled the homeless man who had asked for help. He told Sam that his gift was the most generous donation the center had ever received and would cover expenses for the rest of the year. Upon Sam's request, they announced a few weeks later that the lab would be renamed the Dean Ashton Computer Lab.

When Sam was done helping those who had offered a hand when he was in need, he was left with a little under one million dollars in their account. After a long family discussion that lasted an entire weekend, they had all agreed that they couldn't stay in Philadelphia anymore. Every sight, smell, and sound now reminded Sam of his ordeal and what he'd put his family through. He had refused the offer to be reinstated in his old job. Although he hadn't lost his love for teaching, he could never teach in that high school again.

Sam had put the condo up for sale while Victoria called a head-hunter to find a new posting. The offers for Victoria came in from all across the country. Every major city in the United States with a children's hospital was in the race, and they competed against each other to woo her. After about a week of discussion, they had agreed that putting almost three thousand miles between their former life and their new one would be the best way to move forward.

They purchased a nice little house right on the beach in Encinitas, and Sofia had immediately taken to living near the ocean. They walked on the sand every weeknight after supper, and she took surfing lessons on the weekend. Victoria's new hospital was only a fifteen-minute drive from their beach home, and she could drop off Sam and Sofia on the way to work.

Sofia was about to start middle school in a few weeks. Being far away from her old life, she could make new friends and not worry about her father's misadventures affecting her social life. They looked at schools and settled on a middle school with a strong athletics program. They had put a basketball net in the driveway, and she practiced her jump shot with her mom every evening to be ready for the team's tryouts.

After Sofia's visit with the school's admission's office, they had walked across the street to the senior center and community recreation building. They wanted to check out extracurricular activities for Sofia and job opportunities for Sam. When they entered and looked around, Sam saw a posting on a billboard that caught his attention. The large, fluorescent pink sheet was an ad to find a tutor for the senior center to teach basic computer skills.

Sam had inquired with management, and after a few calls back and forth, they had agreed to hire Sam to take charge of the classroom. The manager had informed him that they couldn't pay him the salary he was used to as a full-time teacher, but Sam replied that he would gladly work for minimum wage. He was happy to teach again but was content to work only two or three hours a day, at least until he could figure out what he wanted to do with the rest of his life. He didn't want any attachments for the moment.

All Sam Brighton wanted now was to live a quiet and peaceful life with his family. The simplicity of beach walks with his wife, of basketball games and homework sessions, of meeting new people and growing in their little community. After all he'd been through, Sam was ready for the simple life—and he would enjoy it.

ACKNOWLEDGMENTS

First and foremost, I would like to thank my wife Veronique for her unwavering support. Your love and encouragements pushed me towards this life-long dream of writing my own novels. I would also like to thank my children for their never-ending love. Special thanks go out to my father and my brother, both avid readers, who transmitted their love of books to me at a very young age. To my good friends Nath and Dee, who were my first readers and critics, I could not have done this without your help. Thank you to Ryan Hyde for your legal counsel. To Chris, Lawrence and everyone at Sunbury Press, thank you for bringing this project to life.

The final thanks go out to you, the reader. Without you, none of this could be possible. I hope you enjoyed reading this story as much as I enjoyed writing it.

ABOUT THE AUTHOR

Simon Landry was born in Montreal in 1979. He graduated from Laval University with a bachelor's degree in education in 2003. He has since then been teaching high school mathematics. An avid reader, Simon decided to plunge into creative writing in 2017 during his spare time. *Chestnut Street* is his first published novel. He currently lives with his wife and two children in Montreal.

www.facebook.com/simonlandrybooks